twisted QUEEN

A FIVE FAMILIES NOVEL

PENELOPE BLACK

for eleanor
who sat next to me while I wrote most of this book.

PLAYLIST

"Dome" by Firewoodisland
"Holocene" by Bon Iver
"Make it Holy" by The Staves
"you broke me first" by Tate McRae
"Riverside" by Agnes Obel
"Colors" by Black Pumas
"You There" by Aquilo
"Rain" grandson, Jessie Reyez
"Hush" by The Marias
"Take Me to Church" by MILCK
"High Enough" by K.Flay
"I Feel Like I'm Drowning" by Two Feet
"As the World Caves In—Wuki Remix" by Sarah Cothran, Wuki

chapter one

Madison

The sun heats my skin, the bright rays red against my closed lids. Warm summer wind sweeps over us, stealing strands of my hair and sending them tickling my cheek. Cicadas sing, punctuating the perfect afternoon as I let myself sink into the feeling of contentment.

"Open your eyes, little star."

The rumble of my father's voice slides over me like my favorite quilt we're laying on, warm and comforting.

My lips twist to the side. "The sun's too bright. I need to wait for a cloud to pass over."

The breeze twirls over us in a lazy pattern, rustling the leaves of the nearby weeping willow tree. It's one of my favorite trees, and even though Mary begs off with claims of allergies, my dad and I always picnic right by it.

I keep my eyes closed and enjoy the feeling of the uneven ground beneath the quilt, our snacks already packed up in the picnic basket.

"You can't walk through life with your eyes closed, waiting for the clouds to pass by before you're ready."

My brow furrows as I crack an eyelid. My hair catches on the quilt as I turn my head to stare at my father. He's laying down with his arms behind his head, his eyes open and staring unblinking at the sun. But that's not what has my attention. It's the fact that he's dressed in a black suit. My dad always looked sharp in suits, but he hated wearing them, said he felt they were strangling him.

"Did you change? I swear you weren't wearing that before." My voice trails off.

He turns to look at me, his eyes so similar to mine. His smile falls a little on the left side, as if weighed down by sadness.

He's smiling at me the same way he did when he told me my aunt Kathleen was in the hospital. She was my favorite aunt who wasn't really my aunt at all. Aunt Kathleen was my dad's cousin. They grew up together and remained close throughout the years. My heart seizes inside my chest, the action painful and violent.

I jerk up to a sitting position. "What's wrong? Is it Mom? Mary?"

Dad doesn't sit up, he just stares at me from his relaxed position on the ground with sadness carved into every line on his face.

"Tell me what's wrong!"

"You already know, my smart little star."

I rake my fingers through my hair, pulling it away from my face. "No, I don't. I don't understand why you're dressed like that or why you're looking at me the same way you did when you told me about Aunt Kathleen or—" I cut myself off, and shift onto my knees. The thread from the quilt squares digs into my knees, and the urge to flee, to figure out what's going on, holds me prisoner. Determination slides through my veins, and I stand up.

Before I can get further than an inch, Dad holds my arm. His grip isn't firm or harsh, but the familiar connection stutters my heart. I feel my brow wrinkle as I stare at his tanned hand against my arm. Something inside my chest squeezes painfully, and my eyes fill with tears I don't understand.

"It's not your time, Madison. You're not supposed to be here."

At the sound of his voice, a single tear slides down my cheek. Raising my head, my gaze roams his features as I sink back down to the quilt.

"Dad?" My voice cracks on the vowel and realization floods my body. My lip quivers and my eyes fill with tears. "Dad, is that you?"

He squeezes my arm in a familiar gesture of affection that constricts my heart. Love shines from his gaze, the sheen sparkling in the sunlight. "You can't be here now, sweetheart. You have to go back. I'll be here when you're ready."

"What? No, I want to stay with you." I shuffle forward on my knees, desperate to hug him.

He stops me with gentle hands on my arms. "Wake up, Madison."

Even as I shake my head, a desperate plea on my lips, the edges of the image around me fade to black like someone lit a fire to the paper this scene was crafted on. I stare in horror as my father's gaze stays on mine, unwavering in attention and love.

chapter two

Leo

The incessant beeping grates on my nerves, but I force myself to sit still. To endure the torture that is inaction. There isn't anything *to* do. I don't have any answers, just a roomful of questions. And until my brother wakes up and tells us what the fuck happened in the time we were apart, I can't do anything.

The idiom *in the blink of an eye* isn't new by any means. And with a family like mine, I'm too familiar with how quickly things can escalate. How life can change to death with the snap of a finger. Add in an asshole father who expresses himself with violence, and you might say I'm more than familiar with these situations.

But this time it's different.

Because for the first time, I don't have my brother to look to. I'm not ashamed to say that I usually defer to him in *family* situations. He's a fucking made man—of course he knows more about this life than I do. That was an option that wasn't afforded to me. Not yet, at least.

I'm out of my fucking element here, and I'm not too proud to admit it. I don't know where the fuck to even begin to look for the person responsible, but I know one thing for sure: I'd rather pluck my own eye out than go to Angelo for help.

That man doesn't do anything for free, and even though Matteo's kept me sheltered from the family business, he didn't barricade me completely. There were times that I'd faced Angelo's personal brand of *help* before, and I'll never make that mistake again.

So until I can figure out what the fuck to do, I sit here in this sterile hospital room that smells of disinfectant and stale coffee.

And wait.

Dante's prowling the halls and presumably dealing with things in only the way he can.

Matteo was in surgery for a few hours, and thank fuck, they repaired the worst of the damage. His Kevlar vest saved his life. He's fucking lucky he started wearing the new slimline prototype from his friend in the Brotherhood. Now, it's just a waiting game to see when his body decides he's ready to wake up.

Meanwhile, every second that ticks by is another one stacked against us. It's another minute that my fucking girl is missing.

I've watched the footage a hundred times, and still, I don't find anything new. Two dead-men-walking in ski masks shoot Matteo and take Madison, but not until after they smash a gun over her head.

The way her body slumped over is an image that I don't think

I'll ever get out of my head. It's like someone pulled her plug, and her electricity just stopped. The way her body just crumpled to the ground will haunt my dreams for years.

My stomach rumbles, reminding me that I can't remember the last time I ate. I had a coffee with Madison, but that was hours ago. Dante left about an hour ago under the guise of food and fresh clothes and whatever else he has to do to secure this area of the hospital. Imagining him prowling the white hallways with a scowl and blood splatter and startling every unsuspecting nurse brings a smile to my face.

The smile fades when the feeling of Matteo's blood, cooled and sticky, on my shirt scratches against my skin. Blood doesn't scare me—you don't grow up Angelo Rossi's son without becoming very acquainted with blood. And, hell, it's not even the first time I've had Matteo's blood on me. Years ago, I broke his nose in a misguided attempt at showing him I'm ready to join the family business.

I rest my head in my hands and stare at the off-white linoleum floor, idly tracing patterns in the brown speckled design while my mind wanders away from my fucked-up childhood. I can't stop myself from thinking of her again, wondering where she is and hoping she's okay.

Madison's strange run-in with the bathroom, the apartment, the safe house. While I could normally write off the coffee shop incident, I read somewhere once that there's power in threes. And I have to believe that it counts toward the three, otherwise, there's another blow just waiting to rain down on us.

And I don't know what the fuck to do next.

Everything inside my gut urges me into action. The need to look for her pounds in time with my heartbeat, but the last time I got up to leave, Dante blocked the door. Said he can't look for her, protect Matteo, and rescue me all at the same time.

Asshole.

We compromised: I stay here, and he can focus more energy on finding her.

I really need Matteo to wake up and tell me what to do. He's always been the one with the big plans, the grandiose ideas. He never let me in on any of them, always trying to protect me.

Maybe it's time I don't give him that option anymore. Maybe it's my time to step up and help.

"Leo?"

The sound of Matteo's voice has me springing out of my chair and rushing to his side. "Shit, Matteo. You scared the hell outta me. Let me call a nurse."

He grabs my arm with a weak grip, halting my movement. "Maddie?"

I shake my head. "Let me get a nurse."

His grip on my arm tightens. "Where is Maddie?"

I glance between his grip and his eyes. Despite his pale pallor, fire reigns from his gaze. Fuck it. He needs to know, and the sooner he can help us piece together the events, the better.

"She's gone. Whoever shot you took her. We've got some guys on it, only the ones Dante trusts. We need your help figuring out what happened."

He nods with a grimace, letting go of my arm. I rush to press the call button for a nurse. She arrives a minute later and checks his vitals, briefly explaining what happened. Matteo's eyelids droop after a few minutes, and the nurse wraps everything up with a promise to stop back soon. I resist the urge to snap at him to stay awake so I can get some answers. It's not fair, but the increasing need to find my girl drums inside my veins.

I pat his arm. "Rest now, brother. I'll look out for you."

It's been hours since Matteo woke up. He's been dozing off and on, and he's currently awake and bitching about whatever horror movie Dante could find. The television screen is small and on the other side of the room, so I don't know why he's even complaining. It's probably just to make himself feel better, productive.

"How much longer do I have to sit here? I fucking hate hospitals," Matteo grumbles. It's a variation of the same thing he's been saying since he woke up like he didn't just have some doctor rooting around in his shoulder today. Neither Dante or I answer him.

The door creaks, but I don't bother looking to see who it is. Nurses have been coming in and out to check on one thing or another, and each time, Matteo gets a little crankier. So this time, I'm going to just ignore the whole thing.

"Surprise," a voice too deep to be our current nurse's says.

I jump out of my chair and stride toward him, relief pumping through my body with every beat of my heart. "Jesus, Rafe. How did you find us?" I shake his hand and pull him in for a one-armed hug. "It's so good to see you. It's been too long since we've all been in the same room together." I look between Rafe and Matteo with a smile stretching across my face. "Damn, I'd forgotten how much you guys look alike."

"That's what happens with twins," Dante drolls as he stands up and crosses the room.

"They're not identical, asshole." It's an old line we've been using since they were kids. It's true, they're not identical, but at least they look like brothers. That's more than I can say for myself.

"You too, you too. Someone want to tell me what the fuck is going on?" He claps me on the back twice and strides toward the hospital bed.

Dante stops next to Rafe and pulls him in for a one-armed hug and claps a hand on his shoulder. "Good to see you, man."

"You too. Wish it were under better circumstances though." Rafe rolls his eyes before pinning his gaze to our brother in the hospital bed.

"Were you followed?" Dante asks, ever pragmatic. He walks toward the window and lifts up a blind to look into the hallway.

"Nah. But if I were, I led them on a merry chase all over the city. How are you, brother?"

"I'm fine. But what are you doing here? It's not safe—"

Rafe's eyebrows rise to his hairline. "Safe? I think that ship has sailed when you landed in the emergency room with a gunshot wound. Now everyone's going to know the elusive Matteo Rossi can be pinned down, if only by a bullet."

"I meant safe for you, you asshole. Now get the fuck outta here. If Dad catches you—"

"Yeah, yeah, yeah. I'm not afraid of dear ol' Dad," Rafe interrupts.

Matteo grits his teeth. "Yeah, well, you're not the brother he'd take it out on."

Three sets of eyes pin me with a stare so heavy I square my

shoulders to weather it. I tip my chin up and raise a brow, giving each of them a pointed look. "Don't worry about me. I'm not the brother who got shot. And I'm not the one who's been away for years."

Rafe's face loses some easygoingness and hardens. "Good. Now that it's settled, someone start talking. What exactly did I see on my security feed? And where the fuck is Raven?"

Matteo holds up a hand and glances between us. "Wait. Back up. How did you even find me?"

"Raven?" I ask at the same time, leaning against the wall. Confusion clouds my caffeine-and-food-deprived brain. Was there someone else there?

"Who do you think called the paramedics?" Rafe smirks as he stares at our brother.

Matteo's gaze flicks from Rafe to Dante to settle on me. His brow wrinkles as he says, "I thought it was you."

I shake my head a few times. "No, we got there a minute after the paramedics." My mind whirls with this new information, and my heart rate picks up as if it knows something I don't.

Rafe folds his arms across his chest and stares between the three of us. "Now that's cleared up, let's move on. Because we're on borrowed time with Raven."

"You son of a bitch," Matteo swears under his breath. "How?"

Rafe shrugs. "How does anything happen? Boy meets girl, boy saves girl, girl thanks boy *generously*, boy's been looking for girl for weeks."

My head spins with their sidestepping conversation in code. It might as well be French for all I can follow. One of them always backs down, it's just changed over the years as to which one it is.

And who the fuck is Raven?

They trade a few more barbs, but there isn't any real heat in them, and I'm too preoccupied to field their conversation, anyway. There's a beat of silence, and then it's like an explosion of sound ripples through the air as realization smacks me in the face.

"Let me put it this way, brother. If you got Raven killed, I'll put a bullet in you myself. And this time, I'll make sure you're not wearing a vest," Rafe continues without missing a beat, flashing a smile at our brother with more teeth than heart.

"The fuck did you say to me?" Matteo snarls as he pushes up off the bed without a grimace.

"Sounded a lot like a threat." Dante pushes off the wall and crosses the room to stand next to the hospital bed.

"Back up. Raven?" I clench my hands into fists and stay on my side of the room with the wall at my back.

Rafe looks between the three of us, a cruel smirk slashed across his face. "Oh, didn't you know? That girl's mine."

chapter three

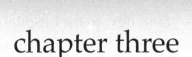

I catapult into consciousness, my body jerking and my eyes flashing open. It's dark around me, but not pitch-black. A low humming noise is beneath me, and I taste metal on my tongue—blood.

My chest aches with grief so profound I'm unconsciously searching for my father before I realize it. I bite back a sob when reality crashes into me with the force of a semitruck. Like salt in an unhealed wound, the crippling feeling of being alone settles over me. And I know inside my soul that wherever I just went, I really saw him. I don't remember much more than a few moments, but it's enough to bring the pain of his absence to the forefront of my mind.

I blink several times, exhaling a breath that subdues some of the grief enough for me to take in my surroundings. It's the kind of dark that's muted, not quite stealing your sense of sight. Panic squeezes my heart tight, and I take some comfort knowing that it's me and not my sister in this predicament. Mary's been afraid of the dark since she was six. This would be her nightmare.

As long as I don't end up in one of those cages underwater, with sharks swimming around me, I can get through this. Whatever *this* is.

I have to. There is no alternative, at least that's what I tell myself as my fear threatens to take the reins.

My body sways and jostles in an unmistakable way, and the rough material of a blanket over me scratches my skin. I must be in a car.

Oh, shit. Am I in another van?

I quell the urge to rip the blanket off and give myself away. If I am in a van, then I probably only have one shot to make it out of here without getting seriously hurt—or dying.

I call on my calming, meditative breathing techniques for a few precious moments. Low murmurs of unrecognizable voices reach my ears just as the pain in my head makes itself known with a vicious throb.

I press my hand to it out of instinct, but all that does is coax a gasp from my throat. The side of my face is wet and sticky with what I'm guessing is blood. The details are kind of fuzzy, and the how isn't nearly as important as the need to escape, so I shove it down to deal with another time.

Blood sticks to my fingertips, and like some magical switch, flashes of memories slam into my brain. It's like one of those flipbooks we had as kids, and single images of what happened appear before my eyes, fast enough that it feels like I'm watching the whole thing play out again from a bird's-eye view.

Oh my god—*Matteo*!

He was shot, and they—they just left him there! Helplessness rises up my throat, and I choke down the sob threatening to explode. I send a prayer to the stars to watch over him until he gets help. I have no idea how much time has passed, but I can only hope that Leo and Dante came back in enough time.

The thought of him dying is incomprehensible. Realistically, getting shot at that close range by what seems to be a *murder for hire* spells death. And that may be true for some people, but not him.

Not Matteo Rossi.

Larger than life and powerful enough to command a room with a single look.

No, that man cannot die. I'm not nearly done with him yet.

I refuse to believe he died. And I just know that I would know it, somehow *feel* it if he died. He's alive. He has to be.

I grasp that belief and repeat it as a mantra for the next thirty seconds. Then I slowly peel down the blanket, careful not to make any sudden movements and snag someone's attention.

The wool material itches my nose and the urge to sneeze seizes me.

These damn sinuses are going to get me killed, I curse inside my head.

I close my eyes and concentrate on not sneezing, keeping that reflex locked down tight. The urge to sneeze rushes through my system and I manage to contain it to an incredible soft noise, my eyes scrunching up tight and my shoulders jerking upward involuntarily.

Opening my eyes, the first thing I notice is that it's still dark in here—darker than I expected. I slide the scratchy blanket further down my body, turning my head from side to side to take in my surroundings. I was right—I'm definitely in a vehicle. And unfortunately, it seems like some sort of custom van. I think it's safe to assume I'll never willingly get into another van again. Not after everything that happened.

There are boxes on the floor around me instead of a second row of seats, caging me in, but I don't want to risk sitting up to get a better look. Not yet, at least.

I glance around, noting some sort of black film over the window across from me. That explains why it's so dark in here. It looks almost like a thick plastic, the street lights barely breaching it to let in dim light.

Shifting up onto my elbows, I caution a glance toward the front of the van, where the voices are coming from. They're talking too low for me to make much out, and the radio covers the rest of it. I blow out a breath, the air stirring the loose hair in front of my face and think about my options.

They're seriously lacking.

What's a girl that's used to being in control of her life do in a situation where she has little of it? And what if it's a life-and-death situation?

She does something unpredictable, that's what.

A kernel of an idea sparks inside my mind, and just that is enough to dampen some of the mounting anxiety swinging from my neck like a two-ton weight. Before I can do anything, I need to get a better idea of where we are. If we're on the highway, I'm going to have to go with plan B, but if we're on a side street, I'm fairly confident it'll work.

Regardless, it's the only plan I have.

I strain my ears to the low conversation a few feet in front of me and push up to a sitting position. The boxes and the wide bucket driver and passenger seats offer me some concealment. The element of surprise will buy me a few precious seconds, and it'll have to be enough. The blanket slides off of me when I shift into a crouch and balance on the balls of my feet. I've never been more thankful for sneakers than I am right now. In fact, when this is done, I'm going to write a strongly-worded thank you note to the brand for their perfect sneakers.

My legs feel stiff and my head spins, but I push it all down and focus on what I have to do next.

I swivel my head from side to side with a slowness punctuated by the thundering of my heartbeat. It sounds like a drumbeat echoing inside my body, calling upon some long-buried primal instinct to survive.

There's nothing outside of the homemade blackout windows that stands out inside here. The material adhered to the window ripples and distorts the view. I look over my shoulder and see two people in the driver and passenger seats, the back of their heads indistinguishable in the low light.

I shift forward, placing a hand down in front of me with my eyes on my kidnappers. A bead of sweat slides down my throbbing temple, my adrenaline spiking so high I have to swallow past the nausea. I count to five with my eyes glued to the front of the van, praying the stars are on my side right now and the men didn't notice me wake up.

Their murmuring continues without a glance in my direction, so I push up a little from my crouch and get a glimpse out of the windshield.

Shit.

I was hoping for city blocks, but instead, I see the long stretches of concrete with the occasional factory or warehouse.

If I pull this off, I'm just as likely to be picked up by another psychopath in this neighborhood. At least my hands and feet aren't tied this time.

And what a seriously messed-up thought that is. I'm definitely going to need therapy when this is all over.

I sink my teeth into my bottom lip as I debate what to do.

Fuck it.

I exhale a breath as quietly as possible and quickly crab-walk toward the sliding door of the van closest to the sidewalk. The sounds of Bon Iver start, and one of the men murmurs something before turning the volume up. I take it as the sign I was looking for and curl my fingers around the handle and yank it toward me, anticipation thrumming inside my body and coiling my muscles.

But the door doesn't open. I yank it again; the noise of the plastic handle releasing sounds like a thunderclap, second to only the blood rushing in my ears. My hands shake as I try for a third time, my gaze scanning the door.

The locks!

With a triumphant smile, I grasp the lock and yank it up, unlocking the door. I pull the handle again, and this time, the door unlatches and slides open.

The pinging noise and the overhead light flashing while the van is in drive might as well be a bullhorn for the attention it gets.

"What the hell?" the driver yells, swerving the car to the right.

"Ah, fuck, pull over."

"Goddammit. We cannot let her get away," the driver grumbles.

"You honestly think I don't know that?" the other guy snaps.

The car swerves again, righting itself before it slows down. I don't stick around to hear anything else as I hold my breath and leap out of the half-opened door. My lashes flutter closed without conscious thought, and I pray that I don't break anything as I tumble out of the moving vehicle.

I land on my side with a bone-jarring thud. I don't bother muffling my yelp, my shoulder screaming at me as I roll several times. The pain is agonizing and all-encompassing. It feels like I just went through a salad spinner, but like one with pebbles that feel like blades against my skin, leaving pieces behind.

I stop on my back, my chest heaving as I stare at a starless sky and will the world to stop spinning. Nausea churns in my belly, threatening to leave my lunch all over the pavement.

Move, move, move. The word echoes inside my brain, commanding my muscles to obey. With a groan of agony and determination, I roll over onto my stomach and push myself onto all-fours. The pain in my shoulder screams at me, and my left arm buckles underneath the pressure.

I grit my teeth and use my right arm to push up to my feet just as the noise of squealing tires reverberates in the still night air around me. Headlights slash across the street, highlighting the warehouse and factories on either side of the street. It's a ghost town.

I spin on my heel and start running. I'm directionless and dizzy, stumbling more than I thought I would. The desire to put distance between me and them hammers against me. I need a miracle—a good, kind person to help me.

My heart throbs in time with my shoes slapping the cracked and dusty pavement. The dim, yellow circles of light from the street lamps leave most of the streets shrouded in shadow. My hair whips around me, tangling in my eyelashes. I don't bother to fix it, just swipe it out of my vision with the back of my forearm.

The roaring engine sounds like a herd of lions breathing down my back, and I know if I turn around and look over my shoulder at them, it'll be my downfall. I'll trip, or they'll be closer than I expected, and it'll psych me out. For as much as I don't enjoy horror movies, I refuse to become a real-life example of those stupid victims who die in the first ten minutes because they look behind them.

I'm so busy focusing on not looking behind me that I miss the figure running at me until it's too late. The dark shadow hones in on me like a missile, drawing a panicked noise from me as terror coats my skin.

One of the men from earlier charges me, his face somewhat visible as it's cast in a strange yellow light. His balaclava mask pulled up to rest on the top of his hair.

I pivot away from him at the last moment, but I'm not quick enough. His arm comes down around me like a band of iron, knocking the wind out of me as he grabs me and lifts me off my feet. I kick out and feel my heels connect with his shins as I claw at his hands. They're wrapped tightly around my middle, crushing my ribs and squeezing the air from my lungs.

"Shut the fuck up." His words are low and laced in malice. "I swear to fuck, we better get double for all this hassle, or I'm going to fucking kill him myself."

He drags me backward, ignoring my desperate kicks and claw-like swipes. I fight like my life depends on it. We cut through the beams of light from the van's headlights, which stopped moving with a squeal of the tires.

"Hurry the fuck up, Dave," my captor snaps. "I'm tired of this shit. And I want to catch the rest of the game tonight."

"Fuck off, Jared, I'm right here," the other one, Dave, grumbles without any real heat.

"Yeah, well you're too fucking slow. I told you we should've just put two in her back at that apartment. Would've saved us a shit ton of trouble."

"You say that now, but I don't want that sick fuck siccing his goons on us because we took care of two when the contract was just for one. Do you?"

"Whatever. Let's just get this fucking over with. You got it?" He shifts his hold on me and swings me around to face the other guy. The headlights give him just the right kind of backlight where I can't make out much of his features, only that he's tall and dressed in black—both things I already knew.

He frog-marches me closer and when we're about a foot in front of the other guy, he comes into focus a little more. And that's when I properly lose my shit.

"You don't have to do this! I promise I won't say anything. Just let me—"

"Jesus, would you shut the fuck up already." The guy holding me, Jared, shakes me hard in his grip.

My teeth clamp shut and the words get stuck in my mouth for a moment. Icy tendrils of fear wrap around me, so potent and heavy, I think I black-out for a moment. I redouble my efforts, squirming and kicking and scratching with everything inside of me, ignoring my screaming shoulder and every scrape and bruise as if they don't exist. I become someone else—some*thing* else.

Long gone is the girl who loved ballet and afternoon tea from vintage teacups and in her place is this creature determined not to become another statistic.

But I'm no match for the strength of two huge assassins. And as one closes in on me with a syringe in his hand, I send a final plea up to the stars.

The syringe pricks my neck, and he depresses the plunger, injecting my veins with whatever fucked-up cocktail of drugs is in there.

I bare my teeth at him as a single tear rolls down my face, vowing to seek revenge if I make it out of this whole.

"You sure this'll work?" Jared asks.

"Snagged it from the girl I'm seeing. She's a vet at South Shore."

Unconsciousness doesn't come quickly like the movies suggest it does. It's methodical, slowly stripping you of your faculties one by one, so you feel the agonizing torture of your body being turned against your mind.

"Yeah, well, you better hope it works," Jared grumbles as he adjusts his hold on me. "Because I'm not going to chase her down again."

I promise retribution with my gaze, but it doesn't matter, because no one is looking me in the eye anyway. Jared flips me over his shoulder a second after my legs give out, letting my arms and torso hang over him as he calmly walks back to the van. Like this is a normal occurrence for him, which I realize with a start, it probably is.

"So, you heading to Eddie's for the game tonight?"

Black spots creep along the sides of my vision, darkening it like a vignette.

"Yeah. I'm meeting Harry and a few guys there after we clean up this fucking mess you made." Jared rearranges me, shoving his shoulder into my gut, expelling the air from my lungs in a puff.

"Yeah, yeah. You'll be singing a different tune when we ransom this one back to the senator," the other guy, Dave, says with a chuckle.

It's the last thing I hear before the blackness crowds my vision, and I can't hold on any longer. My lashes flutter closed, and like the rest of my body, they refuse to obey my command.

Three seconds later, and I'm floating in a sea of endless black.

chapter four

Madison

I rouse from my drift along the lazy river of endless black space by the repeated cadence of whatever I'm currently on. I wiggle my fingers, but they don't listen to me. The disconnect between my brain and my body is still firmly in place. I beg my eyes to open so I can get a sense of what hell I'm currently in, but they refuse. Nausea churns in my gut, and I'm not sure if it's from whatever they injected me with or I'm motion sick with the movement.

My fear preys on my vulnerabilities and conjures up metal shipping containers and giant ships and other girls in cages, headed toward a fate worse than death.

I curse my imagination and my sister's love of true crime, and focus on my breathing. In and out, nice and steady.

After a moment, the panic recedes to a more reasonable level, and I'm able to figure out that someone is carrying me. I hear mumbled words and feel the rumble of his voice against my body.

I bet that same guy is carrying me again. Dave. No, Jared.

Jesus, does it really matter his name? a small voice inside me reasons.

Before I have time to properly freak out about where he's taking me, we stop moving. Someone bangs on a door, the noise loud enough that I would've flinched if I had any control over my movements.

The door squeaks as someone answers it, and a growl precedes his words. "Just what the hell do you two think you're doing?"

"Well, see, the thing is, *boss*, we ran into a little hiccup."

"That's hardly my problem. And there's no reason to show up on my doorstep at this time of night. I have neighbors, you know."

"What's the matter, Senator? You don't want your neighbors knowing the color of your bathrobe?"

"Or maybe he doesn't want to be spotted with us, Jared."

"Now that seems more likely, Dave." He shifts to the side, the movement sending my stomach lurching.

"Jesus, get inside before someone sees you," the guy, a senator, I guess, hisses. And I finally place his voice. It's Senator Hardin— also known as Blaire's ex's dad.

There are rumors about him, but most of them involve backroom deals that benefit the upper one-percent of the wealthy—not hiring hit men.

"Not a word until we're inside my office," Senator Hardin says with a huff.

My hair sways from side to side as Jared carries me over his shoulder into Senator Hardin's house. I keep my breaths even as a tingling sensation pricks my fingertips. It feels like a cross between the feeling of pins-and-needles when your hand wakes up after falling asleep and when you accidentally touch a light socket.

I listen to the footsteps around me and try to keep track of the path we've taken inside. The moment I can get my body to actually cooperate, I'm taking my chances and running. I'm pretty sure the senator lives in a gated community in a neighborhood not too far from Blaire.

The squeak of hinges is the only clue that a door closed.

"Alright, you have thirty seconds to convince me not to kill both of you for fucking this up."

The man holding me shifts his weight for a moment before he walks a few paces and sets me down. I'm laying down on my side, on some sort of love seat—all hard cushions and scratchy fabric against my skin. But I don't even care because for the first time in what feels like years, my eyelids open. My dark-red hair is wild and covers half my face, concealing my cracked lids. I resist the urge to blow it out of my face, but I don't want to tip them off before I'm ready to move.

And it would be nice to get as much information as I can to give to the cops when I finally get free of this whole thing.

Unless you tell Dante first, a little voice whispers in my head. I can't help the image that flashes before my eyes of the senator and his two goons bleeding on the floor under Dante's thumb. Vengeance slithers through my veins, bolstering my courage.

My grandma always told me I was meant for great things, and my eight-year-old heart took it as gospel that I was the next prima ballerina or leading role on Broadway. But getting out of this unscathed would be enough for me. I'd consider myself fulfilling her prophecy if I can survive this.

I *will* survive.

So far, it hasn't been nearly as bad as I had feared, but that could all change in a heartbeat—and depending on the man in front of me.

Senator Hardin wears a light blue pajama set with white pin stripes and a dark blue bathrobe. He's standing behind his desk, this giant wooden monstrosity with ornate carvings that look out of place in a room this small. Dale Hardin is known for boasting his ancestry links to the Sons and Daughters of American Revolution, claiming his family has ties to the founding families.

I wouldn't be surprised if this desk was actually from the early 1900s, back when wood desks were real and not the particle board crap they sell now. It would be almost beautiful in a nostalgic, historic sort of way if I wasn't staring at it while I waited for a bunch of men to decide my fate.

What a cruel plot twist fate has thrown me.

But I'm adaptable and smart and fucking determined.

I watch as the senator shifts his weight from one foot to the next before crossing his arms over his chest. "You have ten seconds to explain why there's an unconscious girl on my one-of-a-kind designer chaise before my personal guards make you disappear."

The words are barely out of his mouth before the door opens with a quiet creak and two sets of legs appear in my peripheral vision. I'm assuming it's the bodyguards he spoke of.

I watch as Jared widens his stance. "See, the thing is, Senator, Dave and I always have a fail-safe. You know, a backup plan in case someone decides to fuck us. But before we get to that, let's talk about this pretty little red package here."

"I paid you to take care of someone, not bring me—"

"Exactly," Jared interrupts. "You commissioned us to take care of *one* person. Your details were explicit, so imagine our surprise when we showed up and found another body there."

"It's probably just some hooker. Why didn't you just shoot her too? What the fuck am I gonna do with some bitch? And why the fuck did you think it'd be a good idea to bring her here?" Senator snarls the words through clenched teeth.

"Let me rephrase: You paid for one hit. Not two. And as far as what to do with her, that's entirely up to you. We can take her off your hands for you . . . but that's going to cost you."

Their cavalier attitude about my untimely death should startle me more than it does, but I'm going to chalk it up to the fact that my adrenal glands are probably tapped. I'm in the middle of a prolonged triage on what the hell to freak out about, and right now, that doesn't even compare to the very real possibility that I might die here.

Without the full use of my body on a gaudy chaise couch in the office of a shady government official.

It sounds like the plot of an episode of a prime time crime show.

"How much?"

"Double," Dave says.

"Double? Are you out of your fucking mind? I'm not paying you to take care of some street rat bitch."

"Well, see, she doesn't look like a street rat at all to me. Does she to you, Jared?" Dave uses that tone that sounds like all he's saying is *fuck you* but politely.

"Nah. She looks more like some rich bitch who'd fetch us a pretty penny. I figure we'd be certifiable heroes finding some lost little park avenue princess in the clutches of the depraved senator's basement," Jared adds.

I hear the senator sputter and if I could, my eyebrows would be in my hairline.

"Is this—is this a shakedown?" Disbelief colors the senator's tone.

"Just a friendly reminder. Our price just went up—triple."

"Triple? Why the fuck would I pay you triple *now*?"

"Because now you have to factor in our convenience fee."

"More of an *in*convenience fee, really," Dave says.

I watch the senator's face turn red as he sputters again, doing a shitty job of tamping down his rage. "Get the fuck out of my house before I kill you myself. Russel, take care of the girl. Tom, escort these men off my property."

I wouldn't be surprised if *off my property* is code for *six feet under*. It looks like Senator Hardin's going to pop a blood vessel if he doesn't calm down soon.

A pair of legs moves closer until they stop right next to my head. It takes a ridiculous amount of effort to hold still as my adrenaline spikes—again. I close my lids and focus all my energy on listening for clues as my limbs prickle with awareness.

"Ah, before we leave. I believe you owe us payment."

"You'll get it once I get proof-of-delivery. Russel, turn her over. Let's get a good look at her and see if we can use her for anything before we take her to the farm."

The farm?

Sweat beads along my hairline as my adrenaline climbs higher, igniting a prickle of sensation along my limbs. My fingers twitch with the need to move, to get the hell out of here.

Large hands clamp around my shoulders and turn me over. It takes everything inside of me not to flinch at the contact. I force my chest to rise and fall with steady breaths, and I pray to whoever is listening for no one to notice the tremor in my hands.

"What's wrong with her?"

"Just a little dog tranquilizer," Dave.

There's a beat of silence before the senator asks, "You gave her a *dog* tranquilizer?"

"You didn't pay us enough to inquire about our methods. You paid us to execute a job, which we did. This shit right here is outside the original scope of work."

"Sir. You better take a look at this," the voice close to my head says over some rustling.

I feel the strap of my small crossbody purse tug around my neck, and my heart clenches at what I have inside. My wallet is in there—with my address. I'm struggling to remember what day it is and if my sister and cousin are home.

"Fucking incompetent assholes. That's the last time I ever ask Sal for references. I could've sent my son to do a better job than this. And it cost me a hundred grand," Senator Hardin murmurs.

"Sir?"

"Madison Walsh. Why does that name sound familiar?" There's a moment of silence. "Goddammit. This isn't some street whore. She's a St. Rita's girl, which you fucking imbeciles would've known if you'd taken thirty seconds to search her. Her goddamn student ID is right here."

There's a beat of silence, and a bead of sweat slides down my neck and into the collar of my shirt. My muscles tense involuntarily as I wait for someone to catch me or shoot me or something.

"The fuck do we care? A hit's a hit," Jared says. I wish I could open my eyes to read the people and the room a little better. But if they're going to kill me, maybe it's better to not see it coming.

"Fuck. Fuck. Fuck. Okay. It's okay. I can fix it. I can." His voice trails off, and I hear footsteps in a pattern that suggests he's pacing.

"So you want us to take care of her then?" Dave asks.

"Tom, I thought I said to get them the fuck off my property?" Senator Hardin sounds just shy of manic as he barks orders around the room. Shuffling footsteps fill the room before the door creaks twice—I'm assuming Tom escorted Jared and Dave out.

"Sir? What do you want us to do with the girl?"

"Shh. Just shut up and let me think," Senator Hardin snaps.

I call back on my yoga practices and feel each muscle flex and release, gently waking them up so we'll be ready when the moment is right.

After a few minutes of quiet, the footsteps stop abruptly. "Okay. We're going to drop her at the Hawthorne estate. When my son dated Blaire, I had a full work-up done on her and her family. Blaire's a St. Rita's girl, and they're probably close enough in age that she'll recognize her. That way we can keep our hands clean from any retribution from the Walshes."

"The Walshes, sir?"

"Yes, *the Walshes*, keep up, Ken," the senator sneers. "I can't be sure she's not related to them. They're a powerful family, one you don't want to piss off."

"Apologies, sir. I didn't recognize the name."

"Of course you didn't. You're not supposed to—that's the whole point." The Senator straightens the lapels on his bathrobe several times in a row, nearly obsessively. "If they find out that she's here, like this, they'll demand retribution. And with the re-election coming up, I can't afford any hits."

"Won't she recognize you, sir?"

The senator tsks. "That's why *I'm* not going to be the one who drops her off. You are. And dispose of her purse too. Then it'll look more like she drank too much and got lost or something," he trails off, mumbling something too low for me to hear.

"What if she talks, sir?"

"Well I guess it's a good thing she never saw us, isn't it? If she talks, it'll only incriminate the two idiots who brought her here. And that might save me the money and trouble of taking care of them myself. So the way I see it, it's a win-win." The bodyguards murmur their approval. "But just to be sure, here."

I don't have time to prepare before a pinch pricks my neck. My heart beats faster when I realize that I've just been given another tranquilizer. My fingers tingle and black spots dance around the edge of my vision. I can't contain the groan as I start floating down the lazy river of black fog again.

chapter five

Madison

I float in that space between full consciousness and . . . something else. It's not quite dreamland, but it's ethereal and fuzzy. Like all those times Lainey, my sister, and I took disco naps after stuffing our faces at our favorite brunch spots.

It feels safe here, comforting, even. And I'm hesitant to leave this place. The details around why I'm here are indistinct, but if it's one thing I do remember, it's an overwhelming feeling of sadness and fear. It's a visceral feeling, unlike anything I've ever felt before.

So why should I leave this safe, warm, comfortable place for a place filled with darkness and terror?

Even as I start to toy with the idea of staying here in this calm, restful place, something sharp tugs low in my gut. A flash of instinct that tells me I can't stay here.

For a moment, I allow myself the freedom to do something selfish, to stay here, where I'm protected.

Almost as soon as that thought crosses my consciousness, it gets ripped away, and the faces of my loved ones flash before my eyes.

My twin sister, the other half of my being.

What would I do if I never saw her beautiful smile again?

And what would *she* do if she never saw me again?

I know her on a level that most people will never have the chance of knowing anybody. We shared a womb together for nine months and we shared a home—a room, even—together for every month after. I understand her need to be independent, to make her own name for herself something outside of mine.

She's forever been second, always after me. Mary literally comes after Madison in the alphabet, and she sat behind me in every class, ceremony, and award luncheons. She's never been in the spotlight, and up until recently, she never showed any interest.

But I know my sister, and I know that no matter how hard or how far she runs to separate us, she'll come back to me.

Can I really do this to her? Could I really abandon her like so many others have abandoned us already?

Low murmurs filter through the sticky cloud of consciousness. It's too quiet for me to make out any words, but something tickles the back of my mind, urging me to open my eyes and wake up.

Another face flashes before my eyes, my best friend, my cousin, Alaina.

I can't even begin to imagine what she's been going through. But I know it's been tough. I know it's taken a toll on her physically and emotionally.

Could I be another person she loses?

It's terrible, but the thought of never seeing them again is the one thing that urges me from my peaceful existence, floating in endless black.

I suppose I shouldn't be surprised that I'm attracted to darkness or that it calls to me. After all, look at the men I'm attracted to.

The thought of them sends a pang through my heart, piercing it swiftly.

My muscles seize with the need for action. I've never been one to sit idle by the sidelines, so I'm not really sure why I'm so content to stay here now.

Years ago, after my dad died, I allowed myself an endless amount of time to be still. Inaction was a gift I gave to myself. But then I realized if I didn't step up, nobody would.

My mom was incapable, and my sister was inconsolable. And with my dad gone, who else was there but me?

I'm not sure if I'm missing some sort of life lesson here, or if the stars are providing me with another opportunity to shine. But I know one thing for sure.

I'm not ready to leave them behind yet.

Consciousness is a funny thing. It's not instant, it's not like the movies make you think where you just snap your fingers and you're awake.

I made the decision, I'm ready to go back, I'm ready to face whatever it is the kidnappers have in store for me, and yet, here I am, still floating in this abyss.

I will myself to open my eyes, to twitch my fingers, to constrict my muscles, to do something—anything.

But nothing happens. Murmurs filter into my endless black, and I strain my hearing to recognize anything. A plea for help sits on the tip of my tongue.

Suddenly this darkness isn't so comforting and warm. It's constricting, pressing in on me from all angles, pushing against my lungs, and squeezing my head between its mighty fists. All at once, I feel the air being sucked out of my lungs, as if I'm trapped in the deepest, darkest parts of the ocean.

And then my fears creep up on me. Long, creepy tentacles curl around my ankles and hold me immobile to the sandy bottoms of my own nightmare prison.

So I swim. And claw. And crawl.

I claw my way through nothing, an invisible oppression that feels never-ending.

"Madison!"

I jerk at the sound of my name, whipping my head around to look for the face behind the familiar voice. Blackness greets me.

"Maddie!"

My heart pounds, and I double my efforts to reach the top or edge or end of this hell I'm trapped in. Fear tiptoes up my spine and anxiety slithers over my skin as I strain to hear their voices again. What if they're trapped in here with me?

"Madison!"

I pivot to the right, certain the sound came from right next to me, but I don't find anything, just endless nothingness.

My limbs feel weighed down; my coordination sluggish as I look around in vain. My lungs scream for air, and I struggle against an invisible foe.

"Raven. Don't you dare stop. Keep going."

My heart skips a beat at his insistent tone, so I shove everything else down and focus on his voice.

And I don't stop.
I can't.

chapter six

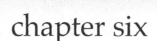

Madison

With the last vestiges of my strength and sanity, I continue to wade through. For what feels like forever, I'm climbing, swimming, crawling—trying to break free.

And suddenly, I see a tiny pinprick of white light, a beacon of hope. I run toward it, at least, I think I'm running.

The circle of white light grows larger and larger until everything around me is white. It's bright enough to sear my eyelids, especially after the pitch-black.

I squint against the harsh light, but I don't let myself stop. I keep moving forward on this endless white. I wonder for a second if this is some sort of metaphor, and some sort of test I have to pass before I can rejoin the land of the living. Or the conscious, I should say, *right*?

Would I know if I died?

The question flits across my mind like a stone on a lake and pulls me up short. I really should've thought of this before.

What if I'm dead and this is . . . it?

I'm not really sure that now is the best time to have an existential crisis, especially considering the last moment of consciousness and clarity I had, I was being injected with some sort of tranquilizer that left me immobilized.

And yet here I am, pondering the very existence of our souls.

With that thought heavy on my heart, I succumb to my exhaustion and stand still for just a moment, heaviness blanketing me like a twenty-pound quilt. My shoulders jerk under the weight, and a groan slips from my lips.

A very tangible sound that I can not only feel but hear.

And the fact that I can hear it, and that I can feel it. And then I feel my face scrunch up in pain is so euphoric I want to cry. Surely if I can feel myself, then I can move, right?

Exhaustion tugs me with its iron grip, dragging me back to the land of oblivion, promising comforts again. But then I hear the telltale sound of heels clicking on a hardwood floor, the noise focusing my mind. And with just a few sharp clacks, everything slams into me at the speed of a train.

The safe house, the intruders, the kidnappers—the senator!

I peel my eyes open, my lashes sticking to one another as panic flies through my nerves like I'm on that terrible zero gravity ride. The need to flee infuses every fiber of my being as dizziness overtakes me. My breaths come loud and labored as I blink several times.

My vision takes a moment to clear and the space in front of me comes into focus. Something white obscures my vision, and I have a half of a second to doubt my own sanity. Am I in one of those dream inside a dream things? Am I inside a cloud?

"Oh, thank god."

Wait a second, I know that voice. I've heard it almost every day for the last several years. Turning my head to the side, big blue eyes framed by lashes too long and voluminous to be real fill my vision.

"Blaire." My voice comes out in a croak, and a cough wracks my body before I can say anything else.

"Jesus, Madison. Here, drink this." She thrusts a bottle of sparkling water in front of my face, the cap already off with a paper straw.

Using my elbow as leverage, I shuffle up into a semi-sitting position. My fingers tremble as I reach for the water, and Blaire gently bats my hand away with a tsk. She brings it toward me, and I sip while she holds the bottle in front of my face.

The water is the perfect temperature, cool enough to quench my thirst but not too cold to irritate my throat. I take another sip and give myself a moment to calm my racing heart. My adrenaline starts to wane, leaving my hands shaky.

Giving myself another moment to catch up to what the hell is going on, I shuffle to lean back.

Blaire sets the bottle on the marble coaster on the nightstand next to the bed. She doesn't say a word, but I can feel her gaze like a physical touch. It burns against my skin, full of accusations and a fierce need for answers, but underneath that is genuine concern.

She waits exactly five seconds, enough time for me to settle back into the white, overstuffed pillows cushioning my back. It seems I'm in one of her many guest bedrooms, this one decorated in a white theme.

I guess my cloud guess isn't too far off, I think with a smirk.

"What the hell is going on, Madison?" Blaire's sharp gaze pins me to the comfortable bed, and I sigh.

I allow my eyes to fall closed for a second before I turn to look at her. I don't even know where to begin to answer that question. And honestly, I'm not even sure what the hell is going on. So I ignore it.

She stares at me as she drums her fingernails against the side of the wooden chair she's sitting on. It's next to the bed, and I idly wonder how long she's been sitting there, watching me. At a quick glance, she looks the same as always. It's the persona she's spent years cultivating, tweaking it with such brilliant subtly, it's no wonder she's feared as much as she's admired.

But since that day she cracked her armor open a little, I've been able to read her better, pick up on the little things. She looks picture-perfect with her jet-black hair artfully curled into beach waves and her designer clothes. But if you spend a second looking at her, like I am now, I easily spot the chipped polish on her fingernails, the wrinkles in her linen skirt, and the smudged mascara underneath her eyes.

All of which add up to her sitting in that uncomfortable chair and watching me for quite some time.

I feel the corner of my mouth tug up into a half smile and murmur, "I knew you cared."

Blaire huffs and shifts in her seat, fidgeting with cuffs of her short-sleeved linen shirt. "Don't be ridiculous. Of course, I care. We're . . . friends. Besides, I didn't want you to die inside my house. Do you know how many favors I'd have to pull to cover that up?"

A laugh slips free before I can stop it, and something in my chest aches with the movement. I grimace and sigh. Something doesn't feel right, and now that the adrenaline is wearing off, I'm feeling the effects of my half-cocked escape plan.

"You're going to be sore for a few days, but Richard was already here."

"Richard?"

She quirks a brow and stares at me for a moment. "Yes. My family's physician. For as much as we pay to keep him on call, he came right away. He relocated your shoulder and treated your road rash and the gash on your head."

With gentle fingertips, I feel around the tender spot on my head. A sharp prick of pain pulls a hiss from between my teeth. The neon green-and-blue tee I'm wearing distracts me from the pain. It's so bright, I wonder if it glows in the dark. But more alarmingly, it's not what I was wearing. I cock my head to the side as acid pools in my gut at the idea of someone undressing me while I was unconscious. "And my clothes?"

"There was no way I was letting you on Mother's two-thousand thread-count Egyptian cotton white sheets covered in dirt and dried blood. The clothes are from last year's spring collection I had in the back of my spare closet. And I did it alone, so don't worry."

In an ironic twist, her obvious discomfort at explaining her act of kindness eases my own uncertainty. Warmth settles into my heart, and I smile at my friend. "Thank you. I don't know what you did or how you did it, but thank you for helping me."

She huffs and rolls her eyes. "You're a valuable asset to me—at least that's what I told my mom when she asked why the hell there was an unconscious girl on our front porch. And she promised not to tell my dad, so we're good."

My brows scrunch together and I stare without seeing at a point over her shoulder. I refocus on her and ask, "How did I get here?"

"Well, I was hoping you could tell me. What the hell is going on and where have you been lately? And should I call my father's private security? I have it on good authority that they can make someone disappear for the right price."

She talks so casually of permanently removing someone that it eases what's left of my fried nerves. But something she says triggers a memory loose, and I jerk forward. My hair falls across my face as I throw back the blankets covering me. I don't even blink at the matching neon shorts I'm wearing, even though they're bright enough to stop traffic at dusk.

"I need to go. I have to find Matteo. And Leo, Dante."

Just as my legs swing over the side of the extra-tall platform California King bed, Blaire places a hand up in front of me—the universal sign for stop—and pins me with her infamous stare. But I stopped being intimidated by that look two kidnappings ago—and oh my god. I can't believe I just made some joke about that, even if it was in my head.

I rub the side of my head as I try to concentrate on what to do next.

Blaire's oblivious to my inner turmoil. I feel her gaze on me for another second before she speaks up. "Back up. Who are you talking about? Is that who you've been with this whole time?"

I shove to my feet, my bare toes sinking into the plush soft white rug underneath the bed. "Yes, no—it's complicated." I sigh, cutting myself off.

How can I explain the drastic and unexplainable turn my life took since the night of the masquerade?

"Sit down, Madison. Talk to me, let me help you."

The understanding and concern shining from her gaze has me

second-guessing myself. Without Lainey and Mary, I'm flying solo here. And I'm not naïve enough to think that I can take on the likes of the hitmen or assassins or whatever they are by myself. And I didn't forget whose house they carted me to, drugged and carried like a Christmas ham.

And I really, really need to find Leo and Dante—and *Matteo*.

I bite the side of my lip and release a breath. I don't even let myself think about the possibility of Aries, I haven't seen him in too long. Should I still be considering him? My mind drifts away in a little bit of a fuzzy pattern, and I really wonder if I should be concerned about it.

I shake my head a little to the left and refocus, biting the inside of my cheek before releasing a breath. "Alright. But I really need to make a call. Where's my phone?"

She hands me her phone already unlocked. "Here, use mine. You didn't have a phone or a purse when you got here."

My brows wrinkle. I could've sworn I had my purse around me still. I shake my head, my temple throbbing as I try to recall what happened before I woke up here.

"They must've taken it," I mutter.

"Who?"

I ignore her question, intent on calling one of my men. Staring at the keypad on Blaire's phone, my heart plummets with a sinking realization.

I don't know any of their numbers by heart.

"Shit." I look from the phone to my friend, my lifeline right now. "I need to find someone and I don't remember any numbers. But I need to find Matteo Rossi. He was—he was shot." I choke on the last word, coughing to clear my throat as sweat breaks out on the back of my neck.

"Shot? Jesus, okay. Sit down and drink this while I send a message," she says as she reaches over and grabs a to-go iced coffee cup. "Iced pumpkin spice latte."

I lean forward. "You'll find him?"

She takes her phone back and starts scrolling. "If he's in the city, I'll know within a few hours. If he's in the state, I'll know in twelve, and anything beyond that, it'll take a few days. But don't worry about it, we'll find him."

Relief fills me like an inflating balloon, hope swells at the uncharacteristically earnest look on her face. Some of the panic squeezing my chest exhales. Blaire has the kind of pull that people only aspire to have. If she says she'll find him, then I know she will.

She shakes the cup from side to side in a gentle motion, as if to entice me to take it from her.

I accept the coffee as the gift it is and bring it to my lips for a sip. Smooth, creamy espresso and coconut milk hit my taste buds, and she's right, it's a damn good latte. I shouldn't be surprised that she had someone make a specialty latte—one of my favorites.

And yet, I am. I don't often get taken care of. And if I'm being honest, it feels nice for someone to look after me for a change.

I sit back on the bed with a sigh and bring the coffee to my lips for another sip. Sweet notes of pumpkin and caramel burst on my tongue. My soul heaves a sigh of pleasure. It's the simple things in life, I suppose. Or maybe I'm being philosophical again, and in the midst of an existential crisis, no less. I'm not entirely sure I'm having one, but I can't say for sure that I'd *know* I was having one, either.

Hmm, something to think about later, I suppose. Blaire snaps her fingers in front of my face twice, and I startle, giving her a wide-eyed look.

"Are you okay? You were just staring at nothing with a strange look on your face."

"I'm fine. I'm just, well I guess I'm a little fuzzy, but thank you for the latte. It's really good and thoughtful."

She waves a hand in the air as if to brush off my thanks. "It's nothing. I thought you might need the caffeine and the sugar. And Barbara makes the best lattes within a twenty-mile radius."

"How do you even know she's the best within twenty miles?" I ask around a smile before I take another sip. From over the rim of my cup, I watch her type into her phone.

She quirks a brow at me. "Do you know anyone else serving pumpkin spice in the middle of one of the hottest summers on record?"

When I don't say anything, she puts down her phone and sits back in chair in one move. "Now, start at the beginning."

chapter seven

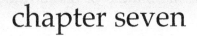

S he allows me a quarter of my perfect latte before she dives in. We both know I'm stalling, but she doesn't call me on it right away. I use the few minutes to collect my thoughts and figure out a way to explain this situation that's more likely to be the plot of an action movie than my actual life.

How can I explain it to her in a way that not only will she understand but that she won't judge me?

Am I really that worried about someone judging me for my interest—and involvement—with several men? If I was so worried about it, would I have even entertained the idea?

I think briefly of my cousin Lainey, and her relationship with three men. But more importantly, how happy she's been with them.

Blaire makes an impatient noise in the back of her throat.

The corner of my mouth tips up. "I'm surprised you waited that long."

"Stop deflecting. What's going on, Madison? I haven't seen you at any of the usual places. Where have you been?"

"It's—" I sigh, cutting myself off. "Before I begin, I need your word that this doesn't leave this room."

Blaire stares at me. The corners of her eyes tightening. She doesn't move, but I don't back down. In fact, I take a slow sip of my latte, enjoying the way it perks me up as I think of anything other than the worry churning in my gut about Matteo. Barbara really does know what she's doing.

She drums her fingernails against the arm of the wooden chair she's sitting in as she crosses her legs at the ankle.

"I'm not sure I can make that promise, Madison. If I think that you're in danger, or there's something I can do to help you, I can't promise you that I won't intervene."

I nod a few times, the movements slow as I trail the condensation down the cup with the tip of my index finger.

I tilt my head and look at her—really look at her. A weight sits on my shoulders, heavy and imposing. And I mentally weigh the options of confiding in someone who's not my sister or my cousin, someone who maybe wouldn't empathize.

Who wouldn't understand my complicated relationship with four very different men.

And aren't they the root of everything? The eye of this storm I've found myself trapped in?

"Alright. I suppose you're asking for me to trust you."

She tilts her head to the right, her posture ramrod straight as she looks me over. "Don't you already?"

I hold her gaze and will myself to focus. I'm scared, and I need her help to find Matteo. That's the truth of it, and I'm in a limited position here. I don't know who I can trust, outside of the men I need to find.

And she's my best ticket at finding them.

It's been forty-five minutes since I opened my mouth and filled Blaire in on the wild and seemingly outlandish story that's been my life for the last few weeks.

My latte is long gone, and my stomach started growling a minute ago. I'd be embarrassed if I hadn't just laid out my secrets for the gossip collector. With a jolt, I realize I have no idea what time of day it is, or even what day it is. I have no idea how long I've been gone, and the pressing need to find Matteo is riding my nerves hard now that I filled Blaire in.

Outside of her sending a message, I haven't heard anything in at least an hour.

"Okay, so let me get this straight."

Her posture has changed dramatically since I first woke up, no longer is her back ramrod straight, crammed into the wooden chair. Now she sits next to me on this oversized, overstuffed bed with more pillows than one person would ever need.

She had another latte delivered to the room about fifteen

minutes ago by someone I didn't see. She twirls the nearly empty cup between two fingers.

"You've been seeing four different men. For the past—how long again?" She looks over to me with a raised brow.

I shrug a shoulder. "I don't know. What is *seeing*? I mean, technically, Matteo and I are exes. We aren't *seeing* each other—"

"He was your first call when you were in a life-or-death situation," she interrupts.

"Well, I mean, I don't know if I'd call it *that* exactly."

"You were kidnapped and stranded in the middle of a burning building. What would you call it?" Her tone conveys the skepticism in her gaze.

My chest hitches when I think about it like that. He was my first choice—the only choice at the time. Now, I might have more than one option. Even though I hope I'm never in a situation like that again, there's something warming about that knowledge.

"I'd call it complicated."

"But you both said *I love you* right before some guys stormed that apartment." She says it like a statement, not a question or clarification. Like she's just patiently leading me to the conclusion she already reached miles ago.

I nod my head a few times and loll my head along the backboard to look at her. "I know it sounds like I'm getting around, but it's not like that. I like them."

"Of course you do. Who doesn't want a bunch of hot men panting after you? That's literally why we summer in the Hamptons."

I bite my lip as I think about her choice analogy. A year ago, I would've spent at least a month in the Hamptons with her and other girls from school. I never really strung anyone along, but I never minded a little harmless flirting. It's a lost artform, a necessary step that too many people skip.

"What about your mystery man who's been crashing the summer events?"

I lift a shoulder and let my mind wander to Aries for just a moment. Finding out his name is my priority after Matteo.

"Yeah. Him too."

She waggles her phone in the air. "I can find out who he is with a few phone calls."

"Where's the fun in that?" My grin grows wide.

"And you're really not going to choose?" Her voice gets high-pitched at the end of her question, high enough that it brings a smile to my face. I don't know if I've ever seen Blaire flustered, and I'd say this is as close as she gets.

A laugh bubbles up from my chest, easing some of the tension. "No, Blaire. I'm not going to choose."

"And they're all just . . . just *okay* with this?" Her eyes widen, and her mouth drops open as she stares at me.

"I mean, I'm not really sure. I think?"

She blows a breath out, puffing her cheeks for a moment. "Honestly, Madison, it sounds like the plot of some really bad action film. The kind with a hot girl who gets herself into trouble and needs to be saved."

"I know." I don't let the sting show on my face. I know those movies. The ones where the love interest is of no value to the heroes of the film. She's just there as eye candy.

"But if you think that's bad, you should listen to what happened to my cousin Lainey."

She shakes her head as if to clear it. "Okay. But before we dive into that, let's stay focused. So, what happened then?"

"Right." I pause and think of my words carefully. I was dreading this part of the story.

Despite what she said the other day about having some plot to take him down with her mom, I can't say for certain that her history with Dale Hardin won't cloud her reaction.

Trepidation skirts down my back, and I blow out a breath, exhaling the air slowly. A vintage-looking oil painting with a modern frame snags my attention across the room. So I use it as my focal point and talk to it as I recall the events at the Senator's house with as little emotion as possible.

I detail what happened when I woke up, how I felt, and what I heard and saw. But I leave out the really scary parts, and I try to make it as impersonal as I can.

Stick to the facts, I remind myself.

It's almost like an out-of-body experience as I hear myself explaining how I saw Matteo get shot, how I fought like my life depended on it, how they overpowered me in the end.

All the grief and terror melts away under the weighted blanket of detachment.

I tell her the dark thoughts I had, the deep-rooted fear that squeezed my heart in a vice-like grip. How I thought that I was going to die.

But fate had other plans.

And then, how I woke up in the back of a van, scared and afraid. And all that fear and terror just carried with me, only now it was amplified by adrenaline.

I hear the words tumbling out of my mouth like I'm reading some sort of book, emotionless and without inflection. In some ways, I think it's easier for me to recount everything this way.

I hear myself explain how I was given some sort of tranquilizer by the masked men, but I'm not really sure what it was that either malfunctioned or its intention was to just paralyze me.

I recount the bone-deep dread unlike anything I've ever felt before when my mind was conscious but my body betrayed me, paralyzed and unable to respond to countless demands I shouted at it.

The lack of power, the complete vulnerability at being at someone's mercy.

I've never been much of a gambler, but I always trust my instincts. And right now, they're screaming at me to keep the senator's involvement to myself.

It's quiet for several moments after I finish talking. The moments turn into minutes, and they start adding up.

Ten minutes go by, and I still don't make a sound. I'm waiting for her response or reaction, I suppose.

I realize with a start that this is my truth. And it's so very different from anything I would've expected. It's dark and gritty and overwhelming.

And it makes me feel . . . less than.

Damaged.

Other.

A single tear slides down my cheek, splashing against my collarbone. Another one follows it. I roll my lips inward to stave off the sob that's threatening to erupt from my soul.

Something inside cries for the girl I was a month ago. She was strong and independent and *whole*.

Each encounter claimed part of me, robbing me of my naïvety of the underbelly of society. Ripping away my faith to see the good in everything.

The well of grief seems endless, but I know from experience it isn't. I know it'll pass, as all things in life do.

Without a word, Blaire reaches over and curls her hand over mine. She squeezes my hand once.

I didn't know I was waiting for something until now. But I think I was waiting for her acceptance, her understanding, and her belief in me.

I turn to look at her at the same time she looks at me. Not for the first time, the emotionless mask that she so often wears is gone. Sometimes, she wears it for so long, I worry it's going to become permanent. But right now, all I see is a vulnerable, compassionate, kind-hearted woman who I'm lucky to call a friend.

A tear rolls down her cheek as she stares at me with conviction.

"I'll take care of them for you, Madison, of that I can promise you." The promise in her words is fueled by the conviction in her tone.

I nod as another tear rolls down my cheek. With each tear that carves a path of pain down my face, the horror of the recounted events feels a little less loud.

I didn't realize how much I needed someone to believe in me at this moment, to be on my side. How much I needed someone to offer me the kindness and the care that I would so readily offer anyone in my position.

I squeeze my fingers around her hand.

"Thank you, Blaire. I don't know what I would do if I woke up on someone else's doorstep. I don't know where I would be. And given the way my life has turned out the last few days, few hours—however long I've been here—I hazard a guess it wouldn't be anything like the kindness you've shown me. Thank you."

"Of course. You don't have to worry about that, I'm always going to be here for you. And I promise I'll take care of those men that hurt you." Rage sparkles from her eyes, and my responding smile shouldn't be as pleased as it is.

I can't help it. There's something intoxicating about revenge.

Before I can say anything else, there's a knock at the door.

Blaire sighs and wipes the tears from her cheeks, checking to make sure her face is perfect. She slides a finger underneath her bottom eyelashes, catching any smudged mascara.

I don't even want to look in the mirror to see what kind of mess I look like. Raccoon eyes from old mascara and a bird's nest of a hairstyle. Anybody who comes in this room can just forgive me, or they can turn the other way, for all I care.

But Blaire doesn't have that luxury.

She hops off the bed and adjusts her clothes, smoothing out nonexistent wrinkles on her shirt. She smooths her hair back off her face and tucks away any flyaways.

I watch in amazement as she visibly straightens as she puts herself together.

The moment the mask slides over her face is instant. The air around her changes, and I bet if I could see auras, hers would've just changed. She crosses the room, grasps the ornate brass door handle, and pulls the door open.

"Excuse me, Miss. I'm sorry to interrupt but there's someone insisting on speaking to you."

Blaire sighs through her nose, the noise conveying more than her words could. "Can't this wait, Henry? I'm kind of busy here."

"I'm sorry, Miss, but he insisted. And he's been here for the last thirty minutes. He said if I don't get you right this second, he's going to, and I quote, *kick the door down and go room to room to find you*. Would you like me to call the cops, Miss?"

"No, it's probably some kid thinking he has a stake with me because I flirted with him at the party two nights ago. I'll take care of it." She looks over her shoulder at me. "I'll be right back, okay? It's better if I just handle these things and instill fear firsthand. Just make yourself at home, and when I get back, we'll figure out your next steps. Okay? You're not alone, Madison."

"No problem. I'll be here. Maybe we can check for news about Matteo when you get back?" I hold my breath while I wait for her answer.

"Of course," she murmurs as she leaves.

The door catches on the rug, leaving it cracked open. I exhale a breath and stare up at the ceiling, feeling emotionally drained.

chapter eight

Ares

I clasp my hands behind my back as I stand inside the ornate foyer of the Hawthorne Estate. I suppress the annoyance that's trying to escape my chest and look at the overabundance of wealth in the foyer. Distaste curls my upper lip before I can reel it in. It's a motherfucking foyer. Why do people need inlaid pearl handles and four-inch crown molding—and are those fucking diamonds imbedded in the floor?

I scuff the toe of my shoe against the white-and-black mosaic pattern on the floor. A smudge streaks across what I think is black onyx, and I smirk. There's something about these small rebellions that quiet the raging storm inside me to a tolerable level. Enough to pretend that everything's fine.

Sure, everything's fine. My brother's in the hospital, and I have two more hours to figure out where the hell my girl is before he does something stupid that could fuck up years' worth of work.

I roll my shoulders back, my muscles tensing and flexing underneath the expensive fabric of the charcoal Tom Ford suit.

Dress for the part you want.

I hear my mother's voice echoing in my mind, a line she often told me when I was younger. Before she agreed to ship me across the world. Before I splintered from this fucked-up family.

While I'd rather be in sweatpants and a tee, that kind of attire doesn't inspire the same amount of deference upon a single glance.

So I dressed the part I need to be today to get what I want.

What I fucking *need.*

I look around to distract myself. The estate manager didn't want to let me in, but I gave him enough incentive to get me what I want. And right now, that's information. Because even though I said I was content to play cat-and-mouse with her at our shared events, I was waiting for my Raven to come back to me. And I'm nothing if not observant.

Besides, all bets were off the moment those two motherfuckers snatched her from my apartment.

So who better to ask than the queen of Manhattan.

For now, at least.

Her name has been passed around in hushed whispers for long enough to know that she's someone most people fear. Unfortunately for her, I've seen what real monsters look like, and she isn't it.

They hide behind politician's smiles and overpriced suits. Behind greased palms and murder coverups. They flash their ten-thousand-dollar smile and rub elbows with the upper one-percent of society.

True sociopaths who shake hands with lawmakers and famous movers-and-shakers in the world with one hand. And with the other, they clutch a knife, just waiting until you turn around so they can slam it into your back. If they don't stab you, then they threaten your loved ones until they can bend you to their will. They make you their puppet.

But I'm no one's bitch.

So, no, I'm not intimidated by the outstanding show of wealth around me or the rumors about Blaire. Fortunately for her, she has something that I need.

And when I find Raven, I'm going to tie her to me in a move so permanent, she'll rule alongside me. Hell, if Blaire Hawthorne can give me information to find my girl, I might even be feeling generous enough to let her keep the borough.

I don't fucking need it anyway. Between Matteo and me, we've got enough plans in place to effectively have our thumbs in pies across the world.

My phone vibrates in my pocket, distracting me from plans of future domination. I slide it out to check the preview text on the screen. I've sent enough feelers out about Raven's kidnapping that I'd be an idiot to ignore any messages.

It's an address from Seth, a friend I made a few years ago. His hacking skills are legendary, and he has almost as many connections as I do.

My heart fucking stops as the street name sounds familiar.

It jumpstarts with a bang, echoing in my ears as I plug in the address and pull it up on my map app. It takes a moment to populate, and I can physically feel my blood pressure rise as the little blue dot hovers over the red dot—my current location.

My instincts roar in my ears, demanding I tear this place apart until I find her. I glance around, looking for cameras or lurking house staff, my mind spinning with my next steps.

I expected information from my little impromptu visit, but this isn't what I had in mind. It seems someone made a request for information on Matteo's whereabouts from an IP address registered here. People are too lax with their technological security, and thankfully, that helps me today.

Logic prevails and I throw a temporary leash around my rage. I need to be sure she's here before I make a move.

I check my watch for the fifth time in the last five minutes, and I clench my fists before relaxing them. I'm not going to get what I want by throwing my fists around and puffing my chest up like some primate. As much as I hate to admit it, I'm not the king of this jungle and one perceived wrong move, and I could kiss my easy chance of getting my Raven goodbye.

Not that I'd leave her. No fucking way.

It'll just be harder, not impossible.

Outside of this thirty-thousand square foot ostentatious display of grandeur where someone is definitely overcompensating for something else, I am the king.

That's the thing that so many of these people in this upper echelon of society fail to realize. By displaying your wealth in such an unavoidable way, you make yourself a target.

Now, I've found it much more prudent to lie in the grass, waiting, stalking my prey quietly from behind bullshit smiles and overpriced champagne flutes at charity functions where people have more money than sense.

And unfortunately for me, or fortunately for them, depending on how you look at it, I'm not ready to pounce yet. So, instead, here I stand with my hands clasped behind my back inside a two-thousand-square-foot foyer with a Rembrandt on the wall, waiting for a nineteen-year-old girl to confirm the information I just received.

The sounds of heels clacking against the black onyx-and-diamond tile floor precedes her. As I turn around to face her, I swipe my hand over my mouth, concealing my slow-curling smile that feels malicious. I don't want to show my hand yet, and as it stands, I don't know enough about her allegiances to know where she'll land on this—and her culpability.

I make it my mission to know who everyone is and where they stand. But this girl is nothing if not the central hub of information, her personal interests vary depending on the day, so I'm working with half of what I'm used to.

I'll take those odds.

It takes a concentrated effort to keep the pleasant smile on my face and not reveal the snarling mass of rage and testosterone that's trapped inside my chest, swirling and fighting to have control.

But I do. I like to keep all my secrets locked up tight. I'm a vault, really. And I've never been more thankful for my collection of secrets than I am right now.

I should feel grateful, because for the first time in my life, I have a selfish reason to use my network of crows—my connections and informants over the years. I always thought the name was fitting.

When they band together, they're a murder.

And that's exactly what kind of power I wield with them under my guidance. A whispered word hits the right ear, and twenty minutes later, I have information. And if it's not the information I need, it points me in the right direction.

I have a feeling I'm going to be participating in a trade today.

Silence settles between us. I don't know if I was expecting her to greet me with that calculated politeness I so often see her using at the extravagant parties we've co-frequented, but I get nothing. I see why they call her the ice queen. And if I were a lesser man, I might be intimidated, but I grew up with monsters far scarier than anything she could ever dream of.

I feel the time tick by, anxiety tiptoeing down my spine with each second that ticks by, digging its nails in with each pass.

Time is not a luxury I have right now. Despite my mounting urgency, I force my body to relax, consciously unclenching my muscles. I loosen my posture ever so slightly in the way that I've perfected.

It says *hey, I'm not a threat. Come a little closer. Tell me your secrets. Bend to my will.*

So I cut right to the chase and hold her gaze. "I hear you have something that belongs to me."

She stops five feet away and stares at me. The ice-queen gaze, as so many of her peers have referred to it. She tips her chin up and stares down her nose that her daddy probably bought her for her sixteenth birthday without moving any closer. "I'm sure you're mistaken. Everything in here belongs to the Hawthornes." She holds her hands out at her sides, palms up as if to indicate the very space we're standing in.

I nod my head a few times and casually take a step to the side and admire the knock-off sculpture of David.

"A girl."

"You'll have to be more specific. I know lots of girls."

I slide my hands into the pockets of my pants as the side of my mouth curls up in a smile that's anything but friendly as I assess her like the predator I am. She folds her arms across her chest and raises a brow at me.

Ah, so she fancies herself an alpha too, it seems. I rock back on my heels and let a taste of the swirling mass of rage shine through my gaze.

"Are we pretending that you don't have someone stashed away inside your giant empty house that your daddy doesn't know about?"

It's a gamble, but I've picked up a hint of discord in the Hawthorne household, and my money's on dear ol' dad.

I narrow my eyes as I see what I was waiting for. A tightening in the corners of her eyes. It's small, but it's enough. Ah, so I was right. Daddy Dearest doesn't know she has someone—hopefully my Raven—here.

She clenches her jaw. "I'm listening."

"Five-four, red hair, gorgeous. Ring any bells?"

"Maybe."

I sigh, tired of this game already. "I'd be willing to make a trade."

Is that interest gleaming in her eye or just opportunity?

I'm disappointed that someone I thought my Raven could trust would so easily trade her for a favor. But it doesn't matter. Soon she'll be with me, and I'll be able to protect her from everybody, including the likes of Blaire fucking Hawthorne.

Suddenly, everything feels heavy. Weighted exhaustion rolls over me like the fog on a San Francisco morning.

"Look, quite honestly, I'm exhausted. And I don't have the mental fortitude, or the will to go round and round with you, so why don't you just tell me what you want. I'll get back what belongs to me. And then I'll be on my way."

She shifts her weight. "What kind of trade?"

I stretch my neck from side to side and look at her. "Don't mistake my kindness for weakness. I'll just as easily barge in your house and get what I came for without all the niceties. And if you think your little butler would be the one to stop me, you'd be mistaken. You have no idea who I am, or what I'm capable of."

She drops her arms and takes a step forward. Her gaze hardens, anger pursing her lips. "And you have no idea what I'm capable of. You're not taking her."

I raise a brow. "Ah, so you do have my Raven. Nice to see you have some backbone after all. I was worried all those little hushed rumors I heard about you all these years were nothing more than embellished stories from boys who wanted to fuck you and girls who wanted to be you."

"There's always a little bit of truth in every rumor, wouldn't you say, Rafe Rhodes?"

I grin, a cruel slash across my face. "Ah, you've heard of me then. And here I was beginning to think I'd gone unnoticed."

Frustration makes my voice loud, echoing off the plaster walls and domed ceiling above us.

Blaire steps to the side, like she's blocking me from moving past her even though I haven't shifted at all.

My annoyance morphs into anger, and I control my breathing so it doesn't escalate further. The last thing I need to do is clean up another mess.

Apprehension slides along my skin, itchy and distracting. My brother is in an unprotected hospital room, and I'm dancing around the subject of why I'm here. Sure, he has Leo and Dante there. But Dante has other things to do, like track down who the fuck shot my brother and snatched my girl. The only reason I'm not hunting with him is because someone had to retrieve my Raven.

And I'll be damned if I send my little brother to find her.

I open my mouth, done with this shit, a demand on the tip of my tongue when I feel it. A shift in the air, as if the particles had stopped and are now rearranging themselves to accommodate for someone else. The energy moves around me in a different way.

And I find my gaze pulled toward the left, my body following suit, searching, until my gaze collides with hers.

"Aries."

Time stops. I stare at her like she's a mirage, and I'm dying of thirst.

chapter nine

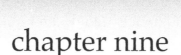

Through the cracked door, the low murmur of voices piques my attention. When Blaire doesn't return right away, I decide to investigate. It beats sitting here in this spare room I've dubbed the cloud, battling my anxiety as I wait for something to happen.

Besides, I'm feeling a sudden need to move, an itch underneath my skin that demands I get up, move, do something. I've never doubted my intuition before, and while it's not screaming *danger* at me, it's still urging me enough that I'm going to take notice.

I feel like I'm fourteen again, sneaking out of the dorm rooms after curfew as I cautiously walk down the hallway on soft footsteps, hugging the wall as much as possible.

I have a half a second to wonder if I'm eavesdropping on my friend's private conversation. But then I remind myself that if she's talking to Dale, Senator Hardin's son, I want to know what he has to say.

Was he in on it? Did he know I'd be dropped off at Blaire's house? Does he even know what happened to me—what his father orchestrated?

There are too many unanswered questions swirling around my mind, and I need answers.

As I creep toward the end of the hallway, the voices get louder, but the recognition I anticipated doesn't quite happen in the same way. I don't hear Dale's voice, but there is something familiar about the masculine voice drifting down the hallway.

Still in the shadows, I listen for a few moments, and then I hear a word that changes everything.

Raven.

My heart leaps inside my chest as I imagine my Aries on the other side of this wall, standing in Blaire's foyer.

I quicken my steps without a second thought of being quiet and rush to the end of the hallway, where it opens up to the atrium-style foyer.

I can feel how wide my eyes are, but what's more alarming is the hope blossoming inside my chest. I can't shake the association I've unconsciously made between Aries and *safe*.

A little gasp leaves me as soon as I see him. Dark-brown hair with natural highlights and long black lashes framing dark-brown eyes. Tall, broad-shouldered, dressed in head-to-toe black. As if he would be in anything else.

He's a prince of darkness.

He can offer pleasure with one hand just as easily as he delivers pain with the other.

His hair is styled back in that messy way that says he ran his fingers through it all day and not *I spent an hour in front of the mirror*.

I don't know if it's because he's one of the four men I've kissed in as many weeks, or because I made myself a promise in the darkest moments trapped in my mind that I'm going to take what I want—and that includes him—or if it's because I just had this conversation with Blaire, and everything feels so fresh, surface-level and ready to burst.

But I can't stop my traitorous libido from perking up at the sight of him. She doesn't give a shit that we've been through hell and back in the last few days, she's ready to climb Aries like her personal tree. And frankly, never get down. The bitch will build a tree house and camp out forever.

"Aries." His name falls from my lips like a prayer.

He freezes for a moment, before he turns to look at me, a slow smile spreading across his perfect face. Afternoon light filters down through the domed atrium ceiling, casting him in a soft spotlight, and I get my first unobstructed glimpse. The intensity I've always felt around him balloons between us as he pins me with his dark-eyed gaze.

He holds me hostage with one look. It's raw and heated—and possessive. A shiver rolls over me, blanketing me in a sort of giddy anticipation.

I witness his transformation with parted lips. One minute, he looks like some long-lost Viking, ready to storm this village to take what he wants. And the next, his eyes shudder and offer me another glimpse of inside his soul.

Relief softens his tensed shoulders as his gaze quickly jumps to scan my body before coming back to my eyes. He reaches my side in three blinks. He slides his hands into the hair at the nape of my neck and tilts my face up to his.

I can only imagine the tangles back there, but he doesn't even flinch. He just holds me with a possessive gentleness I wasn't anticipating.

Backlit by the waning sunlight, I study Aries up close. Long sooty lashes frame dark brown eyes. A starburst of amber forms a ring around his pupil, and I decide it's one of the most unique patterns I've ever seen. It reminds me of a constellation.

I curl my fingers over his forearms, anchoring him to me. He exhales, though it does nothing to alleviate the tension lining his body.

My lashes flutter closed at the euphoric feeling of having him close to me again. For a moment there, I didn't know if I'd ever feel anyone's welcome touch again. And here he is, my mystery man, sliding his thumbs underneath my eyes with gentle strokes and catching my tears.

"I've been looking for you, Raven."

The rich tenor of his voice, like smoke and aged whiskey, washes over me and sparks against my frayed nerve endings. I think I'd recognize his voice anywhere. The corner of my mouth tips up in a nostalgic smile. Those words are reminiscent of the ones I spoke to him in the ladies' lounge.

"You have?" My words are soft, disbelief draping over each syllable.

"Oh, Raven, did you think you could hide from me this whole time?" he asks with a playful tilt of his mouth.

Hope is a dangerous thing. It's destruction masquerading as virtue. And it only takes one teaspoon to poison the well.

And right now, Aries is giving me more hope that I could've ever dreamed of. Even though I know the risks, I can't stop the slow flutter of hope blooming inside my chest.

With my heart beating a rhythm just for him, I push up onto my tiptoes and bridge the gap between our mouths.

I brush my lips across his, once, twice, before I settle back on my heels. It's a touch of affection, one that says *I'm so glad you're here.*

He doesn't press for more, and I'm thankful. With my newfound promise to live life to its fullest, I don't know that I would stop him if he escalated this innocent touch to something more deviant.

I'm keenly aware that we have an audience watching our every move, but I find that I don't care much right now.

"How did you know I was here?"

"I'll always find you, Raven. In this life and the next."

A flush of adrenaline slides over me with his words, leaving goosebumps in its wake.

Two sentences, a combination of vowels and consonants. And yet, they're arranged in such a way, shrouded in conviction and laced with purpose. They're charged.

It feels more than a promise.

A declaration. A binding agreement between two souls that not even death himself can sever.

At any other time, from almost any other man, I'd laugh him off and move on. But there's something about Aries, a magnetism that refuses to be ignored.

And I'm just hopeful enough to stop and listen.

I close my eyes and quietly exhale. I give myself exactly thirty seconds to bask in his attention, his warmth, his promise.

I resist the urge to further eliminate the space between our bodies. Even though every part of me begs to wrap my arms around him. I'm afraid if I do that, I might not let go.

My emotions are so close to the surface. As it is, it'd be so easy to crack and splinter. To let them bleed out all over everyone and everything. And I can't do that.

Not yet, at least.

I have other things I have to do before I can allow myself the time to break down.

He rests his forehead against mine. "We have a lot to talk about, but not here," he murmurs.

I feel Blaire's gaze on us, but I only have eyes for him. His aura is large enough to wrap us up in a protective bubble. As if he's conscious of it, he moves to the side, effectively blocking Blaire's view.

"Are you okay? Are you hurt?"

I have no idea how I look, but probably worse for wear, judging by the way his brow furrows as he scans me again, undoubtedly looking for any sign of injury.

"I'm alright, thanks to Blaire."

"Good, good. Time to go, Raven." He turns and takes a step toward the door.

I pull back a little, still holding his hand. "Wait. I—I need to find someone before I can leave, and Blaire's helping me with that."

"Whoever it is, I'm sure I can find them." He flashes me a smile, but there's urgency behind his eyes, and it's freaking me out.

I tug on our hands again, not to untangle them but to give myself some time to work through the confusion clouding my mind.

"Oh? And just how exactly do you expect to find Matteo Rossi, heir to the five families? Send him a friend request?" Sarcasm drips from Blaire's words, but the silence after them feels heavy.

I jerk my head toward her, my mouth parted in surprise. "What are you doing?"

"Oh, come on, Madison. Everyone knows Matteo Rossi is the illusive heir to the Italian mob. One of the five Italian families that rule the east coast. And if *he* thinks he can locate him so easily, I say we let him. While you stay safely with me, of course." She sneers at Aries the entire time but her words are meant for me.

He takes two steps to end up back at my side, but he's not looking at me. He's giving Blaire a look of pure calculation, mouth flat and eyes blazing.

"As a matter of fact, I know exactly where Matteo Rossi is."

My eyes feel wide as I stare at another instance of two worlds colliding. My lips part on a breath. "What? How?"

He shifts his focus to me, his eyes softening exponentially. "Let's just say we have history. I make it my business to know everything. What I'm more curious about is how you know Matteo."

Blaire snorts, and I can feel the air shift again. She's shoring up her infamous frosty persona, and she's going to unleash it on Aries. "Madison and Matteo go way back. In fact, they—"

I clear my throat to cut her off. "That's not important right now. What's important is Matteo. Is he okay? What happened?"

"He's staying in a private room at a hospital I have connections with. He should be discharged tomorrow."

I squeeze my fingers around his hand and push up to my toes. "Okay, let's go right now. I want to see him."

He searches my gaze for a moment, and I don't know what he's looking for, but I can only assume he's seeing my anxiety and eagerness. I can only imagine what sort of conclusions he's drawing, but I find that I just don't care. The need to see Matteo, to see that he's okay, rides me too hard to care about much of anything right this second.

Without taking his gaze from mine, he laces his fingers with mine and tugs. "Let's go. I'll take you there."

Movement catches the corner of my eye as Blaire crosses the room to stand right next to us. Aries doesn't flinch, keeping his gaze and hold steady. It's exactly what I need right now, and I don't question the how or why of it, I'm just grateful he's here.

"I don't think so. She's a friend. And you're not. She's not going anywhere with you. And just how, exactly, did you come by this information on Matteo?"

Her acidic tone startles me, and I pull my focus from Aries to look at her. "It's okay, Blaire. This is Aries."

She taps her lips with a perfectly painted nail in mock emotion. "So strange, because I thought this was Rafe Rhodes."

A grin tugs up the corner of my mouth. Rafe. I toss his name around inside my head for a moment, enjoying the way it feels to find another piece of the puzzle.

"Rafe? Now that's not what I would have expected your name to be."

"It's short for Raphael. Besides, I like it when you call me Aries," he murmurs as he runs his thumb along the back of hand. A slow sweet up and back down. A simple movement shouldn't be so flirtatious, shouldn't feel this good.

Blaire clears her throat, the noise jarring enough to snap me out of the shared moment. I feel Blaire's gaze, hard and intense, on me, and a lick of shame coats my belly. It's easy—too easy—to slip into that flirtatious role that we so quickly found ourselves in.

"Maddie, you ended up bleeding and broken on my doorstep not that long ago. You're insane if you think I'm just gonna let you walk off with him. You didn't even know his real name."

I bite my lip as I shift to face her. "You know I have to go. I have to find out what happened to Matteo." I pause with a shrug of my shoulder. "And I trust him, Blaire. I don't know how else to explain it."

"Stay here, where it's safe. I've made some calls, and I've got my staff calling around all the local hospitals asking about people who match his description with a gunshot wound. They'll let me know as soon as they find out, and I'll take you there myself."

"No need. I already know where he is. I just came from the hospital. He's at All Saints across town," Aries, because he'll always be Aries to me, says.

Blaire nods twice as she glares at Aries. "Great. Then we all go together, let me grab my purse."

I glance from her clenched jaw to Aries's hand wrapped around mine as I worry my bottom lip. "You've done so much already. And I'm so, so grateful, but I don't want to take up any more of your time."

"It's not a burden, trust me. I'll call for a car."

chapter ten

Madison

Aries escorts me to the town car Blaire called with a hand on my lower back. The collection of ever-growing butterflies don't care that I'm still dressed in a neon tie-dye outfit or that we're on the way to the hospital to visit my ex-boyfriend-turned-boyfriend after he was shot.

No, they don't care about any of that. All they can do is focus on the warmth of his palm on my lower back, soaring around my insides and leaving me with a giddy sort of excitement.

He stays close to my back and slides into the car after me. I hear Blaire's huff of irritation, but my butterflies are still swirling, tangling up with the acidic leeches of anxiety that slowly trudge around inside my gut.

She slides in last and sits across from us. The driver closes the door behind her as Aries scoots closer to me, his thigh pressing against mine. I take comfort in the warmth he's offering me and resist the urge to lay my head on his shoulder. For as much as I've thought about him and as much as he might know my body intimately, I don't really know all that much about him.

I stare out of the tinted window. The city comes alive in a different way when the sun makes its descent. The sky is surprisingly clear, letting the moon glow fat and heavy in the cityscape. It's nearly a full moon, and the last time there was a full moon—on Friday the thirteenth, might I add—some bad things happened.

Let's hope lady luck is on our side this time.

Nervousness swirls in my gut, like a swarm of angry bees. I'm grateful for Aries's presence beside me, even if I don't fully understand why or how he found me. Or how he knows about Matteo.

I have too many questions, most of which are unanswered. The answers I did get only sprouted new questions.

Pain spikes in my head and I hold back a wince. I massage my temple with light pressure, just circling my fingertips over the throbbing area.

The truth is that I don't know what I don't know. It's an unsettling predicament for a girl who thrives with a bit of control. The bottom line is I need more information.

But maybe just not today.

I don't think I can take much more today.

I read an article once saying that your body has a natural defense mechanism. And if it gets overburdened, it simply makes the decision for you unconsciously. Physically, mentally, emotionally—

your instincts take over to protect you.

How many girls have I seen roaming the halls of St. Rita's in a permanent state of numbness or a general lack of care about anything around them?

I used to think they were spoiled or vapid, but I look back on those moments with a new lens. I can't help but wonder what sort of trauma they had faced.

How many times do you face a trauma before it simply ceases to be traumatic? Not because the actions themselves aren't traumatic but just because your mind, your body, your very spirit can't fully comprehend them.

Mom always said I was really good at compartmentalizing. But maybe, maybe I've just been numbing myself.

That's a sobering thought.

And since most things in life are temporary, one day, one thing is going to push me, and I won't be able to numb myself to it. I won't be able to shut up the uncomfortable, itchy feeling that threatens to overtake me, to pull me out to sea from the vicious rip current.

I won't be able to shove it back in a box and throw away the key like I've done so many other times.

And I'll explode.

"I don't make a habit of letting strangers into my car, you know," Blaire says, breaking the silence and my heavy thoughts. She arches a perfectly manicured eyebrow at Aries.

I lean my head back against the seat, turning to see his response. Even if I was feeling up to it, I don't think I need to weigh in. Aries is from the same circles as we are. If he doesn't know who the players are by now, I guess now is as good of a time as any.

He looks up from his phone and regards my friend with a blank expression. "But I'm not a stranger, am I? We've met before."

"Remind me." Her tone is cool. Her armored mask is in full force, not a crack to be found. It's a challenge, and we all know it.

Awkwardness bleeds into the available space inside the car , and I can't quell the urge to smooth out the wrinkles of discomfort that permeate the air. I can practically hear my late Southern grandmother's voice in my ear, encouraging me to ease the tension.

I shift in my seat, the leather sticking to my skin despite the air conditioning at full blast. Satisfied with her apparent point made, Blaire looks at her phone, studiously ignoring Aries next to me. She taps away, no doubt plotting the downfall of the next person who crosses her path. For all I know, she's checking security feeds or asking for updates from whoever she gets her information from.

Aries types on his phone too, his brow furrowed and jaw tensed. My gaze strays to the bridge of his nose. There's a small bump that suggests it was broken at some point before. Not that it deters from his looks, if anything, it only enhances them.

I imagine him as some sort of dark knight, hidden in plain sight by his tailored suits and impeccable taste. I bet he's left a trail of broken hearts and bruised egos behind him.

As if he can feel my gaze on him, he glances up from underneath his long, dark lashes for a moment. It should be a crime for a man to have eyelashes that most women would kill for.

A smirk curls the corner of his pouty lips, but he doesn't look at me or say anything. He just lets me look my fill.

And so, I do.

I scan him from head to toe, enjoying the freedom of looking freely. There's something familiar, comforting even about him.

And in the dim light filtering through the tinted windows of this town car, I'm not entirely surprised to find that he matches up to my internal estimation of him.

I was a little worried that I had built him up so much in my head. And of course, all of the interactions with Leo and Dante and Matteo too.

For a moment, I thought there was no way he could measure up, that I'd fabricated our magnetism, and he might pale in comparison to my memories.

I shouldn't have worried, though. He holds his own space inside my head—and inside my libido. An equal space next to the other three.

The ride from Blaire's house to the hospital felt like an eternity and no time at all. New York City traffic often feels like that to me. Some days, one mile can take an hour.

But we're here now. Walking toward the bank of elevators in the underground parking garage of the hospital.

Anxiety and anticipation fight for dominance, turning my gut into a mosh pit. And over all of that chaos, gratitude washes over me like a fine sea spray, misting me with droplets of thankfulness. Not only has Blaire been a surprising ally in all of this, I think we've bonded in a way neither one of us would've predicted.

We board the elevator, and I shake my hands out a little, trying to expel the nervousness. I know Aries said Matteo was fine, but I can't shake the nagging feeling tugging inside my gut. My worry feels like a rising tide, refusing to stop until I lay eyes on him myself.

For just a split second, I lose hold of the tight grip I have on my emotions, and I feel a little unhinged. No matter how many times I try to shove everything back into their compartments, my once perfectly poised and organized boxes are now bursting and overflowing. The material buckles under the weight of everything, the clasp straining under the emotional overload.

Intelligently, I realize this is a coping mechanism. I learned all about it last year in my psych class. And it's one I've had for so long that it essentially infused with my personality. And still, I can't stop.

And in some ways, I recognize focusing all of my worry on Matteo allows me the luxury to not think about everything I just went through. To not dwell on the fact that someone snatched me right inside an apartment that was supposed to be safe.

The elevator jerks to a stop on the fourth floor, and I jump.

"Jesus," I murmur, pressing a hand to my chest and feeling my heart race underneath my palm, desperate.

Okay, so maybe I'm not doing such a good job of compartmentalizing. I'm in uncharted territory, and I don't think our school's fancy counselor covers this kind of traumatic experience. So, for now, I layer bubble wrap around my boxes of trauma and anxiety and force them to stack upon one another in nice, neat, little organizational cubes.

"You okay, Raven?" He steps into me, the fabric of his suit brushing against my bare skin.

The elevator settles and the doors open. I flash him a small smile. "Yeah, yeah, I'm fine. You really didn't have to come with, you know."

"If you think for a single moment I'm gonna let you out of my sight after everything that just happened, you don't know me at all."

My thoughts fumble over one another. The conviction in his voice speaks to the darkest parts of me, enticing them. But there's something nagging at me, a piece that I'm missing.

"Well, she doesn't know you, does she? Nobody does." Blaire doesn't look back as she starts down the hallway toward the reception desk, the clicking of her heels loud in the quiet space.

"She will," he murmurs, staring at Blaire's back.

With a familiar ease, he slides his palm against mine, lacing our fingers together, and leads the way behind Blaire.

She's chatting with someone behind the desk, but their voices are too low for me to make out the words.

"Thank you, Vicki. This way, Madison," she says over her shoulder. She walks around the desk, pushes the doors open, and leads us down another hallway.

The hospital staff offer polite smiles as we pass, but no one questions us.

Isn't it strange how certain memories can be triggered by different sights, sounds, feelings, scents? And when they all combine together, they roll around and mold into something else, something that feels both familiar and new. As we walk down this wide hallway with fluorescent lights buzzing above us, déjà vu washes over me like a splash of cold ocean water. I haven't been in a hospital in years.

I remember when I had to stay overnight when I had to get my tonsils removed. I had a bad reaction to the anesthesia and they kept me for observation. Mom didn't stay with me; said she didn't like hospitals.

I woke up after dinnertime to find Lainey and Mary on either side of me. We watched Disney movies and ate popsicles and jello all night. I think a nurse felt bad for me, so she bent the rules and let them stay the entire night.

My chest aches with a longing so fierce that it steals my breath for a moment. I miss my sister and my cousin.

I squeeze his hand, and he squeezes mine back. A zing of pleasure and warmth crawl up my spine at the feel of his calloused fingertips against the back of my hand.

Guilt weighs me down for a moment, guilt that I found a moment of pleasure after everything that happened.

But maybe that's the point. Maybe one of the things I'm supposed to take from this whole experience is that life can be taken from us in a blink of an eye. And it's only up to us if we want to live it to its fullest—whatever that means to you.

And maybe for me, right now, that means letting the small swarm of butterflies circle inside my stomach at the feel of Aries's hand wrapped securely around mine.

We push through another set of doors to a new hallway. As we near the nurse's station, my steps slow, and I look around, looking for someone to meet my eyes so I can ask for help.

Aries tugs on my hand. "Come on. I know where to go."

My brows dip as I look over at him. I resume my pace walking next to him, Blaire now on my other side. "How do you know which room he's in?"

He gives my hand a squeeze but doesn't answer. I watch his face closely. I see the way the fluorescent lights cut a harsh shadow against his cheekbones.

He licks his lips, and opens his mouth, but before he can say anything, I hear another voice.

"Maddie."

chapter eleven

Madison

The sound of Dante's voice fills the hallway and somehow reaches my ears over the hum of machines and quiet chatter.

Shock holds me hostage, and I stop moving, letting my arm extend as Aries keeps walking. He stops when he realizes I'm not next to him, and even though I can feel his gaze on me, I can't tear mine from Dante.

Stopped at the end of the hallway with two styrofoam cups of coffee, one in each hand, he's as captivating as he's always been. Tall, broad-shouldered, and dressed head-to-toe in black with danger rolling off him in waves.

He looks like an angel of death.

The morbid thought skitters across my consciousness before I shake it away.

I untangle my fingers from Aries's hand without another thought and run the last twenty feet toward him. I know on a subconscious level I should feel a little bit awkward about launching myself at him, but I'm so relieved to see him that I don't really care about how it looks. Not right now, at least.

I inadvertently placed him on this untouchable pedestal, similar to where I put Matteo. And in one minute—sixty small seconds—it was shattered irrecoverably and beyond repair. Somehow, in my mind, I've made this connection that if Dante is okay, Matteo must be okay. It's not logical, but emotions often aren't.

Relief quickens my steps until I'm close enough to look for any signs of distress, red or puffy eyes. Of course, even if he was upset, or weighed down by sadness and grief, I'm not sure he would allow himself to show that. Not here with so many people.

His eyes widen fractionally when I'm a few feet away from him, and I don't slow down. I launch myself at him, wrapping my arms tight around his neck and hugging him. A muffled sob crawls up my throat, and I bury my face in his neck. I inhale the scent of warm, velvet amber, sinking in the comfort he provides.

His arms wrap around me reflexively. I hear the styrofoam coffee cup squeak against the back of my shirt, but I don't even mind.

At this point, what does a little spilled coffee matter when I have dried blood crusted in my hair.

After a moment, I untangle my hands from around his neck and slide down his body. He releases his hold on me enough so I can step away.

I take two quick steps back as embarrassment warms my cheeks.

A lock of hair falls in front of my face, and I duck my head while I tuck it behind my ear. Clearing my throat, I glance at my feet as if to find my courage or my reasoning for why I just jumped into this virtual stranger's arms.

"I—I'm sorry. I don't know what happened. I guess I was just so relieved to see you." A self-deprecating laugh comes out with the last of my words, and I can't stop the sardonic smile that tips up the corner of my mouth.

"You can hug me anytime you want, Maddie. I'm relieved to see you're in one piece. How did you get here?" He doesn't let me answer anything before he says, "I'm assuming he had a part in that." He tips his head to the side.

I glance over my shoulder to see he's looking at Aries, who's just about next to me now. I glance over my other shoulder to see Blaire eyeing the three of us with a curious glint in her eye.

I already see wheels turning inside that brain of hers, but I decide that's a problem for another day. I'm sure she's trying to put together the pieces of what I told her earlier, no doubt eager to watch the dynamics play out.

"Dante," Aries says with a tilt of his head in that stupid masculine way of saying hello that shouldn't be nearly as attractive as it is.

I shake my head a little and refocus. Turning to look at Dante, I ask, "Matteo. Where is he?"

"Come on, I'll take you to him." He turns on his heel and walks backward toward a room.

"And Leo? Do you know where Leo is?"

"This way."

We follow Dante into the private room at the end of the hall, Aries right behind me and Blaire behind him. Adrenaline floods my veins, easing some of my own aches and pains considerably. I know they're going to come back with a vengeance, but for now, I'm grateful for the reprieve.

I follow Dante inside the room, eagerness making my steps light. I'm anxious to see my boyfriend.

Is that what I should even call him?

What do you call someone you used to date when you were younger, then he broke your heart, and then he took a bullet for you? Boyfriend seems like such a small word in comparison to what he is, to what I feel for him.

My man.

That doesn't sound right either. He's more than just my man, he's more than just a man.

He's just *mine*.

I hear him before I see him. The deep, rich tenor of his voice as he argues about something, barking an order to fix the TV.

And then I hear another voice.

Leo.

I'm nearly pushing Dante with a hand on his back, applying a little pressure to get him to move faster. He doesn't call me out on my pushiness, which I'm thankful for. I'm not sure I could even hear him over the roaring in my ears anyway.

He shifts the coffees to one hand as he peels open the curtain, and I get my first glance of the men behind the voices.

"Took you long enough. I've been waiting forever for that fucking coffee," Matteo spits out.

Dante walks into the room, straight for Matteo. He hands him one cup and steps back, still obstructing my view. "Yeah, well, I had to go down eight floors and cross the street to get it, so you better be thankful."

"You're not even supposed to have coffee," Leo grumbles.

Matteo sighs. "You let me worry about what I can and can't handle."

"Yeah, okay, says the guy in the hospital bed with a hole in his shoulder." Leo scoffs.

Dante crosses to the end of the bed, but my feet feel frozen to the floor, as if the soles of my shoes had sprouted roots. Aries walks in but stays on the wall next to the door with Blaire beside him.

My lips part in a quiet gasp when I get my first unobstructed view of Matteo. I can't believe it.

I blink, this slow languid movement, as if fluttering my eyelashes will somehow change the scene before me.

It doesn't.

"Matteo." His name leaves my lips on a breath.

He's dressed in a hospital gown with a gray cable-knit sweater thrown over the top. A sarcastic little scoff slips from my lips as I take him in. Of course he would still look gorgeous in these harsh fluorescent lights and a washed-out hospital blanket. I sniff, choking back a disbelieving laugh at seeing him so—so *alive*. Healthy, even.

"Maddie."

My name leaves his lips like hope personified. As if I'm somehow answering every unsaid prayer he's made. It's enough to sever the roots holding me in place. I'm next to his bed in three quick steps.

My gaze scans him frantically, looking for injuries. Outside of the sling his arm is resting in, I don't see anything else. My hands flutter along his arm, unsure of where to touch him that won't interfere. He has an IV taped to the back of his hand, and tears brim on my lower lashes when I see a shadow of a bruise around it.

Suddenly, I realize I have no idea what day it is. I have no idea how long he's been here or how long I've been gone. I glance to my left to a whiteboard with the date, his vitals, and his current nurse.

Instinctively, I look over my shoulder to Aries.

"It's Wednesday."

He nods, staring at me with his arms folded over his broad chest. I don't even allow myself the indulgence of taking in his frame under these harsh fluorescent lights. Even though part of my soul desperately wants to, if nothing more than to assuage my own curiosity. It's unfair how good they both look under such unflattering lighting.

I slip my hand underneath Matteo's and squeeze his fingers gently. I look at him from underneath my lashes, hyperaware of any signs of distress.

At my touch, his eyes close, and he exhales. Three agonizing seconds later, his eyes open. I've never been so happy to see the dark hazel color in my whole life.

A bubble of emotion rises up my body and gets stuck at the back of my throat—relief, fear, and something I can't quite name yet. I choke back the sob that's desperately trying to make its way into the room.

"Cherry." He flips his hand around and slips his fingers through mine, linking our hands. With his gentle grip, he pulls me closer. I shouldn't be surprised with the amount of strength he has, and yet, I am. He catches me off-guard, and I stumble forward, my hip hitting the side of the bed. I brace my free hand against the mattress next to his shoulder, careful not to jostle him. He tugs on our hands.

"I don't want to hurt you," I murmur, our faces only inches apart.

"You won't hurt me, I'm fine. See? Now come here and don't make me ask you again." His tone gets gritty at the command,

and something inside of me ignites. I press a knee to the mattress and shuffle onto the bed, facing him before I even realize what I'm doing.

He untangles our hands as he sits up. "Are you okay? What happened? Where have you been?" He barely pauses to breathe between questions, his gaze scanning me from head to toe.

Leaning forward, he runs his free hand down my arm, and a grimace tugs at the corner of his mouth. So I lean forward to lessen the strain.

He looks like he just woke up in his penthouse apartment from a full night's sleep, not tossing and turning in an uncomfortable hospital bed with a thin blanket and lumpy pillows.

"I'm fine, I'm fine."

I stare at the man in front of me as relief and anxiety battle for dominance. My body feels too small to contain such massive experiences.

Tears fill my eyes and my sinuses start to burn as I face the very real possibility that I'm going to start crying big, fat tears. The kind of ugly crying that happens when you can't catch your breath. And I'm going to do it in a hospital room surrounded by my men.

Are they my men yet? The stray thought distracts me from my impending meltdown for a moment.

"Come here, doll," he murmurs, holding out his good hand to the side. I go to him, snuggling up to his side, careful of my movements.

Desperation soaks into my pores. I wish I could fix him, put him back together, so we can leave this place. I worry my bottom lip as fear skitters down my spine. We walked in here so easily. It'd be so easy for anyone to waltz right in.

He curls his arm around my shoulder. "I can feel you thinking."

Sniffing, I tilt my head to look at him from underneath my lashes. "I—I thought you were dead," I whisper. The admission snaps the bar over my vulnerability, and my face crumples. "And then—then I thought I was going to die too."

"Oh, Cherry." He palms the back of my head and guides it to that perfect spot between his neck and shoulder. Almost like it was carved out of him specifically for me.

And that thought makes me cry harder. It's like everything is hitting me at the same time, and for once, I'm too tired to maintain my excellent compartmentalizing. Sobs wrack my body as I expel my fear and anxiety into the stale hospital air. Everyone bears witness to my trauma.

A month ago, I might've been embarrassed.

But now? Now all I feel is comfort and acceptance. It's an intoxicating feeling, one I could get dangerously used to.

Matteo threads his fingers into my hair, keeping his palm on the back of my head. A second later, I feel a hand trace down the length of my arm. I look over my shoulder with a sniff, not at all surprised to see Leo standing there, his fingertips leaving a trail of goosebumps in their wake.

My breath catches in my throat and I wipe underneath my eyes as I sit up. Matteo reluctantly lets go of my hair, and I twist to face Leo. I give him the same courtesy that I gave Dante, which is about five seconds, before I throw my arms around his neck and bury my face against his sun-kissed skin.

He squeezes me to his chest, lifting me off the bed. "Thank god you're alright, baby. I've been crawling out of my skin."

The earnestness in his low voice sends a harpoon to my heart, wrapping around my soul and securing it back to him.

My tears slow but still dampen the collar of his shirt. I'm not ready to move yet. Another tear trails down my cheek, landing against his neck.

"Tell us what happened," Matteo demands.

chapter twelve

Dante

Maddie pulls back from Leo and settles down on the bed, effectively sandwiched between the two brothers. I run my hand down my face, exhaustion from the last few days finally catching up to me.

Or maybe it's relief.

It's such a foreign feeling, one that's tangled up in a web of feelings I normally lock down. It's not conducive to wear my heart on my sleeve. In my life, those emotions are exploited and used to hurt you.

Look at what happened with Maddie and Matteo. Although, it seems there was a grave error in the whole thing, something still doesn't quite add up.

And in my quietest moments these last couple days, I war with myself. There's a part of me that intellectually knows Matteo couldn't have predicted it, couldn't have done anything differently. Those motherfuckers ambushed him at a place that should've been secure.

Still, I can't stop thinking about what I would've done differently.

Could I have done anything differently?

Could I have saved her, spared her from the trauma that will ache like a bad knee every time it rains?

In my most selfish moments, I imagine myself as some sort of fucking superhero, defeating all the odds—and there were a fucking ton of odds—and saving the day.

Just as quickly as those treacherous thoughts come, I dismiss them. I love these assholes like they're blood. Even Leo, when he's not a pain in the ass.

I watch the way he is with her now. His feelings for her are written all over him, from his protective posture to his possessive touch.

I smother a smile behind my hand. The kid's stepped up in the last few days, I'll give him that. Matteo's been shutting him out of family business for years, but I think the kid's ready to step in.

I understand he wants to shield him from the life, but I have a feeling that Leo's not going to take no for an answer any longer.

Especially not now with Maddie here.

She changes everything.

Movement from the corner of my eye pulls my attention. I grab for the gun tucked into the back of my pants on instinct. A split second later, my brain reconnects with my body, and I let go of the handle.

Maddie's friend, Blaire Hawthorne, the unofficial gossip of the under-thirties in the five boroughs. She was reaching forward to snag a coffee from the table. With an eye on the scene in front of her, she pulls out her phone and starts tapping.

I arch a brow and exchange a look with Rafe. He nods in return, so it seems we're in agreement that there's something else here.

I'm not surprised he walked in with Madison. He said he was going to find her, and that asshole considers honor his top personality trait, which is fucking ironic if you ask me. He deals in secrets and extortion, which is just about as opposite of honor as you can get.

Except, everyone he's gathered intel on deserves what they're going to get. Mostly, at least.

But I am surprised that he let the friend tag along.

Bottom line: I need more information and I'm not going to get it boxed in a hospital room. The ticking of the clock above my head grates on my nerves, only amplifying the need to leave.

Maddie shifts on the bed and licks her lips, the action pulling my attention to her swollen mouth and red-rimmed eyes.

She's exquisite.

She's a black pearl in a sea of diamonds. Infinitely more precious and rare.

And even dressed in someone else's clothes with tears for another man drying on her face, I can't stop the covetous want from coursing through my veins.

It's a visceral need.

Madison

I exhale a breath, letting the motion bleed some of the tension in my body. I can do this. I told Blaire what happened, I can tell them too. It's just words. Just a string of words to make a sentence. And a few sentences to sum up my experience.

And the rest, those pesky emotions that keep rising up like the Pacific, they can just stay buried.

For now.

I settle onto the bed, drawing comfort from the warmth from Matteo behind me and Leo in front of me. My mind tries to distract me with visions of a very different situation where I'm sandwiched between two brothers, but I shake it to get back on track.

"I was at Blaire's house. She was helping me find Matteo, helping me figure out what happened. And then Aries showed up like some sort of dark avenger," I murmur.

I turn to face Aries, our gazes colliding. The heat in the room rises as he stares at me with all the intensity of the sun.

"How did you end up at Blaire's house?"

Leo steals my attention with his question. I clear my throat and glance at him before refocusing on a scuff on the floor. "It's a long story."

"We've got time, Cherry." Matteo's voice is low next to me.

"Don't push her," Leo snaps as he shuffles even closer to me. I thread my fingers through his in appreciation.

Blaire pushes off the wall she's been leaning against and takes a step into the room. "I'll tell them, Madison."

My head snaps up, and I take in the earnest look on her face. "I appreciate the offer, but I can—I'll tell them."

She eyes me for a moment, quiet but always calculating, before she nods. "Alright."

"Why don't we take this conversation somewhere more . . . private?" Dante asks, his gaze on Matteo.

I turn to look at Matteo. "When are you discharged?"

"Now," he growls the word out as he reaches around me to free himself from the IV. Leo makes a noise in the back of his throat, but Matteo's a flurry of movement now, applying pressure to his hand.

"Shouldn't we wait for a doctor or something?"

"Nah, the only way we could get him to stay here this long is the promise of finding you. And heavy pain killers." Leo smirks at me.

His words shake loose some comprehension, and I twist around him to see Blaire and Aries. They're not next to each other, but closer to the wall than to me. Embarrassment flushes my cheeks. "I'm sorry, I should've mentioned it earlier, but I'm good here. These guys will make sure I'm taken care of."

Aries walks backward until his back hits the blinds on the window by the door. He folds his arms across his chest and leans against the wall, holding my gaze. "I'm good."

"And miss all this?" Blaire waves her coffee in the air. I blink a few times and glance around. Where the hell did she get that coffee? "Besides, where are you going to go? It sounds like Matteo's apartment is off-limits. And you can't go to the dorms, that'd just be asking for trouble."

I lick my lips and try to rethink my next actions. "What are you saying?"

"I'm *saying* that I think you should come back with me."

"Absolutely not."

"No fucking way."

"No."

All three responses come at the same time. Only Dante is quiet. I look at him now. His silence is a weapon, one that I imagine he utilizes often. He holds my gaze as they talk around us.

"Why not? It's obvious you can't look after her. I can. I have the resources and desire to do it," Blaire reasons.

"Bullshit. I could've walked right in your mausoleum of a house and found her myself, but I was doing you the courtesy of ringing your doorbell. That means that any fuckwit with half a brain can do it," Aries growls out.

"Bro. Did you just call yourself a fuckwit?" Leo's tone dances with mirth.

"Fuck off, Leo."

Leo chuckles. "Damn. I've missed you. Don't stay gone so long next time, yeah?"

Something about the familiarity piques my interest, and I turn to watch the exchange.

Aries shrugs. "It wasn't my call. It never fucking is."

"Yeah, well, it'd be nice to have someone on my fucking side for a change," Leo grumbles.

I smooth down the fabric of my shirt, pressing against the tightness in my chest.

Matteo pulls the sweater over his head with one hand and whips off the hospital gown. His bare chest is a work of art. Chiseled muscles he didn't have two years ago and more tattoos than I would've guessed. It's almost unfair how attractive he is, the white bandage around his shoulder just adds to his allure.

"Are you fucking kidding me? Since when haven't I been on

your side?" Matteo tips his chin up as he stares at Leo.

Dante clears his throat and steps into the room. "Let's table this until later, yeah? I've got a place we can go."

"Yeah, just keep pushing me aside. Business as usual. Ain't that right, brother?" Sarcasm and something else, something deeper, drips from Leo's words.

"Is there something you want to say to me, little brother?" Matteo asks.

In my peripheral, I catch Blaire with her mouth literally hanging open, gaze locked on Matteo. Something hot and acidic sloshes inside my gut.

I push off the bed and stand up. "Stop. Just stop." Everyone turns to look at me, and I fight the urge to smooth out my clothes again. A reflexive move I haven't been able to break myself of for years.

I point to Blaire. "You. Stop staring at him."

She jerks her gaze away with a scowl, a light pink dusting her cheeks.

"And you. How do you know them? And how did you find me?" I ask Aries with a thumb over my shoulder toward Matteo, Leo, and Dante.

The skin around Aries's eyes tightens and he purses his mouth before he pushes off the wall, the blinds creaking in protest. I watch him as something inside my chest tightens. Apprehension rolls over me like a hot, sticky breeze as I track him across the room.

Matteo has a black hooded sweatshirt on, his arms folded tightly across his chest. His lip curls up into a snarl as Aries stops next to him and turns to face me.

I fumble for a moment as the scene starts to move pieces together in my mind.

Same height.

Brown hair, even if Aries's has been highlighted by the sun.

The same strong jaw—the one that Leo has too.

But their eyes, their eyes are different. Matteo's are hazel, forever changing depending on his mood. Right now, they're brown, darker than I've seen before.

And Aries, his eyes are a light golden brown, like somehow a light is shining from them.

My lips part and my brows furrow. "I—I don't understand."

"C'mon, Raven. I know you do."

My muscles tense and I shift my weight from foot to foot. "You're . . . related?"

"Brothers."

"*Twin* brothers," Leo offers.

My mind spins, fumbling over too many thoughts flying through my head. I back up until my shoulder bumps someone. I look over to see Blaire's cold mask on as she stares at the two men in front of me—the two brothers.

Little things, small moments in time that I brushed off as coincidence now look different under this light. And I feel . . . I don't know how I feel.

My brows scrunch together as I stare between the men in the room. "I don't understand. Was it all a trick then?"

"No trick, Cherry. Just a coincidence."

"I don't believe in coincidences, Matteo," I murmur absentmindedly.

"A twist of fate then," Aries says.

The phrasing pulls a little of my confusion away like a vacuum, and I look at him. His face, that gorgeous face which I've felt against mine, is serious.

"It wasn't a trick?"

Aries shakes his head slowly as he holds my gaze. "No trick. I didn't even realize you knew my brothers until I saw the security footage."

"You saw what happened?" For some inexplicable reason, my eyes fill with tears.

He nods, the movement slow and somber. "And I promise you, they—"

The door opens, interrupting whatever he was going to say. A nurse pokes her head in. She glances around and fidgets with the edge of the door. "Oh, I wasn't expecting so many people in here. But, uh, I wanted to let you know that person you told me to look out for. You know, that guy"—she waggles her eyebrows in an exaggerated movement—"he just got off the elevator. The gals at the nurses station are trying to slow him down, but he's with some other men. And well, they don't look the rule-following type."

"Thank you, Lori," Dante says.

"Absolutely. You boys take care now," she says before she steps into the hallway, leaving the door cracked.

"Time to go," Dante says as he crosses the room to look out into the hallway. "Fuck."

"Who is it?" Matteo asks.

Fear prickles along my scalp, and I don't even understand what's going on. But whatever it is—or whoever it is—is scary enough to send a ripple of tension through every one of my guys.

"I'll take Raven and meet you at the car," Aries says as he crosses the room to stand next to me.

"I'll go with you," Leo announces, sidling up to my other side.

"Wait. What about Blaire?" I turn to look at my friend. She's casually sipping a coffee and impassively staring at the rest of us.

"What about her?" Matteo asks as he slides a gun into the back of his sweatpants.

"We can't just leave her here to face whoever is out there!" Nervous energy fills the room, sprinkling along my skin.

Matteo sighs and pinches the bridge of his nose before he turns to face me. He brushes some hair back off my face and flicks his gaze between my eyes. "You're my priority, Cherry."

"I'm asking you to make her one right now. For me. Her driver is waiting for her, all we have to do is get her to him safely."

He sighs, letting his fingers smooth the ends of my hair. "Fine. Rafe, you get the girl to her car. Leo take our girl to Dante's car. Dante and I will meet you there. If we're not back in ten minutes, leave without us and meet at the spot."

Dante tosses the keys toward me, and Leo reaches out and snatches them, pocketing them in two seconds.

"You'll be okay?"

Blaire smirks. "I'm fine. Besides, I've got Rafe to protect me." She winks at him, and I have to stop myself from snapping at her. I don't know what the hell is going on with me, but I feel a little out of control when it comes to her and them.

I shake my head and offer her a tight smile. "Be safe. I'll call you soon, okay?"

She nods and she walks into the hallway without a backward glance. Aries curses under his breath, pausing at the doorway to pin me with a heated look.

"He gave you ten minutes. If you're not there in eight, I'm hunting your pretty little ass down again, yeah?"

I twist my lips to the side and nod, stifling the smile on my face as he turns around and stalks into the hallway.

Leo threads his fingers with mine and tugs me toward the door.

"He'll be alright, Madison. But we've gotta go."

I pause next to Matteo, pushing onto my tiptoes and brushing my mouth against his. My hand lands on his chest for balance, and he holds my hand to him with an iron grip. He dips his head to keep our connection and presses his lips against mine harder. It turns my innocent gesture into something more.

Leo's hand in mine grounds me when the feeling of Matteo's lips against mine has me floating above ground. I settle back onto my heels and slowly open my eyes. I didn't realize they had closed until now.

"Don't fucking lose her to anyone, you hear me?" Matteo practically growls. He's staring at Leo over my shoulder.

"Fuck off, Matteo. I've got her. You just worry about fielding dear old Dad, yeah? Ten minutes and we're gone," Leo warns before he's pulling me out the door.

"Dante." I look behind me for Dante, shoving my hair out of my eyes. I'd wanted to hug him. . . or something.

"It's fine, Maddie. I'll see you at the car, yeah?"

I bite my lip and nod, sending a prayer to whoever is listening to keep everyone safe and in one piece.

chapter thirteen

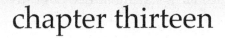

Madison

"C'mon, Madison," Leo encourages as we walk down the hallway.

His grip on my hand flexes before it tightens as he leads the way. It's a good thing too, because I have no idea where to go.

I glance over my left shoulder to see Dante and Matteo talking to one another, never taking their eyes off of me. They wear matching serious expressions, and we're too far away to hear what they're talking about. I hazard a guess that they're strategizing.

As if some cue that I'm not privy to happens, I watch in equal parts fascination and dread as they both visibly straighten and square their shoulders.

A veil of indifference slams over Matteo's face, and the quick transformation has me sucking in a breath. He's lightyears away from the vulnerability of a hospital bed and gown.

Instead, I see him for the show he gives the rest of the world. He's granted me enough time behind the scenes recently, enough to notice the difference.

"This way." Leo's voice is low as he turns right, pulling my attention forward once more.

"Where are we going? I thought the parking garage was the other way?"

"We're taking the scenic route." Leo quickens his pace and tosses a quick glance behind us.

I peek too. I'm not sure if I was expecting some big Italian mob guys to be chasing us with their guns blazing or what, but all I see are hospital staff and a few patients.

"Shouldn't we take the most direct path there?"

"Trust me, Madison. Back stairs, circle around on the second floor to the other staircase, and then double back for the parking garage."

"Okay. And we won't run into your dad?"

"Not if Matteo and Dante do their job and keep him busy long enough for us to get to the car."

I look over at him, my lips parting at the image his profile makes. His strong jaw and dark brows over captivating eyes. His tattoos stand out in the harsh lighting, but somehow, it only adds to his appeal.

A smirk tilts up the corner of his mouth. "I can feel you thinking, you know."

I lift a shoulder and quicken my steps to keep up with his long strides. "I don't understand what's so wrong about seeing your dad right now."

"It's not so much about seeing him as it is him seeing us." He turns to look at me, pointedly aching a brow. "Seeing *you*."

"Why don't you want your dad to see me?"

I'm not even offended at his conviction. I'm pretty sure I don't want to meet the boss of some sort of mafia syndicate, which is something I haven't really had the time to process yet. I'm definitely going to have to brush up on my *Sopranos*.

Oh, and if that wasn't intimidating enough, I'm dating three of his sons.

Is that what we're doing—*dating*?

Shit. I don't even know what to call this . . . this *relationship*.

He must see some of the uncertainty reflected on my face, because in the next moment, he tugs me into the nearest room on the right.

The room is dark and thankfully, empty. The privacy curtain is partially open, and he guides me behind it.

"What—"

I don't get another syllable out before Leo rounds on me, crowding me against the wall. From here, we're almost completely hidden from view, only our shoes from beneath the curtain.

He keeps hold of my one hand, tightening his grip by our sides, and he places his other hand against the wall by my head.

Lust coils in my lower belly when he pins me with his molten dark-green gaze. My lips part and my head tips back almost in invitation without conscious thought.

I hate him a little bit at that moment.

For how easy he makes my heart race. For forgetting where we are and what we should be doing. For disregarding the fact that I'm wearing a matching tie dye hand-me-down outfit with dried blood in my greasy hair while I'm visiting my boyfriend who just got shot by the same people who kidnapped me.

Yeah, it's a lot.

And one slightly dominant move from Leo, and whoosh. It all flies out of my head like it was never there.

I'm not sure if I should be this easy. But maybe that's the wrong way of looking at it.

Maybe this is a gift, how easy it is between us.

My breath hitches as he leans in and skims his nose along my neck, up to my ear.

"Just to be clear, no one is ashamed of you. But if I had it my way, you and my father would never breathe the same air."

I'm stunned for a moment. My normally busy mind completely blank, speechless. His words feel heavy with possessiveness, sending a shiver of arousal down my back.

I look at him from underneath my lashes. "And what about your mom?"

He doesn't hesitate. "There's a special place in hell for mothers who abandon their children to the likes of men like Angelo Rossi."

I lick my lips and swallow past the lump in my throat. It's a loaded statement, and I'm not sure how to unpack it. Or even if this is the right time to start.

"So, no, baby, you won't be meeting my parents if I can help it." His lips brush against my ear with every syllable, and I have to clench my thighs together.

A noncommittal noise comes from the back of my throat, and he takes it as an invitation to continue.

"You're too good for all of them. Too good for all of us, too."

He pulls back to look me right in the eye to deliver the final blow. "But that ship has sailed. You're mine now. And I'm never letting you go."

His words sever the last bit of reservation I had, and I push onto my tiptoes and close the distance between us. I brush my lips against his, sealing his declaration with a kiss I feel all the way down to my toes.

Before it can go further, I pull back a little. "We should go," I breathe the words against his mouth.

He leans his forehead against mine and exhales a breath. My lashes flutter closed as I relish in the simple touch from him.

"I was so worried about you," he murmurs.

It feels more than just words, like his very soul is cracking open before me. Something inside of me clenches at the idea.

He rolls his forehead against mine, just the tiniest of movement, but it's enough to send a prickles of awareness cascading down my body. It's pleasant and enticing. And I have to fight the urge to throw my arms around him. Now really isn't the right moment for more.

"I'm sorry." My voice is quiet but his worry feels big. It could get addicting, his worry—his care for me. I've been worrying about everyone else for so long, it feels almost foreign.

"You have nothing to apologize for, Madison. *I'm* sorry. I never should have let you go alone."

"But I wasn't alone. I was with Matteo," I murmur.

He shuffles closer to me, the sides of his shoes bracketing mine and the fabric of his shirt brushing against me.

His gaze flicks between my eyes, searching for something. "Never again, yeah? From now on, two of us are with you at all times."

"I'm not some little delicate flower, Leo. I can take care of myself."

As soon as the words leave my lips, I know it's not entirely truthful. The painful truth is I was powerless against the two men who snatched me. They had guns and tranquilizers and brute force on their side. I swallow my ego and realize that I need some help.

"I know, baby." He pauses to run his thumb along the back of my hand. "But you are invaluable to me and my dipshit brothers."

He hooks a smile with the last two words, smirking at me with all the charm I've come to associate with him. A little laugh escapes me before I can reel it in.

It's like the moment was getting a little too serious, so he had to make some little quip to lighten the mood. I appreciate him all the more for it. With that feeling fueling my next move, I push on to my tiptoes and brush my lips across his again.

Once, twice, three times.

The need to feel him, to be closer to him pounds at my temples and commands my hands and lips. I slide my lips along his again, a tantalizing tease.

He groans, this low noise from the back of his throat as he presses his mouth to mine more firmly. He slides his hand from the wall to my shoulder and up the sensitive curve of my neck. With his hand on the front of my neck and his fingers on the underside of my jaw, he tilts my head to the side and deepens our kiss.

I groan into his mouth, and use my hold on his shirt to pull him against me.

His lips slide against mine in a way that belies how long we've known each other. He kisses me like he's drowning in our passion and oxygen from my lips is his only cure. He kisses me with familiarity and exploration. It's an amazing juxtaposition.

"What are you kids doing? You can't be in here," the unfamiliar voice snaps from the right.

It pulls me from the web of lust that Leo has ensnared me in. I instinctively rear back only to realize that I'm already up against the wall.

Leo shifts his body to block me completely from view as soon as the first word leaves her lips. I peek over his shoulder to see an older woman in nurse's scrubs scowling at us.

"Did you hear me? I said get outta here."

Leo tenses and the air around us shifts. He leans forward and places a chaste kiss against my lips with deliberate slowness.

"Let's go, baby." He waits for me to nod before he pulls back and guides us out of the room, skirting by the nurse standing in the doorway.

She stares at us with crossed arms, but I decide to take a page from Leo's nonchalance and keep my head high despite the flush of embarrassment staining my cheeks.

He laces his fingers with mine and leads me down several hallways before we reach the stairwell.

He glances at his watch when we hit the first landing. "Fuck."

My adrenaline sputters, a tiny spike in an otherwise tapped pool. "What's wrong?"

"Nothing, we're fine. Let's just pick up the pace, yeah?"

I bite my lip and nod as we pick up the pace to a near jog. Three flights of stairs and another hallway, and we're in the underground parking garage.

It's almost completely at capacity, a sea of red lights above each occupied space. I glance from side to side, panic quickening my breaths.

"Yellow five. This way." Leo tugs me behind him, focused on

getting us to our destination.

I exhale a breath and focus on the back of Leo's shirt and the way his muscles flex and move underneath it with each step. It helps ease some of the panic and paranoia about being so many levels underground.

I'm so busy maintaining my facade of calm that I don't realize we've reached the car until someone snatches my hand from Leo's.

"Hey—"

My protest is cut off when Dante's face gets close to mine as he maneuvers me away from Leo and pushes me against the side of the SUV.

His gaze is wild as he searches me frantically. "You're late. Six minutes late."

I lick my lips, frozen from the feeling of his anger. No, that's not right. It's not just anger—it's fear. Underneath the growly tone is anxiety.

"Do you know what can happen in six minutes with my father or his goons?" Matteo asks from somewhere behind Dante. Backlit by the dim security light and the red occupied lights, I can't see anything but him.

"We're fine."

He doesn't respond to my weak attempt at placating him, but I don't take it personally. I'm still navigating everything about this current situation, so even if I wasn't mentally, physically, and emotionally tapped, I'm not sure I'd know what to do yet.

He stares at me for a moment, his hands on either side of me against the car door and his head lowered to hold my gaze. He nods a few times, and without a word, pushes back and takes a few steps back to round the car and get in the driver's seat.

"What did I miss?" Aries asks as he jogs up to us.

"Nothing. Get in before Dad finds us and we're all fucked," Matteo orders.

chapter fourteen

Madison

Leo holds the rear passenger door open for me, and I scoot in behind Aries. Ducking his head, he ambles toward the seat in the second row, behind the driver's side.

Anxiety flickers in my stomach. Where am I supposed to sit in here? With so many big things happening in my life right now, it feels silly to stress over something as small as seating arrangements, but here I am.

As I pass by Aries, heading toward the third row, he hooks an arm around my waist. "Sit by me."

I halt but don't sit down yet. "But what about Leo?"

"He can sit in the back. I want you right here."

Something about his command sends a prickle of awareness down my spine. His voice has that same growly, commanding quality that Matteo's does, and something about it just works for me in a way I wasn't anticipating.

Leo huffs in annoyance behind me and gently taps my hip with two fingers. "It's fine, baby."

If I wasn't this close to Aries's face, I don't think I would've seen the way his jaw clenches at Leo's term of affection. Is that . . . jealousy? I narrow my eyes at him, but he blinks, and it's gone. I blink a few times and give in, letting Aries settle me next to him.

Leo skirts around me, trailing his fingers along my hip as he sits down in the row behind me.

I still can't believe they're all brothers. It's such a strange thought.

I don't know what's more surprising: the fact that I fell for four different men or that three of them are related. Then, a thought hits me.

"Wait, is Dante your brother, too? A cousin? A long-lost second uncle, twice removed?"

"He wishes," Leo says from behind me, amusement coloring his voice.

"Nah, just a family friend," Dante says as he slides into the front seat and starts the car. "We ready?"

"Yeah, let's go. We've got at least two hours. Start talking, Cherry."

Matteo's command leaves no room for argument, so for the next thirty minutes I fill them in on everything that happened. All of the details that I can remember, most of them fuzzy.

My throat is dry by the time I'm done, and I accept the bottle of water Leo hands me from behind. I don't even question where he got it from, I just accept it with a grateful smile and tip the bottle back for a healthy drink.

"And you told Blaire all of this?" Dante asks as he maneuvers us around a slow driver.

I worry my bottom lip as I think about how to phrase this next part. "Well, almost. There's one thing I didn't tell her."

"Yeah, what's that?" Dante asks when I don't answer right away.

"You know how those guys gave me that tranquilizer?"

"Dead men walking," Leo rumbles from behind me. He's perched in between me and Aries, resting his elbows on the back of the seats as his fingertips skate across my shoulder and up my neck in a soft, soothing rhythm.

"Well, even though I couldn't move, I could still hear. Not the entire time, but long enough to know that Senator Hardin is the one who ordered the hit. And the two men he hired weren't going to take me out." I clear my throat. "They weren't going to kill me, I mean, unless he paid their fee."

I roll my lips inward and swallow down the sticky feeling that threatens to bubble up my throat.

Fear.

It's residual fear.

It sticks to my nerve endings like tar. I wonder how many days before the tar lessens, before it hardens and crumbles off like stale chalk? I guess until then, I just swallow it down and withstand it. One second, one minute, one hour at a time.

I exhale a breath, reminding myself that I'm safe.

Dante glances at me through the rearview mirror. "What did he say? Think, Maddie. Try to recall every word you heard. Nothing is too small."

I close my eyes and will myself to focus. Like recalling a movie, I can remember the sensation of being carried, jostled around by one of the guys, Jared, I think. Once I dive in, the scene starts to surround me. Their scent fills my nostrils, gunpowder and sweat. Their cavalier attitude toward death. Words tumble from my mouth, unbidden.

"Dave and Jared. They talked about meeting up at a bar after they dropped me off at the senator's house. They said something about a bathrobe, and he let them inside. My eyes were closed, but their footsteps were loud on the hardwood floor. The senator led them to his office, and that's where they told him they weren't going to give him a two-for-one. If he wanted me dead, he had to pay them more. Senator Hardin declined and kicked them out. Then they went through my purse and ordered someone to take me to a farm and said something else, but I can't quite remember what." My brow scrunches as I try to recall what happened next. It gets blurry here.

"I'm gonna kill him," Aries says. It's the first thing he's said since before I started my sorry little tale. Conviction laces his words, sending a ripple of energy through the car.

It feels less like four words strung together and more like a declaration—an omen. I wouldn't be surprised if a thunderclap sounded outside, cementing the deal as an unbreakable promise.

"Not if I get there first," Dante mutters.

"I already called dibs days ago," Leo offers.

Matteo whips his head to look between all of them. "Nobody's killing anybody. Not yet."

Leo tosses his hand in the air. "Are you fucking kidding me? This motherfucker shoots you, leaves you for dead, and snatches our girl, and you're saying, what? No retaliation?"

Matteo clenches his jaw. "No, that's not what I'm saying at all. I'm saying *not yet*. We need a solid fucking plan before we go in all half-cocked and get everyone killed. Besides, if anyone gets dibs, it's me." He smirks at Leo before turning around.

"What I still don't understand is why did they bring you to Blaire's? Why they let you go at all?"

"What the fuck kind of question is that—*let her go at all*?" Leo's voice rises at the end, his exasperation clear.

I meet Dante's gaze through the rearview mirror to answer his question. "I don't know exactly. When they looked through my things, I think they saw my student ID, and somehow the senator connected the dots."

"What dots?" Dante asks.

"Well, Blaire used to date Senator Hardin's son, Dale."

There's a pivotal moment here. You know the one, the moment of absolute calm before the storm erupts. That's kind of what it feels like in the confines of this luxury SUV. For a split second, it's as if everything stills. The very atoms in the air stop swirling around, and then it explodes. It shatters in a way unlike anything I've ever experienced.

Somehow, the four of them have synced together so thoroughly, almost like they share conscious thoughts. I can feel the tension rise again, this tangible thing swelling so large that I'm afraid one move is going to pop it.

"Interesting," Dante says in a tone that suggests it's anything but interesting.

The collective mood plummets into something darker, and I bite my lip against the questions on my tongue.

I'm not afraid of them. No, but maybe I'm a little bit afraid *for* them. With everything that just happened with Matteo, I know they're not infallible.

They're not untouchable.

And they're not unkillable.

Fear wraps around my heart for someone other than myself. I've never been cruel or wished someone ill-will. But I live in a city with eight million people in it. Even if I wanted to, I simply can't extend my worry to everyone, so I got used to shutting it out. Offering it to those in dire circumstances or those who were in desperate need. Like, for example, if I saw a man snatch a girl off the street or throw her unconscious body over his shoulder, I'd do something to help.

But otherwise, it's been my duty to look out for just my sister and my cousin. Sometimes my mom.

And the first time in a long time, I feel like I have something really important to lose. I know that this is a moment. I'm at another crossroads.

I can move forward with them down this less-traveled path littered with explosives and weaponry. One that boasts an abrupt ending with one wrong step. But it also has the potential to be full of life-altering passion and otherworldly experiences.

Or I can go back to how things used to be. Back to my dorm room where I spent a lot of time alone. Back to a group of frenemies and acquaintances who would just as soon stab me in the back as offer me a smile.

I honestly don't even know how much safer that existence would be. But I can go back to it.

I know that if I asked them, they would make sure I was safe. And maybe, after a few months, these memories will fade.

But I can't ignore the little niggling notion that isn't how my life is supposed to be. I know everyone naïvely thinks that they're meant for something grand, that their life is supposed to have this gigantic purpose. That they're supposed to rule something, no matter how big or small.

I never felt like that, I guess. Sure, I felt a little adrift, but I was happy to cruise through life, looking for my perfect path.

But now? Now I think I'm facing the path to greatness. It's my make-or-break moment. And I'm going to do it with these four men.

Hopefully.

The rest of the ride to Dante's place in the Hamptons is quiet, everyone lost in their thoughts. Soft string music fills the air. Something about the melody is familiar, but that's as far as I let myself think about it. I stare out the tinted windows, watching the trees sway in the breeze as we drive up the coast.

Cool air blows against my ankles as the air conditioning comes to life. I use this as an opportunity to think over everything, to sort through my feelings. It's more difficult than I imagined. And I desperately wish I had my cousin or my sister here to talk it out with. I don't know if Mary would really understand. But I know Lainey would.

I feel silly, I guess. Not necessarily betrayed, but like, I'm the butt of some sort of cosmic joke. The punchline to five fates twisted up together.

Only, it doesn't feel like I'm a joke. It feels like, maybe, just maybe this is how it was supposed to be.

Maybe I was supposed to run into Aries on the night of the masquerade ball. Maybe I was supposed to trust him to guide me through the chaos that erupted when the lights went out.

It feels fateful, my chance meeting with Leo. He was at an affiliated school for years, and yet, I didn't meet him until after I had unknowingly connected with his brother. What are the chances? Math has never been my strongest subject, but I hazard a guess that they're slim to none.

And what are the odds that both of these men—two men that I've met in the last month—are not only related to each other but related to the first love of my life?

And Matteo. Is it a coincidence that we ran into each other so shortly after I met his brothers? I glance over at him in the passenger seat, his arm in a sling as he types and scrolls on his phone. As if he can feel my eyes on him, he glances over his shoulder at me. He looks guarded and open at the same time.

And isn't that how he's always been? So open with some things like his feelings for me. While keeping an entire country's worth of secrets. Whether by omission or outright lies, they're so tightly knitted and rolled around until they're so insurmountable.

It's what ended us before. Secrets and lies.

My lip twitches at my train of thought. I'm not being fair. I know that he didn't lie about Leo when we were together before.

But he didn't offer the truth either, a little voice whispers inside my head. It reeks of Mary's condescension.

I hold Matteo's gaze for a moment. His lips part, and I can almost physically see the words on the tip of his tongue, dying to be released. Matteo is a fixer. He always has been. I'm sure the inaction is eating him up inside right now. Then again, he could be wielding his phone like this car is his very own throne. I don't really know that much about what he does. And everything I know about the mob is from fiction, and who knows what's based on fact and what's written with liberal creative license.

But I'm still here, in the car with all of them, heading to an unknown place in the Hamptons. That should count for something. I break the connection and look out the window again, effectively shutting him down. It's not forever it's just, I just need a moment.

I don't even know why I'm so upset, really. Okay, sure. He didn't tell me he had a twin brother. But I have my own secrets. When Matteo was confessing his love for me, I didn't exactly tell him about Aries, did I?

And yet, I can't find it within myself to feel shame or remorse. I don't think I would trade any of them for anything. That's a scary, sobering thought.

Okay, so if I'm not angry, then what am I feeling? I sigh, the noise escaping my mouth and taking stress and anxiety with it. My shoulders deflate, and I lean my head against the window, closing my eyes against the coolness of the glass against my overheated skin.

"You okay, baby?" I roll my forehead against the glass, tipping my head toward Leo.

I can't see him, but I can feel his gaze on me, warm and insistent. My mind flashes back to the room at the hospital when his heated stare wasn't the only thing I could feel. A small smile tips up the corners of my mouth. "I'm fine."

"Come back here."

I flick my gaze toward the front and then the back of the car, wary of unbuckling my seatbelt even for a moment. The trauma of riding in the van with those two men still sits heavily on my psyche, threatening to bubble up to the surface in a trap at any moment.

Leo holds his hand out over the seat. "I've got you. C'mere."

When no one speaks up, I unbuckle my seatbelt and slip my fingers into his. He guides me to the third row, settles me next to him, and reaches over to buckle my seatbelt. The whole thing lasts maybe three seconds.

A breath of relief escapes me as I settle into his side. He slings his arm along the top of the seat, across my shoulders. His fingertips swirl patterns across my shoulder. It's relaxing, and before long, I end up leaned against Leo, my eyes heavy.

Surrounded by these men, my dark avengers, I finally allow myself to rest.

chapter fifteen

Leo

When her breath evens out and her shoulders release the tension she's been carrying since I saw her, something inside me settles.

I continue to trace patterns along her shoulder and the curve of her neck. There's something soothing about having her near enough to touch. It calms the raging storm inside me.

"She asleep?" My brother's voice carries from the passenger seat.

I glance up and meet his gaze with a nod.

"Good. She needs it," Matteo says.

"What took you so long to get to the car tonight?" Dante asks, flashing me a look through the rearview mirror.

There's a tone to his voice that I'm not used to. Almost an accusation with a side of . . . jealousy? I smirk to myself at the idea of Dante being jealous. That guy is built like a machine, following Matteo's orders unflinchingly. I'm not surprised my girl could inspire such emotions from him, she's fucking incredible. I don't think there's much she couldn't do.

I look out the window for a moment to cover the smirk. "Got held up by a nurse."

Dante grunts a response too low for me to hear and focuses back on the road.

"What did Dad want?"

Matteo shakes his head. It's a small movement, and from anyone else, it would be nothing noteworthy. But from my brother who never so much as flinches in the face of uncertainty, it might as well be a billboard.

I grit my teeth when he doesn't say anything. The idea that he's *still* sheltering me from what's really happening grates on my nerves.

"I thought we were done with this shit." I sigh, the noise audible over the soft music playing through the speakers.

He turns to look over his shoulder at me. "What shit?"

"You—everyone—shutting me out." I glare at Dante and Rafe too.

Now it's his turn to sigh. "Nobody's shutting you out, Leo. It's just—"

"It's what?" I interrupt him. His exasperation propels me back to a time where I truly wasn't included in anything.

"I don't fucking know." His voice is loud in the quiet confines of Dante's SUV.

My hand stills on Maddie's neck and my first instinct is to check to see if he woke her up. Her chest rises and falls in the same pattern, thankfully. It's safe to say she's exhausted.

I glare at Matteo and he sighs as he wipes a hand down his face.

"I'm sorry, okay? It's just I don't know what the fuck is going on, and instead of figuring it out, I'm running away."

"Don't paint us as cowards, Matteo. We're making the right choice—the smart one," Dante snaps.

"Yeah, well, I've never run from a fight in my life," Matteo mumbles.

As much as their disagreement interests me, I want to get us back on track. "So what did Dad want?"

Matteo's brow furrows. "I don't know. I don't even know how he knew I was there."

"You mean you didn't tell him?" Rafe speaks up for the first time in a long time.

Matteo scoffs. "Of course I didn't fucking tell him. He'd see it as a weakness, and then I'd have to spend the next year watching my six for the knife he'd be dying to put in my back as some sort of lesson."

Rafe snorts. "Not fucking likely. No way dear old Dad's gonna off his golden child."

Matteo laughs, this self-deprecating noise that's more of a scoff. And it holds no mirth. "You guys really have no idea, do you?"

My shoulders tense at his tone. "Well, how would we? You've kept me in the dark."

"I did that to protect you," Matteo interrupts me. "And I'm done apologizing for it. Given the chance, I'd do it again. I'd protect you from this life. It's not one I'd wish on anybody. Least of all you." He pauses for a moment. "And definitely not her."

"We can still get her out," Dante offers in a low voice that just carries back to me.

"We both know it's too late for that. We'll have to come up with something else," Matteo murmurs.

It's one thing to be left out of the family business, but it's hard to hear that he wouldn't do anything different if he could. My brows rise in disbelief with every silent second. "So that's it? Nothing else to say after that?"

"Don't mistake your brother's honesty for cruelty," Dante says. "There's a lot you don't know about that goes on behind the scenes. Things that have broken men older than you—"

"Lesser men, I think you mean," I interrupt him. "And I don't even know why the fuck we're having this conversation. Didn't we already talk about this, and didn't we already agree you're going to bring me in?"

I guess they took my question as rhetorical, but as long as they include me on this shit, I don't really care. I swirl a new pattern along Maddie's arm, letting the soft touch of her skin soothe me. What an unexpected and welcome side effect my girl has on me. I look out the tinted windows, but it's too dark and we're going too fast to really see anything other than green.

"You're awfully quiet, brother," I say to Rafe after a few minutes.

From this angle, I can't see the expression on his face. "What's there to say? I've been excluded from these sorts of family meetings for years. As soon as I can figure out exactly what happened back at the safe house, the sooner I can get my girl out of here."

Silence reigns after his last word. It's a different kind, though, weighted, anticipation and violence brimming in the air.

"Thought you understood back at the hospital room, she's not just your girl," I grit through clenched teeth.

"So we're one big happy fucking family now? Is that what we're doing? And we'll show up to Mom and Dad's house for Sunday dinner with our one shared girlfriend between us? Not fucking likely." Rafe scoffs as he looks out the window.

"Over my dead body. They'll never share the same air," I seethe. "And I've told her as much."

"Oh yeah? And when did you have that conversation? When you were conveniently waylaid by a nurse?" Dante asks.

I lift my shoulder, the one that's not supporting Maddie. "It doesn't matter. Do you honestly want him anywhere near her?"

Matteo pinches the bridge of his nose. "Of course, I don't want him anywhere near her. We also have to be practical. Angelo Rossi is an infected, rotting tree, and with every little bug that lands on his diseased branches, he delivers his poison. He spreads it to every tree, one branch at a time. Before long, the entire forest will be compromised."

"Yeah, and how do we stop it—stop him?"

"We burn the forest down." Dante's words ring with a finality that sends a ripple of premonition through the car. Even Maddie stirs, but she stays asleep.

"But it takes time, time I fear we don't have much of. Dad showing up at the hospital uninvited is a clue, a fucking test. One I would be remiss not to pay attention to. Dante and I did everything in our power to make sure no one knew where I was. Which means what?" Matteo asks, his eyebrows raised.

"Which means he has someone in the hospital in his pocket," I offer, my mind spinning.

"That or the police from the nine-one-one call, which is probably more likely," Matteo agrees.

"Okay, so what do we do now?" I ask, my words tumbling out

quick in my eagerness.

"We have to regroup and quickly. I'll have to be back in the city in less than a week for the next council meeting. So we need to have a plan by then."

He doesn't offer any more information and I don't question him again. The car devolves into silence again, but this one doesn't feel as heavy, each of us tangled up in our own shit inside our heads.

I'm not afraid of getting my hands dirty, and I'm not afraid of my father. The only thing that gives me pause is the well-being of the woman in my arms. So I make her a promise and throw it out to the universe, planting in amongst the stars.

I'll do everything in my power to keep her, so if that means swearing in the family business, so be it.

chapter sixteen

Madison

Gentle hands rouse me from a deep sleep. "We're here, baby."

I open my eyes with a sigh, my lashes sticking together and my lids heavy. "What? Where are we?"

"We're at Dante's place. Let's get you inside and then you can go back to sleep," Leo murmurs. His deep voice is close but not loud.

I blink a few times to clear my vision and see that Leo and I are the only ones still in the car. I look across him out the window to see that Dante, Matteo, and Aries are walking up a grand staircase to a porch that wraps around a gigantic house. House feels too small of a word. *Mansion* feels more appropriate.

It looks like something out of one of those *Town and Country* magazines. You know, the kind you see on the table in the waiting rooms of every dentist office across the nation. The ones that feature the homes that the upper one-percent own.

This is not at all what I was expecting when Dante said he had a safe place in mind for us to regroup.

I tip my head to the side to get a better look at the place. My mouth parts on an exhale. "This is—this is Dante's house?"

"Not what you were expecting, huh?" Leo teases me as I push off his chest to straighten up on my seat and unbuckle my seatbelt.

"No, it's just that when he said he had a place in the Hamptons. I was expecting something a little . . . less."

"Yeah, I know I'm just teasing you. I didn't know he had this place either. C'mon, let's go inside." Leo's voice is warm and dripping with mirth.

I scoot forward and hop out of the car, swiping my thumb along my mouth to catch any drool. I'm a little surprised by how deep I slept, and I'm glad I didn't do something embarrassing, like drool all over Leo's shirt.

I take a few steps and then stop to take in the view. Leo stops right behind me with a hand on my hip.

I can't tear my eyes away from the mansion in front of me to even look at him. I don't really know what to call it. Somehow, *mansion* seems wrong too. It's like something out of a movie with castle-like vibes.

Huge pine trees and sugar maples line both sides of the long driveway, and in the front yard, to my right, is a weeping willow. It might be the biggest one I've ever seen. Butterflies swirl around in my belly when another weeping willow comes to mind. I cut a glance at Leo, not surprised to find his eyes on me and a smirk on his face. I'm sure we're thinking about the same thing.

I can't see too much more of the landscaping as I look around, but I imagine it's breathtaking in the daylight. The night sky is mesmerizing here, the deepest blue with white twinkling lights that feel close enough to touch. The moon sits nearly full, without a cloud in sight.

The outside lights come to life and cast a soft glow around the house. Flood lights illuminate the architecture of the house, and small bulbs line the pathways leading around the property.

"Wow, this is—"

"Incredible," Leo finishes my train of thought. "I can't believe he's been hiding this little gem for so long. Do you know how many times I wanted to get away from the city? I could've been coming here for years."

I knock my shoulder into him gently. "Yeah, well, maybe that's why he didn't tell you. Who would want a bunch of St. Bart's boys up here causing chaos?"

Leo smiles, the affection hitting his dark-green gaze. "Probably the same people who wouldn't let a bunch of St. Rita's girls loose."

A laugh bubbles up, catching me by surprise. I place a finger against my smiling lips, marveling at how wonderful that emotion is. It's almost jarring in how foreign it feels. The last few days have been harrowing, and my heart feels full of renewed hope after being reunited with my men.

I reach behind me and slide my palm into his hand against my hip. "Ready to go in?"

He flashes me another smile, and I wouldn't be surprised if he has a string of broken hearts in his wake. That thing is lethal. The perfect combination of boyish charm and confidence.

He threads our fingers together and walks toward the house. "Yeah, I don't know about you but I could use something to drink."

My stomach chooses that moment to let out a rumble. Warmth flushes my cheeks and I place a palm over my grumbling stomach.

He laughs and tugs me along behind him. "Okay, okay. Drink *and* eat."

Multicolored stonework wraps around the bottom third of the house and light-gray siding covers the rest. I'm pretty sure there's a turret or two on the side of the house, lending to the castle vibe.

Tall bay windows frame the front door and a bunch of windows cover both sides of the front of the house. The driveway goes off to the left, where I imagine there's a multi-car garage. With a house this size, I wouldn't be surprised if there were two garages— enough to fit ten cars.

We hit the wraparound porch and walk through the open front door that's easily twelve feet tall. Wooden French doors carved into a sweeping archway, it's an intimidating entrance. Voices carry from further inside, and as one, Leo and I head in their direction. A few lights are on, but even in the dim lighting, I can see this place is a palace in the true sense of wealth.

The walls are white and tall, with thick quarter round on the bottom and ornate crown molding at the top. One of the most elaborate glass chandeliers I've ever seen offers a soft glow, sending prisms of light across the floor. And to my right is a wide staircase leading to the upper two levels.

Wonder pricks at my senses, the need to explore gently luring me to the dark depths of this place. I would never do it without asking permission, of course, but I have a healthy appreciation for new places like this. And just enough curiosity to appreciate the history.

A short hallway later, and we get our first glimpse of the living space. It's an open-concept, so the kitchen space bleeds right into the dining area and they both flow into the living room, which is easily the size of an apartment.

A whole wall of windows leads from the living room to the backyard patio. The curtains are open, so the moonlight's glow ripples on the surface of the pool off the patio. Yard lights illuminate the backyard every ten feet or so, but I can't see much more than the pool from here.

I can feel how wide my eyes are as I spin around to take in the space. Low-profile chairs frame a velvet couch that looks more like a bed than a traditional couch—the seat cushions are deeper than normal. A blond wood coffee table is between the couch and the wide fireplace, with a seventy-inch TV above it.

The dining room table is long with enough room to seat twelve people, and it matches the coffee table. A metal bowl sits in the middle of the table, but otherwise, it's empty. There's another living space on the other side of the dining area, but it's bare. Only an office desk with a tall-backed fabric chair and a large, empty bookcase fill that space.

I finish my spin to find Dante and Matteo a flurry of movement in the kitchen. They're murmuring to one another as they gather ingredients from the fridge and the pantry. It looks like they had the same idea as we did.

Leo brushes his hand against mine as he walks in the kitchen, heading toward the sink. He washes his hands, drying them on a nearby towel that has an embroidered goat on the front. "Alright, what are we making?"

Dante turns and tosses him a few deli-wrapped items from the fridge. "Sandwiches. It's about all I have right now. We'll get a grocery delivery tomorrow morning."

"Perfect, our girl's hungry. You like tomato and lettuce on your sandwiches?" Leo asks me.

My stomach growls again and I smirk. "Yeah, that sounds amazing. How can I help?"

"Why don't you grab the plates? They're in the cabinet next to the fridge," Dante says as he sets down a handful of condiments.

I skirt around the island and wash my hands in the farmhouse sink. It's a perfect mix of modern, and surprisingly, farmhouse chic, not exactly what I would expect for Dante's style, but I'm finding out new things about these men every day—every minute that I'm with them.

And so far, I really like what I see.

I press my wet fingertips against the inside of my wrists. My grandma once taught me that trick if you needed to cool down or stop the spins. Place a cool washcloth on the back of your neck or run your wrists under cool water. Of course, then my grandpa always mumbled about never sleeping with your socks on.

Sometimes, when I'm doing the most menial of tasks, like washing my hands, a memory strikes like lightning. In this case, it's my grandparents. It's been years since I've seen them, and while the ache for them is still there, it's lessened over the years. Now, instead of depression lining that memory that the cool water on my wrists evokes, fondness coats it. I can still hear her sweet southern voice ringing in my head as I put my wrist underneath the cool tap water and just exhale.

Of course, my stomach chooses that moment to grumble out a quiet request—a demand, really. I can't remember the last time I ate. I shake off the memory as I grab the plates and place them on the island. Matteo finishes slicing up some of what looks like homemade bread.

The whole thing seems like a seamless, instinctive choreographed routine, and it sends a swarm of butterflies a flight. Hope blossoms in the center of the roost, shining a soft glow on the possibility that this can work. A relationship between me—and all of them. I roll my lips inward as I take in the scene for a moment.

Before I get carried away with fantasies about coming home to Matteo cooking us dinner every night, Dante places a sandwich on a plate and slides it toward me. "Ham and turkey."

"You should've asked her if she wanted that first," Leo grumbles.

Dante just stares at Leo for a moment before he resumes assembling another sandwich. I wave a hand in the air, brushing off his protest. It's sweet of him to look out for me like that, but honestly, I'd eat anything right now.

"This is perfect, thank you." I grab the plate and slide on to one of six stools on the other side of the island.

Leo brings his plate and two bottles of iced tea and sits on my right. "Here, thought you might like this."

I reach for the bottle, our fingertips brushing against one another with a little spark of affection. "Thanks."

"Anytime," he says around a grin.

Matteo and Dante stay standing on the opposite side of the island, facing us, and we all tuck into our meals. After a few bites, my stomach settles down a little, and I feel a little more like myself. I didn't realize just how hungry I was.

"Where's Aries?" I ask, looking at the fifth sandwich in front of me and taking another bite.

Leo sets down his bottled iced tea. "I've been meaning to ask: Why do you call him that?"

I finish chewing the bite I just took, but before I can respond, I feel it. The smallest change in the air, the barest whisper of touch along my shoulders, a second before I hear him.

"None of your business, kid." Aries's voice comes from behind me. He pulls out the stool on my other side, shifting it closer to me. With an exhale, he settles onto the stool, his thigh pressing against mine. I bite my lip like I'm the heroine in some historical romance novel, getting those telltale tingles at the feeling of his suit-pant-clad thigh pressed against my bare one. I almost giggle at the whole thing, but I'm able to swallow it down with a sip of iced tea.

Aries nabs his plate and dives in. It's quiet, only the occasional murmur as we all eat. The silence isn't heavy or charged, it's comfortable, and it only feeds my hope further. Despite knowing how dangerous hope can be, I revel in the possibility.

chapter seventeen

Madison

D ante pulls out a bottle of whiskey from a cabinet above the refrigerator. There's a sea of bottles up there, and most of them look full. He grabs five modern-cut highball glasses from another cabinet and brings it all to the island. "I think we all could use a nightcap," he says as he pours two fingers in each glass. He glances at Aries. "Everything taken care of?"

"It's sorted. For now," Aries replies as Dante slides a glass to him.

Dante slides the remaining glasses to each of us as I patiently wait for someone to fill me in. I cradle the glass in my hand and look at each of them from beneath my lashes. When it becomes apparent that no one is going to offer anything else, I decide to assert myself.

"What's going on?"

"Nothing you need to worry about." Matteo takes a healthy sip of his drink.

Irritation spikes in my bloodstream, and I debate on whether or not I have the energy to dive into this tonight. I knew that starting a relationship with multiple men would have some growing pains, and I knew that any sort of relationship with men of their *connections* would also have some unique challenges.

But marrying those two concepts together might be a bigger task than I anticipated. Luckily for everyone, I love a good challenge.

I take a small sip of the whiskey, wincing as it burns a path of fire down my throat. I set my glass down and stare right at Matteo. "Right, well, I thought we agreed to be more honest with one another if we want this to work."

"And what is this, exactly?" Aries asks.

I tilt my head to the side. "What?"

He motions between me and them with his index finger and a glass in his hand. "This. You. Them. And me."

I take a deep breath and swivel the stool to face Aries. "I'm into them. And you. So I want us to date. All of us. More accurately, you'll date me, and no one else." I keep my gaze locked on Aries, even though I see Matteo and Dante shift out of the corner of my eye.

Aries whistles under his breath, the noise low and equal parts astonishment and sarcasm. I wasn't sure a single noise, a half whistle, no less, could sound sarcastic, but that's the best way to describe it.

"Is that right?"

I tip my head up as my heart beats harder in my chest. There's a very real possibility that Aries will walk away from this—from me. But I promised myself that I would take those chances, and I like to think I'm a woman of my word. "Yes."

As he slouches in his chair, he spreads his legs apart even further, and his knee slides between my legs. My breath hitches, but I don't take my gaze away from his.

Aries can play my body better than most men—all the men in this room can, really. But if he thinks reminding me of that fact will deter me, he's wrong. All it's doing is turning me on.

"I realize you didn't know about them." To be fair, he didn't really know about me—he didn't really even *know* me. "The thing is, I'm not going to choose. I want all four of you. And I make no apology for it. I'll understand if this isn't what you want, but I selfishly hope you'll stay." I sink my teeth into my bottom lip as I think over what I want to say. His gaze is glued to my mouth, bolstering my courage. "And I understand I'm being unfair by asking you not to see anyone else but me. But I *am* asking that. I can't explain the magnetic pull I have to each of you, only that it's there and it's the realest thing I've felt . . . ever." I pause and make eye contact with each man in the room.

I swivel in my stool to make eye contact with Leo. It's important for me to see their faces in this moment where I declare my wants and desires. A lethal smirk tips up the corner of his mouth on his too-handsome face and his eyes dance with glee. He's enjoying this. Whether he's enjoying watching his brother squirm or me, I'm not sure. I wonder if he still thinks he can win me over. He talked a big talk in the coffee shop days ago. God, that seems like a year ago now and not a week.

But I meant what I said then.

Just because he's being charming, just because I like seeing a playful Leo, I hold his gaze and say, "I'm not going to change my mind and pick one of you. But I'll enjoy every minute you spend trying to persuade me otherwise."

I raise an eyebrow halfway through my declaration, and he reads the challenge for exactly what it is.

His smirk turns into a wide grin as he drags his teeth over his bottom lip. "Alright, Madison. I hear you."

"It's been a long day. Maybe we should table this discussion for now," Dante offers. "Why don't I show you to your room, Maddie?"

I give in and do what feels natural. Leaning forward, I brush a kiss across the corner of Leo's mouth. I'm gone in a second. It's not meant to linger or to be taken further, but a small reminder. An acknowledgement of our unspoken and insinuated agreement.

Before I can slide off my stool, it's swiveled around, so I'm face to face with Aries again. His legs land on either side of mine this time, bracketing me, and holding me hostage. Not that I'm complaining. He leans forward, and I notice the difference instantly. Long gone is the arrogant, lazy playboy persona and in its place is the face of a mafia boss's son.

Determination and raw hunger.

I feel my lids lower as lust crawls over me like a heavy mist. It's almost as if everything else fades away. He leans toward me, close enough that I could tip my chin up ever so slightly, and his mouth would be on mine. For a breath, there's nothing else that I crave more than that. I yearn to feel his mouth on me again.

But I'm coherent enough to realize that he has to be the one to make the first move here. I've laid down my cards. Now it's up to him to either accept them or move on. The way he looks at me tells me he's not moving on. And I can only hope that it's not a cruel trick.

"What are you doing to me, Raven?" he whispers.

I smell whiskey on his breath and something inherently him—like a day spent in the sun at the beach. He leans in further, pushing some hair off my face with his fingertips.

"Hmm?"

Even though it's a question, I know it's more rhetorical than anything. So I don't answer. Instead, I taunt him and tilt my head to the side, just a fraction of a movement really, and lick my lips. It's enough. His hand stills on the side of my head, threaded in my hair by my ear.

He exhales a harsh breath across my lips. There's a war going on inside my Aries, and I get a front row seat. Someone clears their throat, and I remember we're not alone.

That's the thing about Aries and I. Is it natural chemistry, or something more?

I often thought that I was meant for great things. I think everyone does. When you're younger, you're told stories of greatness. It's the ultimate American dream. But as you grow older, you realize it's a tall tale, a fable meant to inspire. Instead, all it does is lead to feelings of inadequacy and most likely, substance abuse.

But when I look at Aries—when I look at Matteo, Leo, Dante—and when I have their attention on me, it feels like I could do anything. They make me feel weightless and alive. Buoyed by that fickle bitch, hope.

"It's been a long day. Let's call it a night. We'll regroup in the morning and talk strategy over breakfast," Matteo says.

Aries stares at me for another moment before he huffs a disbelieving sort of sigh and shifts back into the stool, though he never moves his legs, still keeping me trapped between them.

"Come on, Maddie. I'll show you to your room now," Dante offers as he walks around the island.

I slide my palms up Aries thighs, stopping a few inches from where my hands really itch to explore and use him as leverage to shift off the stool.

His corded muscles flex underneath my touch. A perverse sort of thrill runs through me at the idea of finally seeing Aries, finally *feeling* him without any clothing between us. He's starred in some of my fantasies since the night we met, but I have a feeling my fantasy version will pale in comparison to the real thing.

All it would take is a swivel of my hips, and I'd be in his lap. Lust coils low in my belly at the idea, and it's fueled even more by knowing that we have an audience.

I had no idea I was into voyeurism. And maybe I'm not, unless it's the right audience.

I flick my gaze from where my hands are on his thighs to his eyes, noticing his clenched jaw and his too-still frame. So he's just as affected. Good.

With deliberate slowness, I move out from between his legs, letting my fingertips trail across him as I cross the room to stand next to Dante.

"Perfect. I could really use a hot shower," I tell Dante, never looking back, despite feeling the heat from three gazes.

chapter eighteen

Madison

We cross through the open floor plan of the living room to the hallway leading to the other side of the house. Or maybe it's a great room—I get a little fuzzy on the proper room titles. Considering this is the biggest living room I've ever seen, I can't tell when it stops being a living room and morphs into a great room.

And oh my god—I can't believe I'm rambling inside my head about the room names. I'm going to blame Aries. He scrambled all my senses.

As if he can sense my mind is caught up, Dante asks, "All of us, huh?"

Despite the numerous pep talks about owning my own desires, I can't stop my body's initial reaction or the flush that accompanies it. The tops of my cheeks feel warm, and they only get warmer at Dante's insinuation. I'm ninety percent sure he didn't mean *all of us* like that, but I kind of did.

I clear my throat and look at him in a futile attempt to read his mood. That man's emotions are locked down so tight, it's hard to gauge his reaction. It kind of makes me want to do something to provoke him though. Nothing too wild, but something crazy enough to shock him out of his emotional straightjacket.

"Yep."

Apparently, my single word was the right response, because I get my desired reaction. He smirks, this little smile playing along the corner of his mouth. He runs his fingers across his jaw, scuffing his five o'clock shadow.

"Alright, I guess we can talk about it more tomorrow."

I bite the inside of my cheek and look over at him as our steps slow. We pause in front of another staircase. This one's smaller than the one in the front foyer.

"We can, but I'm not going to change my mind." I let myself linger over his features for a moment, looking for any obvious signs of distaste. His expression remains carefully blank, his black hair falling across his forehead in a way that makes my fingers itch to brush it back.

Instead, I slide my hand along the ornate wooden handrail, and turn around to head upstairs. A hand on my wrist stops me.

Pivoting on the ball of my foot, I turn until we're nearly eye to eye, close enough that I can see the silver specks in his dark eyes. They look as mesmerizing as constellations in the sky. And any question I had dries up on the tip of my tongue as the look in his eye holds me hostage.

He keeps my gaze, never wavering, just stares at me, and somehow, it's one of the most intimate moments I've experienced. My body unconsciously arches toward him as if we're opposite ends of a magnet, and some sort of otherworldly force is pulling us together. It's a magnetism I can't deny, not that I would ever want to.

His fingertips brush small, soft strokes on the sensitive skin on the back of my wrist. It grounds me as if his very presence and that simple touch roots me—not to this house or even this city, but to him.

I wet my lips with my tongue, my breaths coming in heavier than they were a moment before as anticipation tingles in my fingertips.

But just like with Aries, I'm not going to be the one to make the first move. Not when it comes to this. My stomach clenches, and I can't tell if it's because I'm nervous or excited—or maybe a bit of both. I resist the urge to roll up onto my tiptoes to close the gap between us.

After what feels like an agonizingly long minute, Dante steps forward, and with his free hand, he brushes my hair behind my ear with a tenderness that soothes me. "Why were you late earlier?"

His question throws me for a moment. The foggy residue of lust clouds my brain when I ask the one word barely more than a murmur.

"What?"

He slides his hand to the back of my head, keeping his fingers threaded in my hair and using his thumb to tilt my jaw upward. "At the hospital. Why were you late?"

"Why does it matter?" I counter, my brows scrunching low.

"Because everything you do matters."

I exhale and try to wipe the grin off my face before it fully forms. I have a sneaking suspicion that Dante is jealous. I wonder what it would take to get him to let his jealousy out to play a little. And what sorts of things would settle him back down. Wasn't I just asking fate to give me an opportunity to get to know this man better? Asking for a reason to push his emotions closer to the surface?

Well, here it is, I think to myself.

My grandma used to say that jealousy burns hotter than any sort of hellfire. Guess I'm about to find out if that's true.

With my mind made up, I push up onto my tiptoes. "Did you wish it was you?" My lips slide against his with every word.

He tightens his hold on the back of my head, not to the point of pain, but enough to let me know I struck a nerve. "You let the kid inside that pretty pussy? Hmm? Is that why you were late meeting me?" His words are crass but he delivers them with a gentleness that belies the meaning behind them and only serves to bring my libido to life.

I'm going to indulge myself and taunt him, stirring his jealousy with a hot poker. Sure, I could easily point out that there was only a fifteen-minute window, but his possessiveness feels like a salve to my bruised soul. I don't know why or how, but I've decided to stop questioning things, if only for tonight.

This is the rawest emotion I've seen from him, and I'm not about to waste it. I can only hope that this doesn't backfire and push him away. I have to believe that this is where I'm supposed to be. With them.

I flick my tongue out and trace it along the edge of his lip. A quiet curse falls from his mouth. "Are you jealous, Dante? Do you wish that you were the one who pulled me into an empty hospital room and pressed me up against a wall and shoved your—"

He uses his grip on my head to arch my neck. A gasp leaves me before I can stop it, cutting off my words. The small show of dominance sends a spike of arousal through me, slow and languid.

"Is that what you think, Maddie? Do you think I'd be satisfied with a quick fuck inside a hospital room that reeks of death and decay? A place that any stupid motherfucker could walk in and see you? Is that the kind of man you think I am?"

"What kind of man are you then, Dante?"

He slides his mouth up the column of my neck before biting down on my ear. He uses his teeth just hard enough to make me feel alive. "I'm not the hero, baby girl."

"Good thing I don't want a hero then," I pant out between breaths.

"If we do this, there's no coming back from it, yeah?" He pulls back to study my face for a moment, looking for something. "Because I already know I'll never have enough of you. Not ever." He bites the words out in the harsh whisper as if the admission pains him.

My heart beats hard and fast in my chest as lust crawls through my nerves, making me feel both heavy and weightless. Desperation to feel him against me claws at my veins. I push up onto my tiptoes again, straining against his hold and aching to feel his skin on mine.

For once, it feels like the universe is listening.

Dante must see whatever he was waiting for on my face, because he nods once before he lowers his head. He drags his mouth along my jaw ending his exploration with his lips against mine. He groans almost instantly, the noise deep and low—*and primal*. It sets off a chain reaction in my body. And nothing else exists—not the events of the past few days, not the uncertainty of what I have to face tomorrow—nothing.

For right now, in this moment, it's just me and him.

He releases my wrist, and I instantly wrap my arms around his neck, pressing against his chest. With a hand on the back of my neck still, he slides his other hand under my ass and lifts me up, spinning and crushing me against the nearby wall. We're halfway up the staircase, a precarious position to take our relationship to the next level. But I don't know that I could stop even if I wanted to.

He attacks my mouth with the same fervor I've heard he does everything in life, with an intensity that most men have never even dreamed of. It's intoxicating. I can taste his passion on his tongue, his lust writing every touch, every nip, every press.

He grinds his pelvis against mine, and I moan when I feel the hard outline of his cock right against my pussy. My hips roll against his, causing that delicious friction.

He gives me the illusion of control for another few seconds before he tilts my head to the side and deepens the kiss on his terms. Something about the way he so easily manipulates my body sends another flame of lust through me.

"It's one thing to know about it, but it's an entirely different thing to see it *in person*." Matteo's voice comes from behind Dante, and I flinch at how frosty it is.

I'm not embarrassed, and if I had time to really think about it, I might find some humor in the situation of my one mafia boyfriend catching my other mafia boyfriend shoving me against a wall and ravaging my mouth. But as it stands, I'm too turned on. *Growing pains*, remember?

Dante doesn't move from his spot in front of me, but I have

to assume he knew Matteo was coming. He pulls back with a lingering, soft kiss against the corner of my mouth. But he doesn't remove his hand from my ass or the back of my head, and I don't untangle my legs from around his waist.

Tipping my head back against the wall, I catch my breath. The sound of our combined breathing feels loud in the expectant silence. I roll my head along the wall, my hair catching on the rough texture. It's only then I remember that I probably look a mess—and his walls are white.

"Shit."

"What's wrong?" Dante asks, giving me his undivided attention.

I cringe. "I just remembered that I have dirt and dried blood in my hair. I should probably take care of that before I stain anything else."

"I'm not afraid of a little blood, baby girl."

My skin feels tight, and I can't take my gaze from his. I'm a second away from throwing *all* my inhibitions to the wind when Matteo clears his throat again.

"Everything okay, Matteo?" My voice is a little breathless. My heart's beating so fast, it feels like it's going to beat right out of my chest. And I swear to God, I can feel my heartbeat in my clit.

"I'm a man who is used to getting what he wants, Maddie." Matteo's voice is close, but I can't see anything beyond Dante's broad shoulders.

A muscle jumps in Dante's jaw, and my gaze zeroes in on the way he must be grinding his molars. I'm distantly aware that I'm behaving a little out of character. I'm not sure if I should seek some therapy for my reactions to their jealous or possessive grumblings.

But there's no denying that I like it. I think I might more than like it.

I'm high on Dante's kiss, my own lust swirling in the air around us, permeating this little bubble we've created around us. And so I ride that wave, that high even further.

Tipping my chin up, I let my lips brush across Dante's cheek as I tell Matteo, "I remember who you are." I lightly scrape my teeth against his jaw, and it has the intended effect. A low groan slips between his lips, and I swear I feel rather than hear Matteo's mood shift into that red haze.

People often say there's a thin line between love and hate, but I'm starting to wonder if there's a parallel between lust and possessiveness. Lucky for me, I've always been a good dancer. I'm confident I can tap dance right along that fine line, pushing and pulling each of my men over and back again. Never maliciously, but just enough to get my blood boiling—and theirs.

The air around us heats up with our collective arousal. It's coated in thick possessiveness, dominance. I let myself entertain the idea of letting Matteo and Dante have me at the same time. The thought sends more than a small thrill through me. It feels like a promise—a prophecy.

Dante's hand flexes on my ass. I don't know if he feels it too, or if it was an unconscious move, but I take it as an invitation. With my gaze fixated on his lips, I slowly roll my hips against his impressive bulge.

I brush my mouth along his neck, reveling in the tremors that wrack his body with every press of my skin against his. It's empowering and intoxicating. Dante shifts me in his hold, propping me up higher against the wall, and I finally see Matteo. His eyes have darkened to a molten black. Or maybe that's just my imagination. Either way he looks like some sort of avenging angel, ready to take his reward for saving the city again. With his arm in a sling and dressed more casually than I've ever seen him, he almost looks like anyone I would pass on the street. It's impressively deceptive. He's more like a chameleon than I ever gave him credit for. He's lethal on the best of days.

But today, like this, when I'm still riding the high of simply being alive, rejoicing in the fact that he is too, and allowing myself the freedom to explore my own desires and needs, I don't know if I can resist him. I don't know if I can resist any of them—I don't want to.

chapter nineteen

Matteo

I slide my hand into the pocket of my borrowed sweatpants and stare as impassively as possible at my best friend with his hands and *fucking mouth* all over my girl.

She's taunting me with her prolonged eye contact and breathy groans. Her red hair stands out against the white paint behind her like a beacon. She's a fucking siren, and I'm powerless to tell her no—for now, at least. She's absolutely stunning, and I hate that I'm not the one putting that look of bliss on her face.

A potent combination of rage and jealousy burns black deep inside my gut. People often mistake red as the color of rage. But when you grow up at the hands of Angelo Rossi *and* his friends, you learn to harness your emotions and turn them into weapons. I learned very early in life that your emotions can be a weakness and how quickly they can be used against you.

Love made me its bitch when it comes to Cherry.

And now I need to figure out how to turn it into my greatest strength. I have very few weaknesses, and she's my ultimate Achilles heel.

Angelo will destroy her if given even the slightest chance. I need to move up my timeline—and fast, which means I need my second at my side and not dry fucking my girl in the foyer. I know that motherfucker heard me, his senses are practically supernatural. The only conclusion is that he's provoking me. My trigger finger itches with the need to assert my dominance, but I tamp that shit down and focus on a better outlet for my frustration and aggression.

I sigh, but they don't come up for air. Jealousy eats at me, an oily mass that sticks to the inside of my gut. The kind that burns hot and bright and fast.

My toes hang off the edge of the canyon of swirling darkness that rests inside of me. It'd be so easy to jump in, to give myself over to years of conditioning and learned patterns of behavior.

But those were things I did to survive, and I did most of them with Dante at my side. I consciously take a step back from this swirling mass of darkness that lives inside me. It's an unending cavern that's been growing unchecked for years. I almost feel bad for whoever pushes me over the edge, I don't even know what I'm capable of if gone unchecked.

But even though I recognize my jealousy, it doesn't mean I've lost my head completely. This is my friend—my best fucking friend. And no, I don't really want to kill him even though I would do so much more to anyone else who put their hands on what's mine.

I bite the inside of my cheek in frustration. Now I have to amend that fucking thought too. Goddammit, I haven't had enough booze for this mess yet. I've been so focused on finding her, everything else got pushed to the backburner—including the fact that she's interested in my best friend and my brother.

Brothers, I correct myself silently.

What are the fucking odds that one petite redhead storms into all of our lives like a certified wrecking ball? Or that the same woman somehow ensnared both of my brothers, who I sent away from this place—from this *family*—to keep them safe? She's obliterating everything I thought I knew about myself and about this world.

Dante repositions her, shoves her against the wall with a thump, stealing my attention again. I was doing a fucking good job of ignoring the building jealousy in my gut, but with that overtly move, I lose what little control I had left on my patience.

"Dante, a word," I snap.

He takes his sweet fucking time pulling away from her, and she looks at me with kiss-swollen lips and glassy eyes. Jealousy surges inside me, demanding penance. But there's something else underneath. A perversion, a twisted sort of satisfaction slithers through my veins at the sight of her so thoroughly mussed up.

Her cheeks are flushed, and I know for a fact it extends down her neck and across the top of those perfect tits. He finally sets her down on her feet, holding her steady for a moment. I grind my molars at the amount of care he's taking with her. I should be glad that he's treating her so kindly, but I'm not a fucking robot, and the fact that my best friend—who kills people for a living—treats this woman like she's made of glass fucks me up a little.

My lip curls up in anticipation of his smug look of satisfaction. Instead, his face is carefully blank. I smirk at him and tip my head back with a nod of appreciation. I should've expected this from him. I knew he was sniffing around her, but I had no idea it was to this degree.

For nearly my entire life, Dante has always had my six. He's the perfect second. But Maddie changes everything, and I have to wonder if my second just found a new boss.

He's smart enough to play it like a game, and that asshole is winning. Maddie clears her throat, pulling my focus to her. Again. I'm going to blame my distractedness on the pain meds I'm still on.

"Oh, well, this is a little awkward, isn't it? Lainey told me there's going to be some bumps in the road to this sort of thing. So speaking of which, can I borrow someone's phone? I really need to call her and Mary." She looks at Dante first, and I flatten my lips together to stifle the words I want to snap out.

He slides a phone from his pocket and hands it over without hesitation.

"Thanks," she murmurs. "Now about that shower." She raises her eyebrows as she looks at Dante.

"Bedrooms are on the second floor, to the left. The master suite is the last door at the end of the hall. That'll be your room while we're here. It has an en suite bathroom. Help yourself to anything."

She flashes him a secretive grin that tips up the corner of her lips before she places a hand on his bicep and brushes a chaste kiss against his lips. I frown at the jealousy spiking in my gut, acidic and oily. She descends the stairs until she's right in front of me. She gives me a small smile before she brushes those plush lips against my cheek. I turn my head as she pulls away, our lips just barely touching. Her breath hitches, and she lingers there for a moment.

I feel like fucking pre-pubescent boy right now, vying for her attention and chaste kisses. What the fuck is going on with me? I'm the underboss of the entire Rossi family crime syndicate, and I'm over here simpering over some girl like a middle schooler.

Her smile blossoms into a smirk before she spins around and climbs the stairs two at a time. We watch her go up, both of us silent. I count to ten, and even though I don't hear a door close, I figure she's out of earshot.

I pivot on my heel, purposely leaving my hand in my pocket to project nonchalance, and stare at him. My best friend, my brother in all but blood. "You gave her your fucking room?"

"How do you know it's mine?" He wipes his thumb underneath his mouth as if he's cleaning up after her. That asshole knows exactly what he's doing, but I guess I'm the bigger asshole because I let it bother me.

"Coy isn't a good look on you, man," I snap.

He smiles at me, mirth dancing in his gaze. "Ah, but has anyone told you green is your color?"

"Fuck off, Dante."

"I'd rather fuck—"

My patience snaps like a rubber band. "If you value your life, you're not going to finish that sentence. I've been lenient, *real fucking lenient*, but I'm fucking done for the day, yeah?"

He shuts down, not an expression on his face. "Sure thing, boss."

I pull my hand from my pocket and scrub it down my face. Exhaustion beats against my skin. "Don't do that, man. This isn't like that."

He nods. "Things are changing, Matteo. It's on you how you want to play it, but know that she's now a priority for me as well. She's made the list."

He looks at me for a moment, making sure I understand the

severity of that statement before walking down the hall.

Fuck. Dante's infamous list. It's a short one, and on it are the names that he'll happily offer his services for. I still remember the day he stood up to Dad and flat-out told him he wouldn't offer any of his expertise to anyone but me.

It's unending loyalty, and in our life, a promise you don't take lightly.

chapter twenty

Madison

Ipad down the hallway with an extra sway in my hips, bolstered from all the affection. I peek into the rooms of the open doorways as I pass them. I can't see much, only enough to know that they're bedrooms just like Dante said. Pushing open the last door at the end of the hall, my breath catches in my throat at the sheer size of this bedroom.

I flip on the light switch and soft canned lighting illuminates the space. Fifteen-foot vaulted ceilings with a metal and wood art-deco-style chandelier. Sliding glass doors on one side of the room lead to a balcony overlooking the backyard. Blond hardwood floors and a muted gray plush rug. Light cream-colored paint on the walls make the large space look even bigger.

There's a modern-style fireplace in the corner, set halfway up the wall. Though it's not lit right now, I imagine it's quite cozy. A fifty-inch flat screen picture frame TV is mounted on the wall across from the biggest bed I've ever seen.

It looks like someone pushed two California king platform beds together to form one massive bed that sleeps seven. The quilted headboard is gray and low profile with cream and gray linens to match. And what's most interesting is the two throw pillows on top of the bed. I brush my fingers across the crushed velvet of one throw pillow, enjoying the way it swirls to a lighter color with every swipe.

This has to be the master bedroom. Everything in here screams luxury, and I really wonder who originally lived in this house. What kind of people needed a bed this size? I bite my lip at the obvious answer right in front of me.

Maybe someone who had multiple someones? A little laugh slips out. I hope it was a reverse harem. The world needs more of them if you ask me.

I eye the bed with interest. Yeah, I guess I could get used to that. I've never really slept with someone before outside of Lainey and Mary when we used to fall asleep during movie nights. But I think I would like the cuddling, the affection. The idea of falling asleep and waking up in someone's arms everyday sounds really nice. I don't mind being the little spoon for the right person. I laugh to myself again, more *at* myself this time as I walk across the large room into the bathroom.

I flip the switch and soft white light fills the room. My lips part in awe. It's stunning. Shiny gray marble floors gleam from underneath my dirty shoes, almost an entire wall is a three-sink vanity with a huge mirror. It gives more weight to my multiple-partner theory. A large bay window takes up one side of the room with an ornate, clawfoot bathtub in front of it. I eye the bathtub with interest. I've never really been one to take a bath, but I could definitely see myself reclining here, maybe with a good romance book and a glass of something fruity. Jesus, there's even a vaulted ceiling in here.

The shower is across from the vanity—if you can even call it that. It's almost the size of the kitchen in my apartment. It's a walk-in shower without doors or a curtain. I step inside and see that it has a digital temperature control system. There's also a speaker, four shower heads with what looks like specialty settings, a bench, and a handful of shower products.

It's perfect. I set the temperature and step out to undress, leaving my clothes in a neat pile on the floor. I'll worry about clean clothes later. Placing a hand underneath the water, I test the temperature. I'm not surprised to find it's perfect.

Stepping into the shower, I quickly program one of the three open shower heads and angle it so it sprays on me too.

When I step backward into the spray closest to me, a soul-deep sigh leaves me. How many times have I taken for granted the warmth and relaxation a hot shower offers? *Never again*, I vow. I close my eyes and wet my hair, letting the water slide over my skin, washing away the events of the past couple of days. Grabbing shampoo from the shelf next to me, I squirt a dollop in my hand and lather it in my hair.

What a pleasant coincidence, it's the same brand that I use, just a different scent. Jasmine fills the air, along with steam. After shampooing, I condition my hair and use the body wash I found. There's no label, but something about the scent reminds me of

Dante.

After I finish, I'm not quite ready to leave, so I decide to test out the rest of the shower heads. I turn them on and adjust their settings so each one offers a different spray pattern.

I try to relax, but I'm still too keyed up from everything downstairs with Dante—and knowing Matteo was watching.

I sigh against the billowing steam and the feel of the different shower jets against my skin. By all accounts, I should be a mindless puddle of relaxation.

But when I close my eyes, I feel Dante's hands and mouth on me.

I bite my lip as I fantasize what would have happened if Matteo hadn't interrupted us.

Would I have begged him?

Would I have gotten on my knees for him?

Would he have taken me against the wall?

With flashes of Dante in my vision, I detach the nearby shower head. This one is set on a soft, almost pulsating spray pattern, and it feels amazing against my sensitive skin. I bring it up to my breasts and angle the shower head so it feels like someone is gently squeezing them.

With my other hand, I reach up and pinch my nipple, enjoying the bite of pain.

After a moment, I lower the spray and tease myself with slow movements. My chest heaves with labored breaths as I keep my eyes closed tight and imagine it's Dante's hands. His fingers. His mouth on my skin instead.

I turn the handle over in my hand so it's pointing more upward, and angle it toward my pussy. Tingles of euphoria race up from my toes as lust courses through my body at a speed I wasn't expecting.

A low moan leaves my lips at the feeling of the water against my sensitive skin. I rotate it slowly, so it hits every angle.

Water beats down against my clit in a way that reminds me of my favorite battery operated boyfriend back at the dorms.

"Dante," I moan, still caught up in the fantasy. I pretend it's his mouth flicking my clit, his fingers pumping inside of me.

I feel cool fingers wrap around my hand holding the shower head, and my eyes fly open.

"Matteo." His name leaves my lips on a gasp.

He's standing in front of me, dressed in his sweatpants and sweatshirt, sling forgotten. The three shower heads drench him in seconds. He looks at me with a hunger unlike anything I've ever seen before.

"When you come, it's going to be my name on your lips, Cherry." He takes the shower head from me and switches the setting without even looking.

The pressure and tempo increase and the angle changes. If I thought I was climbing that mountain fast before, it's nothing compared to now. I feel like I'm on a roller coaster, and I'm almost at the top of the peak before I plummet.

My feet flex, and I instinctively push up onto my tiptoes, bracing myself for the orgasm that I know is going to detonate.

Matteo shifts closer as water sluices down his face. His hair looks nearly black across his forehead in soaking-wet tendrils. His eyes darken, nearly smolder as he lets me see his barely-restrained lust.

"Fuck yourself with your fingers, Cherry. I want to watch you."

As if I'm a puppet, and he is my puppet master, I slide a finger inside myself. Warmth radiates from my cheeks down my neck, and to my chest. I stare at him as I slowly slide in and out, in and out.

He glances down at my fingers before he looks back at me and shuffles closer. His sweatpants start to sag on his lean hips as they become increasingly wet.

"Two fingers, Cherry. Don't be shy on me now." His voice is husky and commanding. "Slip two fingers in that pretty pink pussy and show me what I've been fantasizing about every single day for two years."

His acknowledgement of our shared past ignites something low in my belly, something more than just lust. It's a need so visceral, I clench my teeth against the rising tide.

I slip another finger inside myself and tilt my head back, trying to stay in the moment and not get lost in the clouds. His heated stare feels like a physical touch, and my mouth parts on a breathy moan.

He continues his assault on my clit as I slide my fingers in and out faster.

"That's it. Good girl." He leans in, grabbing my bottom lip between his teeth and gently pulling. The pressure increases before he lets go and swipes his tongue over my lip, as if to soothe it.

"More," I beg.

It's like that one word was the key to unlocking the door that held him back. And then the next instant, he crushes his mouth to mine. There's no lead-up. It's a full on assault he plunges his tongue inside my mouth.

And in some uncanny way, it's mimicking the tempo of my fingers, so it feels like he's fucking my mouth. I want to lift my leg around his hip, desperate to be filled with more than just my fingers.

I ache to be touched, and I ache to touch him everywhere. But mostly I just ache for him.

He moves forward, pressing as much of his body against mine as he can while still holding the shower head. My fingers stutter in their pace, and I tilt my head back against the tile to maintain contact.

"Come on your fingers, Cherry."

That's the only warning I get. My muscles clench as pleasure so delicious races through my body. Everything clenches at his command as a mind-blowing orgasm rips through my body like a bolt of lightning, hot, bright, and overcharged.

Matteo doesn't move his mouth, and for a moment, we just share the same air as I come down from my high. My lashes flutter open—I didn't even realize I had closed them.

The look on Matteo's face is one I'll never forget for the rest of my life.

It's a longing, so desperate that it calls to my soul.

He doesn't withdraw the shower head, even when I squirm against the feeling of it against my overly sensitive clit. I tried to back away, but I'm already against the wall.

"Have you had enough?" he whispers against my mouth.

It feels like a loaded question, and the only answer is an echo of what Dante just told me.

"Never."

In one swift movement, he withdraws the showerhead, discarding it on the floor, where it sprays against the wall next to us. He slides his hand underneath my knee and lifts it to the bench next to me. He trails his hand up the back of my thigh and sinks to his knees.

My breath stalls as I stare at him.

My dark knight on his knees, swearing fealty to me.

His chest heaves with labored breaths as he curls his hand around mine. He brings my fingers to his mouth, wrapping his tongue around the same ones that were just inside my pussy moments before.

"Fucking delicious," he says on a growl.

I'm practically panting, heaving, trying to get more air in my lungs. The sight before me is liable to give me a heart attack.

He uses his hold on my thigh to spread my legs more, opening me up to him. His face is two inches away from my pussy, and if I didn't just have one of the best orgasms of my life, I might be feeling a little embarrassed. But he doesn't give me time to feel much of anything as he dips his head and licks me without another word.

"Oh, god, Matteo."

My eyes screw shut as he attacks my pussy with the same amount of calculated restraint he shows in life. He leaves no inch of me untouched, swirling his tongue between my folds and circling around my clit.

I'm sensitive from my earlier orgasm, and with each rotation around my clit, my legs shake. Small aftershocks of the explosion I've already felt. I rest my hand on his head, curling my fingers through his hair and hold them there as I shamelessly grind against his face.

He pulls back just enough so I can see my pleasure shine from his face. He licks his lips and stares me right in the eye. "You're the best thing I've ever tasted. And I want more, so you're going to come again."

"No, Matteo, I—I don't think I can," I stammer as he begins all over again. "It's too much."

"It's not," he counters. "Show me how you can be a good girl."

Those two words again, like magic, they unlock something deep inside of me. My body softens on instinct, my hips tilt to open myself up a little bit further for him.

He leans in to continue his exquisite torture on my most sensitive area. He's merciless in his quest for my pleasure. He never lets up, encouraging me to rub myself against his face, and when I'm so close to coming I can practically taste it, he plunges two fingers inside of me and wraps his lips around my clit.

My head hits the tile behind me, and I detonate.

chapter twenty-one

When I finally return to reality, I crack open my eyes to see Matteo push to his feet, licking his fingers clean. The sight of him so thoroughly enjoying me keeps that ember of lust burning inside me. He swipes a thumb under his lips and smirks at me. It's a dirty little smile, full of dark intention. I'm a boneless pile of satisfaction, propped up against the wall with my foot still on the bench.

"That was . . ." I trail off, unable to find the right words to convey everything that was.

"Perfect," he murmurs.

I twist my lips to the side with a nod. "It was perfect."

Leaning out of the shower, he snags one of the plush white towels from the hook on the wall and walks toward me.

I curl my fingers around the towel and pull it toward me. "Thanks."

He doesn't let me take it from him though, instead, he pulls it back toward his chest. "I take care of what's mine."

He dries me off with slow, precise movements, bending down to drag the soft material up my thighs and around the back of my legs. He pauses, his darkened hazel-eyed gaze cutting me in a way I haven't experienced before.

Something in my chest aches, squeezing and sending warm fissures from my heart. It's a look that speaks volumes, one that transcends the "I love yous" we exchanged back at his safe house. It propels it into something else, something on a cellular level.

"Matteo." My voice is a whisper, a prayer, really.

"Forever, Cherry." He takes his time standing up, bringing the towel with him, dragging it across my skin to catch any stray water droplets. It's one of the most intimate moments of my life.

I nod, our faces aligning as he stands up, my words stolen by his vehemence.

He wraps the towel around me, securing it underneath my arms, and the whole time I just watch him. It's been a while since I've had complete access to him—since he allowed me to see him like this.

I'm floating, riding that blissful wave that crashed over every nerve ending and watching him through heavy lids. He reaches behind his head to pull off his wet sweatshirt. It's a move that has no business being as attractive as it is. With his arm laid up, I take it as an opportunity to turn the tables a little.

"Here, let me."

Grabbing the hem of his sweatshirt, I slowly pull it up, revealing his cut abs with each inch. With careful movements, we get him out of his sweatshirt and tee. He lets them hit the floor with a wet smack. If he stares at me, I don't notice. My focus is solely on the outline of his hard cock in the wet material.

Lust and steam swirl in the tiled space around us, and an ember of desire smolders inside me. By all rights, this fire should've been extinguished—Matteo surely delivered more than enough. But it seems one look at him is enough to rekindle that flame.

I send a silent thank you to god or whoever's listening for inventing gray sweatpants, because if I thought gray sweatpants were a gift before, it's nothing compared to how Matteo looks in them now.

I bridge the gap between us, pressing my towel-clad body against the hard planes of his chest just when something red out of the corner of my eye steals my attention. Guilt stabs the lusty balloon I was floating in and brings me back down to earth.

"Matteo, you're hurt."

"It's nothing," he murmurs and slowly trails his fingertips up the back of my arms.

I pull back and look at the red seeping through the gauze on his shoulder. It's not enough to warrant a trip to the hospital, but it definitely needs some attention. "No, you're really bleeding. I shouldn't have let you keep going."

His fingers tunnel into the hair at the nape of my neck, and he gives my locks a tiny tug. My head tips up, our lips a breath apart. "Nothing could have stopped me. Nothing. This?" He lifts his injured shoulder. "This is nothing."

It would be so easy to lose myself into Matteo once more, but I would never forgive myself if my selfish desires caused him more pain or permanent damage. I throw a bucket of ice cold water on my raging libido, the same one that was definitely satisfied not minutes before, and yet perks up and demands more right now. I settle a palm in the middle of his chest and gently push him out of the shower stall until he hits the counter.

"Let me clean you up first, okay?"

He sighs and tilts his head. "Cherry, honestly, it's—"

I tiptoe my fingertips up and brush them across his pouty lips. "I insist. Let me take care of you." It's a parroting of the words he said to me not five minutes ago. Recognition flashes across his face and he nods, acquiescing.

With my palm flat against his chest, I arch a brow and toss him a mock glare. "Stay here while I find some supplies."

He huffs a little laugh, the corners of his mouth tipping up and holds his hands up, palm toward me, in a faux surrender. I make sure my towel is secure underneath my arms and set about looking in the cabinets for some sort of First-Aid kit. It's not bleeding like crazy, but he needs a new dressing for sure. I open the drawers and cabinets underneath the vanity first, but I don't find it.

"Try the cabinet to the left."

I open the tall cabinet on the left, a matching one on the right. An oversized blue bag with a red cross sits on the second shelf. "I thought you'd never been here before."

"I haven't. I didn't even know Dante had this place, but he packs his First-Aid kit the same way every time."

I place it on the counter next to him with a thump. "This seems excessive."

"It's not your standard kit. It's more . . . tailored to our lifestyle." Matteo just lifts his uninjured shoulder in a shrug. "Dante likes to be prepared."

"So you really didn't know he had this place?" I ask while I unzip the bag and pilfer through the contents, looking for what I need. Truthfully, I'm not entirely sure what I need. I don't have a ton of experience with cleaning up bullet wounds.

"No, I really didn't know, but I shouldn't be surprised. Dante likes to have contingency plans for his contingency plans. Most people have a plan A, maybe a plan B. Dante actively has ten plans going at any given time."

"Sounds like someone else I know." I shoot him a smirk over my shoulder.

"Ah, Cherry's got jokes, I see," he teases me.

"Am I wrong?" I muse, looking inside one of the many pockets inside the bag.

"Dante's my second. It's inevitable that we have similar habits."

"Yeah. And what does that mean exactly—your second?" I ask as I stand in front of him, forgoing the supplies for a moment.

He rests his hand against my hip, anchoring me to him. "It means he watches my six. Always. We're a partnership. One that's been built on loyalty and forged in violence."

A shiver of premonition trickles down my back at his words.

I worry my bottom lip with my teeth. "I've never done this before. I don't want to mess anything up."

"I'll walk you through it, Cherry. And you're not going to hurt me. Start by taking off the bandage."

"Everything okay in here?" Dante's voice startles me. Matteo and I both look at him at the same time. Between the last time I saw him and now, he changed into a pair of low-slung black athletic shorts and a black short-sleeved tee. Pride blooms in my chest when I notice his disheveled hair. My fingers caused that perfectly mussed-up look.

"We're fine," Matteo grits out.

"Actually, I've never done this before, and I want to make sure I'm doing it right," I interrupt.

There's a collective pause then. I feel like we're on a Merry-Go-Round, spinning and spinning and spinning. I'm trying to balance in the middle, standing and attempting to divide my time. But some rotations are too fast, sending me flying toward one man.

And here I am, asking them to slow down and venture toward the middle *for me.*

Depending on which way Dante steps, determines everything. He'll either walk into the bathroom or retreat into the bedroom. Both send a loud message, and both are okay. This kind of . . . *relationship* is unprecedented, so growing pains are bound to be rampant. It's not like there are magazine articles about how to invite two of your four boyfriends to shower you with orgasms and attention.

Actually, someone should totally write that article. It'd be so helpful for situations like this. I hold in my snicker, this is definitely not the place for it.

Dante slides his palms up the door frame, his biceps flexing as he pushes against it. He glances from me to Matteo, but I don't pull my gaze from his, not even to attempt to dissect Matteo's look.

Take a step toward me, choose me, I beg with my eyes.

I know he made his choice earlier. I wanted to wait for him to make his own choice, and he did. He made that choice very clear on the stairs, but this is something different. I'm not entirely sure what I'm asking for right now, but I know it's something new, something that I've been fantasizing about for a while.

Hell, I'm not sure if I'm even ready for the whole two-at-once deal, but I know I'm eager to explore a little. I roll my gaze along

Dante's body, my fingers involuntarily clenching against Matteo's shoulders. I swear, their bodies were crafted out of temptation and designed to make smart girls do stupid things.

Like invite one boyfriend to play along with her and her other boyfriend, like we're sitting down to tea or something.

Jesus, calm down, I chastise my inner voice. He's asking If I need help cleaning Matteo's wound, not if I want him to join in a three-way. I heave a little laugh.

Unless you initiate it. Damn, why does that little inner voice sound like Lainey?

I bite my lip as I look at Dante up and down. If that's not an open declaration to my intentions, I don't know what it is.

I know he understands when he leans in further, his shoulder muscles bunching with the exerted force. There's a second of worry that pierces me like a needle, but then he pushes off the door frame and walks into the bathroom, and my mind blanks.

Excitement flutters in my belly as I watch him stroll toward me and settle at my back. Warmth coats me from both sides, and my breath hitches at the fantasy that shutters over my vision.

Matteo's intense gaze sears my skin, heavy with questions and lust. I glance at him from underneath my lashes, unsurprised to find his eyes on mine.

Dante slides his palms over my arms until he reaches my hands. With a little pressure, he releases my grip on Matteo's biceps. Dante keeps his hands over mine as he guides my hands, his skin always in contact with me as we clean Matteo's wound, apply a layer of antibiotic cream, and place a gauze bandage over it. I seal the gauze with tape around the edges, protecting it once more.

"There. Good as new." My voice comes out far breathier than I intended. It's only then I realize that my pulse has skyrocketed and my chest rises quicker with labored breaths. Anticipation tastes like strawberries on my tongue, tart and sweet.

Dante trails his fingers up my arm, over my bicep, around my shoulder, following the curve of my neck until he grabs a handful of my hair and winds it around his fist. My gaze snaps to his in the mirror over Matteo's shoulder. A gasp leaves my parted lips when I see the look of unadulterated hunger on his face.

We left the staircase wanting, both of us needy, longing. I thought my need was satiated. But it was just an appetizer.

And Dante? He's *starving*. He tips my head back and my lids lower without conscious thought. He holds my gaze as he runs his nose along the exposed curve of my neck.

"You smell like me." His lips brush my sensitive skin with each syllable.

Matteo's hands fist the towel at my side as he pulls me more firmly against him. His cock strains against the material between us. "But she tastes like me," he growls out. "Ain't that right, doll?"

I lick my lips, my mouth suddenly parched.

"Is that right, Maddie? Does this pussy taste like him?" Dante talks against this perfect spot behind my ear. It's full of nerve endings, and little bolts of pleasure shoot straight to my pussy with each word.

And that's the only excuse I have for what comes out of my mouth next. "I don't know. Maybe you should find out for yourself."

Growls echo around me, and it sends a flood of arousal to my system. At this rate, I feel like I'm close to the edge already, and no one's really even touched me.

"You hear that, boss? Our girl wants me to eat her pussy. And since you already had your turn, you can sit this one out." Dante smoothes his hand over the generous curve of my ass and along the inside of my thigh, underneath the towel.

My eyes slam shut when his fingertips barely skate over my throbbing pussy, a noise of protest falling from my lips.

"Eyes open, Cherry. I want to see the look on your face when he makes you come."

It's an unexpected command from him, but I don't take the time to revel in his ability to share, I just obey. Opening my eyes, I meet Dante's gaze in the mirror again.

A shrill ringing fills the air, and it takes me a moment to realize that it's not inside my head. Both Dante and Matteo freeze like two kids caught with their hands in the cookie jar before they're tornados of action.

"What's wrong?"

"That's the alarm," Dante explains.

My lust crashes against the cool tile as cold fear slides into my heart. I fold my arms across my chest. "What kind of alarm?"

"Security breach," Dante says as he pulls up his phone and curses. "Kitchen, two minutes. Might want to get dressed."

chapter twenty-two

Everything inside me freezes, my thoughts blanking. "Security breach?"

"Stay with me, Cherry. It'll be fine."

I blink, startled to find him right in front of me. His voice soothes me, and I find myself nodding while my mind spins in a dizzy whirlwind.

"Fuck," he curses low. "Let's get you dressed, yeah?" Matteo reaches behind him to snag the folded clothes on the counter.

I grab the clothes with trembling fingers, either from the pleasure I was riding high or the fear that slicks the back of my neck. Probably both. Almost on autopilot, I slip the borrowed oversized sweatshirt over my head and get a whiff of that classic clean laundry scent and mint. I towel-dry my hair quickly, scrunching it up to absorb as much water as possible before stepping into a pair of black athletic shorts. They're pretty big on me, so I roll them at the band several times.

It's then I remember that Matteo will need help, not that I think he'll ask for it. When I turn around, I come face to chest with a very, very naked Matteo. My gaze zeros in on his hard cock, demanding my full attention. I lick my lips, anticipation thick on my tongue. I feel dazed, hypnotized, almost. A tiny thread of fear winds around my lusty haze. He's huge—bigger than I remember. Like I'll be feeling him for days after he's finally inside of me.

I shift from foot to foot as I envision a very different ending to the little soiree had the alarm not gone off. He makes a low noise in the back of his throat, gaining my attention.

"Eyes up here, Cherry. You keep staring at me like that, and I won't be held responsible for what happens next." His words have that low gravelly tone I love, the kind that makes me jump to every command.

I slowly drag my gaze up his body over his six pack, his chiseled chest, and muscles that look like they're carved from stone. There's no doubt about it, Matteo is a work of art.

Honestly, all four men are, I'm sure of it.

And I can't wait for the day that I get to explore them *extensively*. He reaches behind him and pulls another pair of black athletic shorts off the counter. I don't know where these clothes came from or who they belong to, but my best guess is Matteo brought them in here before he joined me in the shower. And they're probably Dante's since this is his house, even if it's barely lived-in. At some point, I'm going to need clothes that fit. But I file that worry away and focus on now. That's a future problem, my current priority is to just get Matteo dressed and downstairs, so we can figure out what's going on.

I help Matteo shrug on another hoodie, this time a black one, making sure not to scrape his newly applied bandage. Bending down, I gather the dirty laundry into my arms.

"Leave it. We'll get it later." He opens the cabinet to the right, the one opposite of where the First-Aid kit was, and I see towels and other linens stacked on the shelves. All but the very top shelf. That one has a handful of different weapons. I set the laundry on the countertop and stare with lips parted and wide eyes.

Matteo grabs a gun, checks the magazine, and tucks it into his pocket with all the casual grace of someone grabbing a newspaper.

"Why are there weapons in the bathroom?" My brows furrow in confusion. I feel like every time I get an answer, three more questions sprout up by the end of the day. Hell, sometimes by the end of the hour. And I suddenly feel no closer to answers.

"You can never be too prepared," Matteo says as he grabs my hand and intertwines our fingers together. "Come on, let's go downstairs and see what they found."

We walk hand in hand downstairs, and my eyes cut to the wall that Dante had me pinned against. I don't know why, but I had expected to see something there, some sort of proof of our tryst, even as brief as it was. Perfect cream-colored paint greets me.

We make our way through the house and into the open living space. Dante and Leo are already in the kitchen.

"Where's my brother?" Matteo asks.

Leo fiddles with his phone in the palm of his hand, anxiety written over the way his brow dips over his eyes. He glances from me to Matteo and back again. "Dunno. Haven't seen him since you guys went upstairs. He's not answering our calls."

I untangle my hand from Matteo's and pause next to the island. He beelines for the tablets on the counter, all three of them show security footage of what I'm assuming is the property.

Matteo drags a hand through his hair. "Fuck. I thought Rafe said the place was secure?"

"He did," Dante agrees.

"Then what the fuck is going on?" he asks as he scrolls through various screens, looking at different angles. Even with night vision enabled, it's still mostly dark with the occasional tree swaying in the breeze.

Anxiety sinks its claws into my muscles, coiling them tighter by the minute. Cold water drips down my back in slow rivulets, sending goosebumps chasing after them. I feel a tug on my hair, and I turn to see Leo has moved closer to me.

"Don't worry, Madison. No one's going to take you." Leo's words are meant to be reassuring, I'm sure, but they only prove to sink the anxiety further.

"I know. I'm more worried about you guys. And Aries." I nibble the corner of my lip and glance around the kitchen.

He gently tugs again, regaining my attention. "You ever going to tell me why you call my brother the god of war?"

I face him, a smile playing around the corners of my lips. He's trying to distract me, and it's working. I could easily tell him, but it's more fun to make him work for it a little. I lift a shoulder and smirk. "Maybe one day."

"Mm. One day. I like the sound of that. It means you're thinking of the future—one with me in it. I like it."

My nose scrunches up at his charm, a wide grin on my face. "Or it's just words."

He tucks a lock of hair behind my ear, his fingers trailing to the ends. "Nothing is *just* anything with you."

His words seem innocent enough, but he stares at me with intention. My heart skips a beat the longer we look at one another. I step closer to him, ensnared by his dark-green eyes and messy hair.

"And you're incorrigible, Leonardo Rossi." My words are barely above a murmur, but we're close enough that I know he heard me just fine.

"But I'm yours."

My smile falls as the sound of blood rushing in my ears overtakes my hearing for a moment. I hold my breath as I wait for him to smirk and crack a joke. He quietly observes me, never wavering in his attention and never amending his promise.

Because that's what it feels like to me. A promise written in blood and tattooed on my heart.

"Really?"

He shuffles closer, sliding his thigh between mine and bending down to put his mouth next to my ear. "Tell me you're mine."

"I'm yours, Leonardo," I breathe the words. A shiver cascades down his body when I whisper his name, and my lips twitch at the power it infuses me with. I know he told me he likes it when I use his full name like that, but it's nothing compared to how his body acts on instinct when his syllables fall from my lips.

He groans, this low, urgent noise. "Say it again."

I smirk and arch my back, brushing my chest against his. "I'm yours, Leonardo."

"Fuck," he curses as he slides his hands around my back and over my ass in a move so possessive it has me arching my back further.

Slow clapping starts from somewhere behind me, startling me

out of the little bubble Leo and I unconsciously made. After the second clap, Leo spins us so his back is to the person clapping, pinning me between him and the island.

"Dead, dead, dead, and dead. That's what you all would be, had this been a real security threat."

"Rafe?" Leo asks, his arms slackening.

"Hello, brothers."

"What the fuck is going on? Where have you been?" Matteo asks in a voice wrapped in danger.

"Oh, did I interrupt your time with Raven? My mistake."

I move out from behind Leo just in time to catch Aries's mock innocence as he glares daggers at Matteo. "What's going on? There's no break-in?"

Aries faces me, sliding his hands in his pockets. "Nah, there was. But luckily for everyone, it was just me testing out the security measures."

"Okay," I say the word slowly, dragging it out as my brows lower over my eyes. "Why didn't you tell us though?"

He cocks a brow and looks at me, but it feels like he's speaking to all of us. "We're in the middle of rich-prick utopia here without knowing who's friend or foe or in a dozen different pockets already. And in case anyone forgot, someone put a bounty on my head, and caught you in the crossfire. So, no, it's not all fun and games. Not yet."

I flinch from the reminder, shame licking a hot trail down my chest. "I didn't forget. I'm just . . . depleted, exhausted, and emotionally drained."

"That's not what I meant, Raven." Aries blows out a breath and stares at the ceiling. "It's only a matter of time before they realize they got the wrong guy."

"Or Dad comes knocking. Again," Matteo offers.

"Exactly. So we need to get our plan into motion, and the first step was testing the security."

"And what *is* our plan?" I ask Aries.

"I'm working on it," he says with a nod.

"*You're* working on it?" Matteo asks, tilting his head just slightly to the right. "Don't you think that's something we should do together?"

Aries smirks, a cruel slash of his mouth, and shrugs. "Sure thing, brother. You just seemed a little *occupied* earlier."

I straighten at his insinuation, but it's less indignation and more curiosity. I glance between the security footage on the tablets behind me and Aries. Did he *watch me* with Matteo—and Dante? Fizzy feelings of sensuality warm my lower belly at the thought. One glance at Matteo lets me know that he doesn't share my sentiments. His shoulders are tight and his mouth tips down at the corners. He takes a step forward, fists clenched at his side. "Did you—"

Two steps, and I'm in between them. "Is there anything that needs our attention?"

"No," Dante offers.

I nod a few times. "Good. It's been a really long few days, let's call it a night. We can go over everything in the morning." Matteo opens his mouth, but before he can utter a word, I set my hand on his arm. He gives me his attention immediately. "I'm tired, Matteo."

His shoulders lose some of the tension. "Alright, Cherry. I'll walk you up."

"Nah, I'll take her up, boss. You handle your brother," Dante says, walking around the island.

There's a moment of hesitation before Matteo nods and leans in to brush his mouth across mine. "Sleep well, Cherry."

"You too," I murmur, letting Dante slide his palm against mine.

Leo stands in front of me and places a featherlight kiss against the corner of my mouth. "Sweet dreams, Madison."

I turn my head to catch his lips, but he's already backing away. Their open affection surprises me in the best way. I turn, seeking Aries, but he's moved to the wall next to the refrigerator. He leans a shoulder against it and stares at me with guarded eyes. I bite my lip as I regard him. Maybe he's not going to be okay with this *relationship*. Or maybe he's just tired.

"Goodnight, Aries." My voice is low and soft, meant for just him despite all of us within earshot.

He dips his head toward me. "Goodnight, Raven."

My heart feels heavy as I let Dante lead me through the house and back into the room we were just in. I shove all my worry away for another day. I'm past the point of exhaustion, and I don't think I can mentally take anything else.

I beeline toward the oversized platform bed, crawling onto it from the foot of the bed. Once I'm snuggled underneath the covers in the center of the bed, I notice Dante standing in the doorway. My eyes feel heavy, my lids like ten-pound weights. A yawn takes me by surprise, stretching my jaw wide.

"What?" I ask him when I notice his wide grin.

"Nothing," he says as he shrugs a shoulder.

I smirk and roll over. "Goodnight, Dante."

"Night, Maddie. I knew you'd look good in my bed," he murmurs as I drift off to dreamland.

chapter twenty-three

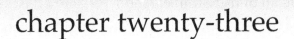

S oft sunshine warms my skin, stealing me from one of the best sleeps of my life. I stretch before I even open my eyes, reaching my arms up high and pointing my toes. The sheets shift and slide down to my hips. Cool air blows across my skin, a perfect combination to the heat of the sun. A low groan leaves my lips when I feel the resistance in some muscles.

A smirk tips up the corners of my lips when I recall why exactly my muscles are so deliciously sore. Never in my wildest dreams would I have expected that to happen—or what was about to happen had Aries not decided to run a security test.

I push myself to a seated position, blinking away the last vestiges of the dream I was having right before I woke up. I don't remember exactly what my dream was about, just that it involved all four of my men. Come to think of it, I was right about to experience some really fun group *activities*, so I'm not sure why I woke up.

A grumble from my stomach vibrates my body. I stare it down with an arched and unimpressed brow. Okay. I guess that's why I woke up then. Hunger should take a backseat to the kind of fantasy I was living in that dream.

I wonder how long I've been asleep. Fat rays of sunshine brighten the room, and I stare at it with fresh eyes. If it's impressive at night, it's nothing compared to it during the day. It highlights the design and craft that went into such a luxurious room. It's the perfect amount of cozy and minimalist chic with understated luxury.

Leaning over, I snag the phone on the nightstand to my right. It illuminates the home screen, showing me it's three o'clock in the afternoon. "Jesus, three o'clock?" My eyebrows hit my hairline. I slept half the day away. I guess I needed the rest more than I realized.

I turn the phone over in my hand, the material cool against my skin. *That's right*, I think. Dante gave me his phone to call my sister last night, but I got sidetracked by Matteo. And then Dante. And then the whole security issue. Then by the time I crawled back into this bed, I was out before my head even hit the pillow.

I heave a sigh, debating on if I should get food or call my sister first. I feel like I need sustenance to bolster me for any sort of phone call with her. But at the same time, the need to call Lainey crawls over my skin like a little ant, irritating and demanding my attention.

Just thinking about the prospect of calling my sister, sort of derails the post orgasmic bliss wave I was riding when I woke up.

I exhale a bone-deep sigh and settle against the headboard, pulling up the phone app.

One person I don't have to worry about calling is my mother. I huff, the noise a little self-deprecating. She's probably sunbathing on some beach somewhere, the only concern for her current boyfriend or her next cocktail. Besides, I don't have her number memorized.

It's a good thing I've memorized my sister's and my cousin's phone numbers so many years ago. I always had an inkling it would be important to memorize them, and I'm so glad I did. After dialing Mary's number, I bring the phone to my ear and listen to it ring for four, five, six times before her voicemail kicks on.

"It's Mary. Leave a message. And I may or may not get back to you."

There's a beep, and my tongue feels tangled, unable to form the words that were just there. I don't know if it's because I just woke up, or because I'm hungry, but I wasn't prepared for this. In a surprising turn of events, hearing my sister's voice brings a wave of longing so fierce that my heart aches.

I miss my sister.

And even though I would never bring her into this—or Lainey, for that matter—I long to have them near. I'd never jeopardize their safety to have my best friends and confidants with me. They've been my sounding boards since before I knew what that really meant. It's such an important role in a teenage girl's life, and I've been blessed with more than one.

I expel a breath, the sound audible in the speaker in my phone. "Hey." My voice comes out garbled, and I have to clear my throat. "Hey, it's me. Maddie. I just wanted to check-in. I lost my phone, so I didn't know if you're trying to reach me, but I'm—I'm okay now. And you can call me back on this number. It's—well, I guess it's my boyfriend's number." I laugh a little bit, the noise more self-deprecating than joyful. And it's only because I know my sister well enough to know that she'll be huffing and rolling her eyes at my use of the word *boyfriend*. "Well, I guess that's a long story, one better left for the next time I see you. I hope you're safe. And I love you. Call me."

I hit the red end-call button and clutch the phone between my fingers, holding it to my chest. I blow out another breath, my cheeks puffing from the force of it. Then I dial Lainey's number. It goes straight to voicemail.

"Hey, it's Alaina, I can't get to the phone right now. Honestly, you're probably better off texting me. Talk to you soon!" She laughs a little before her message ends and her voicemail picks up.

Even though there's a fierce longing in my chest, a smile spreads across my face just hearing the sound of her voice. She always jokes that I'm the optimistic one, but if I am, she's my guiding light.

"Hey, Lainey, it's me. You are never going to believe what's happening to me—or what's happened to me." I cut myself off with a little laugh. "It's a long story, but I lost my phone. I'm worried about you, and I want to make sure you're safe. You can call me back at this number. It's—well, remember that one time I said I was going to start my own collection of men just like you?" I bite my lip, a wide grin spreading across my face. "Yeah, I think I kind of did. Call me when you get this. Love you!"

I end the call and place the phone in my lap. My stomach chooses that moment to remind me that it's empty. So I toss the covers off my lap and slide off the platform bed. At some point during the night, I must have gotten hot, because I'm only wearing an oversized tee. The athletic shorts I went to bed with are on the floor, and I slip them on, rolling the band a few times to make sure they don't fall off my hips.

My nose follows the bacon scent trail all the way down to the first floor and back into the kitchen. All the doors in the hallways are closed, but I don't hear any noises that would suggest anyone was inside.

I wonder how Matteo's feeling. I make a mental note to change his bandage again today as I cross the threshold from the hallway into the wide open space. The sight before me is vastly different than the one I left last night. All four of my men are around the island.

Matteo and Dante are between the island and the sink, Aries leans against the counter by the refrigerator, and Leo sits on a barstool at the island. They're all dressed so similarly, it causes a giddy sort of joy to blanket me. Tees in varying shades of charcoal and black, athletic shorts or sweatpants—again in varying shades of black. They look like some laid-back boy band.

The thought is just ridiculous enough that I wish I could snap a photo for digital, undeniable proof. I tone down my mirth to something much more tame and cross the room.

My nose is assaulted with a variety of delicious scents—bacon, obviously, but also warm, rich coffee, sweet and sugary waffles, freshly squeezed juices. It's an impressive spread.

Dante sees me first, his face lighting and softening in a way that sends a wave of warmth. I tuck some of my unruly hair behind my ear and cross the room to them, stopping behind the stool next to Leo.

"How did you sleep?" Dante asks.

"Like a baby." I flash him a smile.

"You know, I never understood why they said that," Leo chimes in. "Babies do not sleep well. They're up like every two hours." He reaches over and grabs a piece of bacon off of a plate with a pile of what smells like applewood smoked maple bacon.

I squint at him, amusement tickling my senses. "And you know so much about babies?"

He finishes chewing the half of a strip in his mouth and looks at me with a cocky little smile. "There's lots of things I know."

I make a non-committal noise of agreement, but before I can question him further about how he knows so much about babies, Matteo pushes a plate toward me.

"Sit down. Eat. You must be famished."

I place a hand on my stomach. "Actually, I'm starving. This looks amazing. Thank you."

I pull out the stool and scoot around, my legs brush against Leo's thighs as I settle on to the plush cushion of the barstool.

chapter twenty-four

Madison

I don't waste time and tuck into the Belgian waffle with fresh blueberries and crispy pieces of bacon. My first bite of the waffle is perfect—crispy outside and soft inside

"Mango ceylon iced tea." Matteo slides a glass in front of me.

I place a hand to my collarbone, touched at the gesture. "You remembered."

"I remember everything about you, Cherry. I thought you knew that." Matteo winks before he picks up his espresso cup and takes a sip.

Déjà vu clouds my senses. The familiarity of this scene hits me like a bowling ball. It wasn't long after this scene—but set in

Matteo's apartment—that everything spiraled out of control.

Aries pulls out the stool on my other side and settles into it with a smirk, snapping me out of the memory. That's what makes this different—Aries. He's the wildcard, the missing piece of the puzzle that wasn't factored in before. He changes everything for the better, so I'm hoping we don't have any repeats of what happened.

"That reminds me," I say after I finished my mouthful of delicious food. "How did I not know you had not only one brother but two?" I look at Matteo, since he should have been the one to tell me all those years ago.

He sips espresso from his tiny red cup like he doesn't have a care in the world. "You know why, Cherry. We talked about it at the apartment, remember?"

I nod and nibble on my piece of bacon. "Right, because you're in the mob." I tilt my head to the side, raising both brows. "Just like your dad. Right? And what about the rest of you guys?"

"You already know I'm involved, Maddie," Dante offers.

"Right, you're his second. I'm still not one hundred percent on what that means." There's a moment of silence where no one says anything. Collectively, they tense, casting one another wary looks. I set my piece of bacon on the plate. "What? Is it something I said?"

"We don't usually talk so openly like this," Matteo offers with a shrug.

"Okay." I stretch the word out, trying to read between the lines. "We're alone, aren't we?" I look at each of them, subconsciously seeking confirmation that we're safe. "I mean, the whole security breach thing, that was just Aries last night. So theoretically, shouldn't we be able to talk freely here?" I look to Dante, since this is his house.

He nods as he takes a sip of what looks like black coffee. I'm not at all surprised that Dante likes his coffee strong and bold. It suits him. "Hypothetically speaking, yes, we could talk freely here. However, where there's technology, there's always a way in."

I cock my head to the side and idly wipe the grease from my fingertips on the paper napkin next to my plate as my mind tries to play catch-up to a game I didn't know existed last month. "What do you mean?"

"Well." Dante sets his coffee down and folds his arms over his chest.

My eyes stray to the way his muscles bulge and flex underneath his black tee.

"Just as easily as Aries tapped into our network last night, our enemies could too."

The hair on the back of my neck rises.

"Jesus, man, don't scare her," Leo says, setting his fork down with exasperation.

"I'm not scaring her, I'm giving her the truth. She can handle it, can't you, Maddie?" Dante counters.

I look up from my plate and focus back on him, on the way his dark brown eyes watch me with careful expectation and understanding. Something about the way he unwaveringly stares at me soothes some of my anxiety. I nod.

"She can take a lot more than any of you give her credit for," he murmurs.

Warmth sears the top of my cheeks, and I can't help myself for thinking this is a double entendre.

"But that means that they have to find us first. So, while I think it's technically possible that someone could hack into our system, because I haven't had enough time to secure it. I don't think anyone will. They would have to know where we are. And no one does.

Right?" Dante looks at Aries, Leo, and finally, Matteo. All three of them shake their heads.

"Well, they'll know I'm here soon," Aries says.

I cut my gaze to him as alarm rips through me. "What does that mean?" His words sound ominous, and they send a shiver of foreboding through me. There's something palpable in the air, something I haven't been able to label yet. But it's the same feeling I get whenever Blaire has one of her infamous ideas, which are always more like carefully detailed revenge plots, but still.

"While sleeping beauty over here was knocked out all day." He smirks at me before he focuses back on Dante. "I was doing a little research. Turns out, our favorite senator spends his summer vacation in the Hamptons."

"No shit," Leo murmurs from next to me before he forks another Belgian waffle from the stack in front of us and plops it on his plate. He lathers it in butter with a small drizzle of syrup. I watch in fascination as he practically inhales his third waffle of the meal.

"You're supposed to be dead," Matteo says.

"Exactly," Aries interrupts. "Let's use that to our advantage."

"How? By ambushing him where he's undoubtedly surrounded by personal security?" Matteo scoffs.

Aries clenches his jaw and narrows his eyes. In a blink, it's gone and his neutral mask is back in place. "No. By going to the white party. It's a party for the—"

"I know what the white party is," Matteo says, waving his hand in the air as if to brush Aries's words away.

"Not all of us do though," Leo says.

Aries and Matteo glare at one another for a moment before the former switches his focus to his other brother. "It's a party for some of the nation's top one-percenters, the ones who vacation in the

Hamptons or fly in just for the weekend of events. It kicks off with the white party. It's elitist as hell, and more than one backroom deal is done that weekend. I'm told the senator secured an invite this year, and it'd be perfect for a little revenge."

I wait, my eyebrows lifting toward my hairline and my lips twisting to the side to smother the smile that's threatening to spread across my face. The white party. Definitely famous—it's legendary. Although I don't know if I would say only the top one-percent attends. I feel like I've seen tons of people there that don't meet that particular parameter. I'm curious enough to hear the rest of Aries's plan before I interject my own commentary.

"So what better way to show the senator not only that I'm not dead, but that I know he's the one behind the hit than a very public place?" Aries says with a smirk.

"You're going to shake down the senator in the middle of some uppercrust party in the middle of Long Island?" Leo's eyes widen with each word.

"Shakedown is such a common term. I prefer the word *negotiate*." His voice is so smooth. It's no wonder he's been rubbing elbows with some of Blaire's mutuals. I reckon his particular way of phrasing, with that smooth voice of his, and his commanding presence is enough to charm just about anyone.

"Okay," Dante says. "Say we go with this plan. Won't he recognize you as soon as he sees you?"

Aries nods and drums his finger against the side of his mug. It's nearly empty, but if I had to guess, I'd say he seems like a sugar-only kind of coffee drinker.

"Right. Which is why we send in *them*." He looks at Leo and me.

"I'm in," Leo says without hesitation.

Protests spill from Matteo and Dante immediately.

"What?" Aries raises his voice for attention. "Baby bro wanted to dive into the deep end, didn't he? Well, now's the time."

Matteo tips his chin up. "Yeah, and what about her?"

Aries scans me from head to toe. "Didn't you just hear what Dante said? Don't underestimate her."

"I hardly think wanting her to be safe is *underestimating* her," Matteo snaps.

Before it can turn into another verbal sparring match, I decide to wade in. "Actually, I've been to the white party before." Even though my voice is quiet, it cuts through the noise immediately.

Aries looks at me with a raised eyebrow. "I know, Raven."

My mind stumbles for a reply. "How?"

Aries leans forward, draping his arm across the back of the stool and bringing his mouth close to my ear. "There are lots of things I know about you, about others, about what you like to do with others." His lips caress my skin, sending sensitive prickles of arousal through me.

I feel my cheeks heat, but I'm not embarrassed. Well, maybe I'm a little embarrassed by how easily he can turn me on.

He pulls back, and I hold his gaze. There's a challenge written all over him, from his stiff posture to his arched eyebrow. While I've never been fearless exactly, I also never shy away from a good challenge.

"I can do it. I'm sure there will be people there that Leo knows too. I can call Blaire and get us an official invite."

"Make sure it's for three," Aries interjects.

"Three?" Matteo asks with a frown.

"White party is in a few days, and I know you have to go back to dear old Dad tomorrow."

"Tomorrow?" I cut a stare at Matteo.

"Tomorrow." He blows out a breath with a nod and braces his palms against the countertop. "But Dante and I have to leave tonight."

"Why? You just said you didn't have to be there till tomorrow," I point out.

"He's expecting us tomorrow. Which means we have to get there tonight. He doesn't know we left the city. So if he's planning on fucking me over—"

"Why would he do that?" I interrupt him, my heart skipping a beat.

"Yeah, Matteo, why would dear old Dad plan on fucking you over, huh? Should I bring out the spreadsheet, maybe a flowchart. How about just a Venn diagram of his shitty traits as a father and his shitty traits as a boss. Spoiler alert, Maddie, there's like an eighty-five percent overlap." The scorn and sneer in Leo's voice takes me by surprise.

"I don't understand," I murmur, looking between them.

"A conversation best left for another time," Matteo says, cutting Leo a sharp look. "All you need to know for now is that I have to get back, Dante too. My brothers will be here with you the entire time. I'll be back in just a few days."

"And you'll stay then?" I look between Matteo and Dante, settling on Dante to give me the truth.

He shifts his head, a small movement, but it gives me the answer I asked for. When he comes back, it won't be for good. I tuck some hair behind my ear and look at the breakfast spread in front of me. "So walk me through it then. I'm just going to—what? Live here forever? Never going back to my life in the city—to my cousin or sister? I don't understand."

"It's not forever, Maddie, just for right now. Until we know you're safe."

My leg bounces up and down the ball of my foot pushing against the metal rung on the stool. "Okay. You guys have to go back to the city. Leo and I will go to the white party. And Aries." I look at him. "You'll do your thing, right?" I raise my brows at him, waiting for him to explain what his thing is.

I make a mental note to ask him more questions—general and specific. As powerful as our connection is, I don't even know his favorite color. Scanning him from head to toe, I would have a pretty solid guess and go with black, but he continues to surprise me. So I wouldn't be all that shocked if he said it was fire-engine red or green like grass after a lightning storm.

Aries just holds my gaze and nods solemnly. "I'll keep you safe, Raven. You have my word."

"I know," I murmur. "I'm not worried about that."

chapter twenty-five

Madison

I sigh, the sound noisy and full of the nervousness swirling in my gut.

"What's wrong? Are you feeling okay?" Dante asks.

I wave a hand in the air. "I'm fine, just processing. I thought we'd have more time here. Together, I mean."

"So did I." Matteo nods.

Biting my lip, I cock my head to the side. "Wait a minute—I thought you just saw him at the hospital? You didn't want anyone to see him then, but you're going home now?"

Matteo leans back against the sink behind him. "What do you know about the mafia?"

The question catches me off guard, even though it really shouldn't, given our current topic of conversation. I fiddle with the end of the fork on my plate. "Only what I've seen in movies and TV shows."

Matteo nods and runs a hand across his jaw. "Okay, well, most of the shit you see is exaggerated. Or outdated. Some of those movies, they're old school. We don't tie cement blocks to the feet of men who betray us and drop them in the middle of the Atlantic. We have a much more sophisticated way of dealing with traitors, big mouths, and thieves."

I swallow over the sudden lump in my throat and take a sip of my iced tea. "Okay."

"What I'm saying is that there's a reason we don't go around telling everyone our business. A reason we let Hollywood exaggerate and portray us as trigger-happy hotheads. But you don't get to be the boss without getting your hands dirty."

I look at Matteo. "And you're the boss."

"Yes and no," he answers.

I just stare at him, waiting for him to elaborate.

"Our father is the boss. He's the head of the entire five ruling families that make up the east coast outfit, and that's all I'm gonna say on that. Because for as much as they get it wrong—the way society paints us—my father is one thousand times worse. He'd torture and dismember you without blinking an eye, and it wouldn't even be about you. It'd be a lesson to someone else. That's why he can never know about you."

There's a lot to unpack in his statement, but my mind trips up on his last sentence. "Never?" I choke out, horrified. What does that even mean? My heart aches a little bit on the inside, the fist of finality the word *never* carries squeezes around it.

"He shouldn't have said never," Dante says, and Matteo cuts him a dark look. "Well, you fucking shouldn't have. Are you planning on giving her up anytime soon?"

"You know the answer to that," Matteo snarls.

Dante nods. "That's what I thought. So don't freak her out like that." He stares at Matteo for a moment longer before shifting his gaze to me. "What he meant was we're going to keep Angelo Rossi in the dark about you for as long as possible. Because once he knows, everything changes. He's Pandora's box, only sociopathic and violent."

Dante's words send an ominous ripple through the room. My eyebrows shoot up, and I shake my head a few times. "I don't really know what to say. It doesn't exactly sound like I have a choice, do I?" I grit my teeth.

I understand that there's a lot about this I don't know. This is a whole world that I've never been privy to. But even though I know that intellectually, my emotions don't take a backseat. Something dark pierces my heart, not only because it sounds like Matteo wasn't planning on claiming me in any sort of public fashion, but there's no end date. And because they made this choice without me. Shame licks at my heels, hot and quick rising. I tilt my head forward, letting some of my hair shield my face.

"Stop," Dante commands. My gaze snaps up to him. "Whatever you're thinking right now, stop. We're doing this to protect you, and that's the only reason."

"I wouldn't do it if I didn't think I had to," Matteo says.

"I don't even understand what you're doing though. Like what is happening? Why are we even here?" I throw my hands up in frustration, letting them land on the counter top before strumming them against the marble. The soft tap, tap, tap pattern soothes my frazzled nerves and cools some of my irritation.

"There's a lot of things we can't tell you yet, but trust us—trust *me*—when I tell you we're doing this to keep you safe." Matte's voice is full of conviction, just shy of begging me to understand what he's saying.

I nod a few times, small movements, really. "And who keeps you two safe then?" I ask, looking between him and Dante.

"We look out for one another, Maddie. We'll be fine." Dante's assurances soothe some of my anxiety. There's a lot of unknown happening right now, and I do my best not to let it overwhelm me.

I blow out a breath. "Okay, so we have tonight then?"

Matteo nods once. "We leave in an hour."

"An hour? Why didn't you wake me up sooner?" Alarm buzzes in my veins like ants marching in a line, back and forth.

Matteo lifts his uninjured shoulder. "You needed the rest, so I told everyone to let you sleep."

I narrow my eyes at him. "If I didn't just wake up, would you have left without saying goodbye?" I glare between Matteo and Dante.

"Of course not," Matteo says softly. His eyes soften, and dammit, it softens me a little bit too.

I pull on the reins of my anger and tie them up like balloons. "Okay. You guys can't keep me in the dark, okay? If this"—I wave my hand around—"*whatever this is* is going to work, communication is key. I know you can't tell me everything, but this stuff? This you can, okay?" I look at all four of them and wait for each one to acknowledge me. "And I really want this to work."

I clap my hands together. "Let's clean up. We're gonna spend the next hour together in the living room. That big grey couch looks amazingly comfortable."

"Ooh, together on the couch, kinky. I like it." Leo smirks.

I flash him a faux unimpressed look, even though I appreciate his knack for breaking the tension more than he probably realizes. He just smiles at me, his dark green eyes twinkling with mirth. Damn him and his little flirtatious smile. It shouldn't be nearly as charming as it is. I school my face to something neutral.

"Funny," I deadpan.

"Alright, Madison." He holds his hands up in mock surrender before he spins off his stool bringing his plate over to the sink. He doesn't even try to hide the cheeky grin on his face.

I reach out to touch Aries's arm, holding my palm against his forearm. "You too, okay?"

He looks at me out of the corner of his eye before he finishes his coffee and sets it down. "And what exactly will we be doing on the couch in the living room?"

"Spending time together," I say before flashing my megawatt smile. The one that always softens the exterior of everyone who needs it. And I feel like Aries might need it today.

He smirks at me and gives me a reluctant nod. "Alright."

"Perfect." On an impulse, I lean forward and brush my lips across the corner of his mouth. I don't linger, but I swear I hear his swift intake of breath.

We clean up the kitchen quickly, wrapping up the leftovers and sticking them in the fridge for later. As one, we walk into the living room. The couch has a low back but wide plush seats.

When I sink down into the middle one, it feels like someone's giving me a warm, velvety hug.

A low groan leaves my lips. "Oh, this is amazing."

No one responds, but everyone snickers under their breath, standing and staring at me.

"Aren't you guys going to sit down?" I pat the couch on either side of me.

"Dibs," Leo says before I even finish talking.

"You can't call *fucking dibs* on her," Aries says around a scoff.

Leo cocks his head to the side. "Madison doesn't mind, do you?"

My lips twitch as I idly wonder if we'll always have this kind of banter. I shrug and say, "If I could, I'd sit next to all of you."

"See? There's room for all of us," Leo says.

"What are we watching today, Maddie?" Dante waggles a remote control in the air, redirecting the conversation.

"Well, I was thinking about what you said, about how I don't know what Hollywood got right, so why don't we watch a little TV. Let's start with *Jersey Shore*."

I bite the inside of my cheek to keep a straight face. Aries's lip twitches, letting me know that he gets the joke. But fortunately, no one else does.

"We are not watching that."

"And why exactly would we watch that?"

"No."

They all talk over one another, and I can't hold in my laugh any longer. "You guys should see the looks on your faces. Okay, but seriously, how about the *Sopranos*? My cousin, Lainey, said it's extremely informative."

"It's one of the better portrayals in the media for sure," Dante says. "We can start it, but we won't be able to watch too much."

"That's alright, we can binge-watch together later. I love the *Sopranos*."

I flash him a wide grin. "Sounds perfect."

Leo settles next to me on the couch, leaning back with me. Matteo is on my other side, Aries chooses the very end of the couch that curves into a chase, and Dante perches next to Leo. The opening credits roll, the recognizable sound of the *Sopranos* theme song fills the room, coming from speakers all around us. Some I definitely didn't notice until now. I've actually seen a few seasons before, but I wasn't watching with this context. Now, I'll be looking for clues and subtext, glancing at each of them to gauge their reactions.

I sink even lower into the couch, and Leo drapes a light cream, fluffy throw blanket over my legs. It's a smooth move, because it has me scooting closer to him. Our thighs press together, and I become acutely aware of his body. Sugared citrus and sunshine infiltrate my senses—the scent I've associated with Leo.

"Thanks," I murmur as I spread it out over both of us.

He throws his arm over my shoulders, and I take it as an invitation to snuggle in closer. Leo draws swirly patterns on my shoulder and neck, applying light pressure to the base of my neck and into my hairline, like a light massage.

I shift around a little until my legs are straight, giving Leo a better angle. This couch is so big, it's two seat cushions deep and six across. It has to be custom-made. I flex my feet and rotate my ankles, a habit I picked up during my dancing years. There's something so satisfying about stretching and flexing those muscles.

The blanket flutters over Matteo's leg, and I smirk at his raised brow. It gives me an idea though. I flick my ankle again, and more of the blanket lands on his lap.

It's an olive branch, at least, that's what it feels like in this moment. All of us sitting together, even if only for the next hour. It's a start.

And it feels good—really good.

Matteo gives me his attention, his brows barely raised, smirk dancing across his perfect mouth. He surprises me with a warm hand on my ankle underneath the blanket, stilling my movements. Ah, so he's accepting my olive branch, it seems.

I bite back my groan when he drags his thumb down the arch of my foot in measured, slow movements. He pulls my other foot onto his thigh and alternates between them. I feel sort of like I'm melting into the couch, slouching further with each pass of his thumb on my arches.

Leo shifts into the corner where the back meets the arm of the couch, the overstuffed cushions on all sides, and brings me with him. He guides me so my back is against his chest, my head fitting in the perfect spot between his neck and shoulder. His fingers slide into my hair and massage my scalp. My eyes flutter closed before I can stop them.

They're taking care of me. It's a simple thought, an easy concept. Although it's a foreign feeling, this—this feels *right*.

"I thought you wanted to watch this."

My eyes snap open at Aries's low voice.

"Leave her alone," Dante says, an authority in his tone that has my libido perking up.

"It's fine. I'm awake." I shuffle up a little bit. I blink away the hazy feeling of contentment and watch Tony Soprano on screen.

Ten minutes later, my eyelids feel heavy. I blink them rapidly, shake my head a little, and shift positions to wake up. I shouldn't be this tired, I literally just woke up an hour earlier. But my body doesn't care. It demands penance for all the things I've put it through recently.

And Leo's and Matteo's hands lull me into a state of relaxation I haven't experienced in a long time. My eyelids feel like cement weights, each blink taken longer to open and harder to blink. Until finally, I give in and sleep laps at my heels like a sun-warmed ocean water. I let it take me, drifting off to dreamland.

chapter twenty-six

Madison

Gentle hands rouse me from sleep, a soft shake on my shoulder.

"We gotta go now, baby girl." The fog of sleep holds me in its clutches, and my eyes are slow to open. "You fell asleep, Cherry. Dante and I have to go now."

It's then I realize that I'm snuggled up next to Leo. Pushing the blanket off me, I stretch my arms above my head as a yawn takes me by surprise. "Oh, wow. Okay. I'm sorry I fell asleep, guys. I don't know what happened."

"Don't mention it, Maddie. You've been through a lot. Your body needs rest." Leo's voice is next to my ear. It's low and smooth like my favorite hot latte in the fall.

I look around and rake my hands through my hair. "You guys are leaving?"

"Yeah. We were supposed to be on the road forty minutes ago, but we wanted to let you rest a little bit longer."

Something inside my chest cracks a little. "You could have definitely woken me up. Here, let me walk you guys out." Dante's lips twitch, and I'm almost positive it's because he realized how silly my offer was as soon as I did. I'm offering to walk him out . . . of his own house. Like I own it. I shake my head a little to clear the last clutches of sleep and scoot off the couch.

"Sure," Dante says, his mouth twisting into a grin.

I follow Dante with Matteo behind me as we make our way through the darkened large first-floor footprint of the house and into the back hall that leads to the garage. He stops abruptly and spins to face me. A startled squeak slips out before I can stop it.

Dante threads his fingers into the hair at the back of my neck and steps into me in one fluid movement. A gasp leaves my lips at the unexpected move. He rests his forehead against mine and murmurs, "Be safe, okay? Trust Rafe and Leo to keep you safe. We'll be back for the white party."

Without even remembering making the decision, I grab onto his wrists and hold him to me. I close my eyes and whisper, "You be safe, too, okay, and look out for each other. I don't feel good about you guys leaving."

He uses his grip to tilt my head back and to the side, brushing his lips against mine in a move so tender, so soft, my heart splinters a little bit. "We'll be fine, Maddie. We're harder to kill than we look."

His tone is teasing, but it only heightens my anxiety. Maybe it's because I'm not fully awake yet or maybe that's exactly why I can tap into my intuition. I open my eyes and shuffle forward, pushing up onto my tiptoes. "Well, I am worried about you. So promise me you'll be fine."

He tips his face and places a soft kiss against the corner of my mouth, dragging his lips down to my bottom lip where he murmurs, "I can't promise you that. I don't know what the future holds. But I can promise you that I'll do everything in my power to get back to you."

My eyes widen as his words wind their way around my heart and imbed themselves into my soul. My heart pounds with the realization that we're having a moment. No, *the* moment. You know, the pivotal one where everything shifts, magically clicking into place. With my heart in my throat and a tear rolling down my cheek, I press my lips against his. He's quick to deepen the kiss, sliding his tongue in my mouth as he seals his words of affirmation and love and promise with each swirl of his tongue. He tastes like dark chocolate, rich espresso, and something darker, more dangerous. And lethal.

My back arches involuntarily while I just try to keep up with the way Dante is absolutely owning me right now. I give him permission willingly and wholeheartedly, and if I were above us, I swear I'd be able to see a tiny piece of our souls connecting, swirling around us in a way reminiscent of the aurora borealis. He breaks the kiss suddenly, leaving an inch between our mouths. "You have my word."

I nod, the movement small within the restraints of his hold. I can't stop myself from brushing my lips against his once more, this time a soft sort of kiss. One that offers an agreement. He pushes back slowly, releasing his grip on my hair. His fingertips trail down my neck and over my shoulders, down my arms until a featherlight touch leaves my fingertips. Stepping backward, away from me, he looks over my shoulder and says. "I'll be in the car." With one last look at me, he turns around and leaves.

I press my trembling fingers to my bottom lip, pushing against the swollen proof of Dante's intensity and affection. *Love? Could it be love too?* Another tear slowly tracks down my cheek just as Matteo comes to stand in front of me.

He slides his thumb underneath my eyes, softly caressing the apple of my cheek long after he captures the tear. "Why are you upset, Cherry?"

I bring my watery gaze to his, scanning his features and memorizing them. "I don't know. I just have this awful feeling that we shouldn't be apart."

He steps into me, bringing his other hand up underneath my other eye to wipe away any of the fear leaking from my eyes. "We'll be alright. Dante and I've been doing this for a long time. It's just a meeting, a power play. My father's exerting his dominance."

I nod a few times. I know that, he already told me as much. But I can't shake the fear that we're making a mistake splitting up like this.

"My brothers are here, and they'll take care of you. You'll feel better once you get some more rest. We made you guys some spaghetti in the fridge for dinner, it's Dante's recipe, so if you don't like it, take it out on him. And don't let Leo hog it all."

His teasing works, and a laugh bubbles up, taking me by surprise. "Okay, okay," I say around a laugh.

"Okay," he parrots with a grin.

My smile slips and I tip my chin toward him. "Kiss me, Matteo."

His hands slide from my cheeks down my face and settle

against my neck. The move is possessive, dominant, and it makes my breath hitch. Tingles spark in my fingertips as anticipation of Matteo's kiss washes over me. He steps into me further, his body flush against mine and lowers his head to brush his lips across mine in a kiss so sweet it makes me want to cry a little. It's the opposite of what I was expecting, and I think I love him all the more for it. A quiet sigh leaves my soul at his touch.

He takes his time, first sliding his lips over my top lip, then dragging them over my bottom lip with agonizing slowness. It's exquisite torture, and I realize with stunning clarity that I'd happily spend the rest of my life alternating between kisses from the four men inside these walls.

I don't know who moves first, but our kiss intensifies like we're communicating with our bodies now that our words have dried up. All too soon, he breaks the kiss. My eyes are slow to open, my heart beating out a rhythm just for him.

"I have to go."

I nod. "Come back to me, Matteo."

"Oh, Cherry, don't you know? I never left." With a swift kiss to my forehead, he leaves the house—and me.

Matteo

I slam the car door with more force than necessary. My best

friend just shoots me a glare but holds his tongue. Good. I don't know what the fuck I'd do if he ripped into me about something as trivial as a car. It's a thing—something replaceable. Unlike the devious little redhead I just left inside the house. How she captivated all of us, I'll never know. But she's bewitched us like some kind of supernatural creature on those shows she used to watch back when we dated.

I buckle my seatbelt with quick, harsh movements, not willing to tempt fate with such a mundane death. Dante reverses out of the empty garage and drives us down the long driveaway.

"Why didn't you ever tell me about this place?" I gesture toward the yard out of my window.

"I was going to when it was ready."

"Huh. It feels like you don't fucking trust me if you can't be bothered to tell me about a fucking *safe house* you bought a few hours east of the city." I feel the sneer curling my lips. "And honestly, what the fuck were you thinking? This thing is like a neon billboard, just lighting the path to us."

He glares at me before refocusing on the road. "I was thinking that I found that house on a no-reserve auction, and I was very persuasive to anyone thinking of entering a bid. I gave a fair deal, considering the people who previously owned it were bottom of the barrel."

I clench my jaw. "If you say so."

He sighs. "It's a stressful time, but as your best friend and your fucking second, don't take your shit out on me. I'm on your fucking side. Got it?"

I blow out a breath. Guilt sticks to my ribs like honey. "Yeah, I know. Sorry, man. Everything changed when we brought Madison into this."

"It did. But she's smart, and so are we. We just gotta get through this bullshit meeting with your dad."

I lean my elbow against the door and rest my head in my palm. It's too dark to see much of anything, not that I could at this speed. Dante's fucking lucky he's one of the best drivers, otherwise, I'd never let Maddie get in a car with him. He drives like the minimum is ninety-five.

"You think we made the right choice? In leaving her here, I mean."

It's the question that's been weighing on my mind since we got the summons from Dad.

Dante doesn't answer right away. I know him well enough to know that means he's formulating the best answer. "It was the only choice. She'll never share air with Angelo Rossi, mark my words, Matteo."

"You don't have to tell me that. As soon as we're back, we're doubling-down on our original plan. We need to move it up and quickly."

The car descends into silence, the only noise is the low murmur of the radio, too quiet to really make anything out. I turn over the events of the last few days in my head as I mentally prepare myself to see Dad.

chapter twenty-seven

Madison

I stand in the dark back hall, dragging my finger tip over my bottom lip ever so lightly, over and over and over again. We didn't bother to turn the lights on when we walked down here, and now that they're gone, it's darker somehow.

It's quiet on this end, only the gentle hum of the house. Not surprising, considering there's only three of us in this giant house. I allow myself one more moment of trepidation before I send up a silent prayer, asking anyone who's listening to watch over us.

"Hey." Leo's soft voice comes from behind me.

I spin around to face him, dropping my hand down by my waist and offering him a half smile. "Hey."

"I saw a pool out back. You up for a swim?"

My half smile grows into a full one. My hair shifts over my shoulder when I tilt my head. "I don't have a swimsuit."

"Ah, well, you see, I came prepared." He pulls out two handfuls of fabric from behind his back. A ball of black fabric in his right hand and royal blue fabric in his left. I step toward him and rub the material between my thumb and index finger—definitely a swimsuit.

"What's all this?"

"Seems not only did Dante have food delivered today, he got some other *necessary supplies* too."

I arch a brow at him, a smirk dancing on my lips. "Since when are swimsuits a *necessity*?"

He walks backward a few steps, holding the swimsuits on each hand, a wide grin on his face. "Since you buy a house like this."

"Just us?"

"Sorry to disappoint, it's just one Rossi brother right now. Said he had some calls to make for the white party."

His face is unnervingly blank, which is something I don't see too often on him. I cock my head to the side. "You're never a disappointment, Leo."

He smiles, an expression I'm much more accustomed to seeing on his handsome face. His hair looks darker in this light, swept over his forehead in a haphazard way. "So, you in?"

I beam at him, warmth settling inside my chest. "Absolutely."

"I knew you would be," he says. "Now, black or blue?"

I tap my chin with my index finger, pretending to think. "Black."

"Excellent choice. And for the record, you would look amazing in both of them . . . or none of them." He flashes me a cheeky little grin and waggles his brows.

I grab the ball of black material from his hand and playfully swat his chest. "Yeah, yeah. Should we tell him at least where we are? I don't want another security thing to happen." I worry my bottom lip and fiddle with the swimsuit material.

"Nah, I already told him. After he's done with his calls, I'm sure he'll move on to something else, like plotting the downfall of someone or something."

"Then we're all set. Lead the way," I say, wrapping my arm around his bicep and leaning into him. He takes us back through the house and out onto the patio.

"I already checked out the pool area earlier. The pool house is fully stocked, by the way. We can change and grab a drink or snack there."

"A drink in the pool with my hot boyfriend? Absolutely."

His shoulders and eyebrows rise playfully. "Oh, baby, there are so many wonderful things about that sentence, I don't know where to start." He taps his chin with his index finger on one hand. "Oh, how about you calling me your boyfriend?"

"Damn, I really thought you'd snag on the 'hot' thing first," I tease him, nudging his shoulder with mine.

"I already know I'm good-looking, I mean—" He shrugs his shoulders and holds his neutral face for all of two seconds before he starts laughing.

I laugh along with him. "Aren't you supposed to be the charming one?"

He smirks at me and stops in front of the door to the pool house. "Nah, I'm the fun one."

We walk inside the pool house, which for the first time I feel like lives up to its name. This has to be two thousand square feet. I was expecting like two hundred—a bathroom to rinse off and change and maybe a wet bar. But this is insane. I should've known better really. I mean, look at the monstrosity of a main house. You could probably have five families living in that house and never really overlap.

I turn around in the living room, letting go of Leo so I can take everything in. It's a huge living room with a white marble tile floor and a large circular navy blue shag rug underneath the extra-long L-shaped couch. A wet bar runs the entire opposite wall in what looks like a mini kitchen. And a short hallway leads to three bedrooms—each with their own attached bathrooms—a bathroom, an empty room, and a pool storage room.

There's a flat screen television on the wall across from the couch, and behind me is a pool table. Barring the navy rug, everything is done in shades of white and cream, like the main house. Though there are a few more light blue accents in here.

"I'm already in my trunks," he says, pinching his shorts between two fingers and pulling them outward an inch. "So I'll grab us towels, music, drinks, and floaties. Meet me in the pool when you're ready."

"Sounds good," I say before heading toward the last bedroom. Once I'm dressed in the black swimsuit, I look at my reflection in the mirror. Dark smudges underneath my lashes, hair unruly and wild with its waves.

I suddenly feel a little self-conscious without a lick of makeup on and so *not* put together. I target my bottom lip with my teeth. But if they're still here after seeing me like this, I'd like to think they'll still be here even if I don't wear makeup. Besides, who wears a full face of makeup while swimming anyway. I try to shrug my insecurity off, channeling that confidence of my cousin.

I turn to the side and look at my profile in the mirror. It's actually a really cute suit. It's nothing special, really, all black with a little texture to the fabric. It's a one-piece, but it's revealing enough that I feel good in it. There's a low scoop neck in the front, the straps going over my shoulders to dip way low, stopping just above my ass and exposing my entire back. This style shows off more side-boob than my usual ones, but I don't hate it. In fact, I just might get one to keep in my dorm room. Not that I do a ton of swimming, but sometimes I need a suit for pool parties.

It's understated sexy, and more importantly, I feel amazing in it. I smooth my hands over that slinky material on my stomach. Yeah, this'll do.

I make a mental note to ask Dante where he got it so I can get another. It's an interesting coincidence that he found something that's perfectly to my taste. Then again, I've learned that almost nothing in life is a coincidence. You may not understand the reasoning right away, but one day you will. It's kind of like a new take on the *everything happens for a reason* mentality. I don't know if everything happens for a reason, but I like to think that there's a reason for everything.

I fold my borrowed clothes and bring them out with me as I pad through the pool house on bare feet. I leave them on the end table by the door and close the door behind me, greeting the warm air with a smile. Leo's already in the pool, sitting in a giant doughnut and floating with his arms spread wide. His head tilts toward the sky with his eyes closed as slowly, the sun dips even closer to the horizon. Twilight is on the horizon, not that it matters because it's still hot and there are a ton of outdoor lights on this property.

"How's the water," I call.

His eyes snap open, and he whistles low under his breath. "I'm not even surprised, Madison. You look good enough to eat."

"As good as a doughnut?" I tease him with a smirk as I walk toward the pool. I have a little extra sway in my hips, my subtle way of preening under his compliment.

I use the zero-gravity side to wade into the pool. The water's warmer than I expected, as I slowly sink into its depths. Leo hops off the floatie and swims toward me. I stop him with a hand on the other side of the doughnut.

"Here we are," he says.

"Here we are, Leo," I murmur.

"What now, Madison?" he asks, moving through the water and stopping close enough to touch. "What do you want to do?"

His question feels loaded.

With one hand still on the doughnut, I say, "Whatever I want."

His grin spreads wide slowly. "Sounds like it's time for that drink then."

"I'd love one, thanks."

Leo runs his fingertips over my shoulder as he passes me out of the pool. "Any requests?"

"Surprise me," I call over my shoulder and rest my chin on the doughnut.

chapter twenty-eight

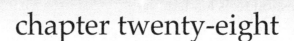

Madison

Soft music plays out of speakers designed into the outdoor pool and patio area. They're hidden so well, I jumped at the first note coming from somewhere by the beach loungers. Leo wades into the water with a tall drink in each hand. "Here ya go. Long Island iced teas."

I accept my glass with a smile. "Thanks."

We settle into a comfortable silence as both of us hang on the doughnut floatie across from one another. I gently kick my legs to keep moving, especially since I can't really touch the bottom here. I sip the sweet concoction, humming with approval before placing it in one of the two cup holders on the side of the pool toy.

"What's your favorite color?"

I laugh and look at him. "What is this? Twenty questions?"

He sips his drink. "Nah, but that's a good idea. Let's play that. And just to make it interesting, for every question you don't want to answer, you have to drink."

I arch my brows at him, excitement drumming in my veins. "Deal, and pink."

"Ya know, I initially thought that too, but now I think black might be more your style."

"Black, huh? And that has nothing to do with the swimsuit I'm wearing, does it?" I roll my eyes with a smile.

He looks at me over the rim of his glass. "Must be a coincidence. Your turn."

I twist my lips to the side as I think. Do I want to ask him fluffy questions or go for the jugular? I look at him staring at me with a twinkle in his eye, and I make my decision. "Pizza or tacos?"

He presses his palm against his heart. "Damn, baby, going right for the kill on the first question?"

I laugh and flick water at him, even though it doesn't land nearly close enough. "That's not even a hard one!"

"Okay, okay. I'll say pizza but I reserve the right to change my mind at any point."

I smirk at him. I'm not at all surprised that we're five minutes in, and I'm already having a ton of fun.

"Childhood pet?"

I shake my head. "Never had one. I've been at the dorms for almost a decade with my sister and cousin, and they don't allow pets."

He whistles quietly. "Damn. A decade away from home? That's tough. Rafe's been gone about that long too."

"And what about you?" I ask.

"Well, I've been at St. Bart's since high school, but we had a cat when I was younger. I don't remember too much, just that she was this little black cat with white paws. I named her Oreo."

I giggle, interrupting him. "Oreo?"

He lifts a shoulder. "I was like seven and I had just discovered Oreos recently. Seemed like the perfect fit." His smile falls as his voice trails off. "But then Dad decided he didn't want to have another mouth to feed, so he locked her out of the house one night after I'd gone to bed. It was the middle of January. She didn't last long in the cold." Barely before the last word is out, he tips his drink up and takes a healthy gulp.

My heart hurts for him. I can't imagine that happening— especially not when he was so young. "Jesus, Leo. I'm so sorry."

He waves a hand in the air. "It was a long time ago. Is it my turn now?"

"I think so."

The song ends and it's quiet for a moment while the next song picks up—"Rain" by grandson. He looks at me, his face serious, and my heart jumps inside my chest. "Okay. This is a serious one."

"Okay." I drag the word out, nervousness coiling in my belly.

He blows out a breath and stares in my eyes. "Marvel or DC?"

I feel my eyebrows scrunch together as I turn over the question twice before my body catches up to my brain. "Oh my god, Leo! I thought you were going to ask me something serious!"

He nods, the gesture solemn. "That is a serious question. And there's only one right answer, so which is it, Maddie?"

I cringe through a smile. "Uh, Marvel?"

"Oh, thank god. I thought we were going to be over before we even got a chance to start." He sighs, this melodramatic production like he's so relieved.

"So what if I said I think Aquaman is far superior to Captain America?"

He looks stricken for a moment before he rallies and plasters his infectious grin on his face. "I probably would've penciled in a weekend of Marvel immersion to help you see the error of your ways."

I laugh, feeling carefree and happy. Leaning over to grasp the straw between my teeth, I take a sip without taking the glass from the cupholder. Leo's eyes flick from my face to my cleavage. I don't even blame him—this swimsuit puts my best assets on display in the best ways. Plus, I like the way his eyes feel on me. It makes me long to feel his skin against mine.

An idea sparks, and I could take the easy way out and blame it on the deceptively boozy iced tea, but that wouldn't be the entire truth. Maybe it gave me a little liquid courage to drop more inhibitions, but the ideas were in my bloodstream long before the booze was.

"Ever been skinny-dipping?" I ask him around the straw against my lips.

He arches a brow as a slow smile spreads across his face. "Nah. I went to an all-boys catholic school, remember?"

"Surely there must've been plenty of opportunities at parties." I trail off, fishing for information.

"Nah, it never interested me," he says, holding my gaze.

I lean forward, decreasing the distance. "And now? Does it interest you now?"

"Everything you do interests me."

Grabbing onto his shoulders, I leverage myself on the doughnut floatie further and lean in to whisper, "Then take off your trunks."

He steadies me with one hand as he wipes his other palm across his face, like he's smothering a smile. "Well, this is the most interesting game of twenty questions I've ever played."

It's the in-between time of day where it isn't quite dark, but it's not sunny out either. There's the perfect amount of light to see one another, which will make this all the more fun. I don't know what's going to happen, only what I hope to do.

I back off and slide into the water, keeping my hands on the floatie. Leo pulls us closer toward the shallower end before his hands disappear into the water. The pink-frosted pool toy blocks my view, not that I'm positive I would even be able to see anything through the water really. He holds up his fist, black fabric clutched between his fingers and water dripping down his arm. Without looking he tosses them to the side, where they land on the cement with a wet plop.

Leo arches a brow and smirks, like he's calling my bluff. Like I'm not the one who suggested this in the first place.

Drowning because I'm trying to undress while in the deep end sounds like a terrible way to go, so I swim to the four-foot-deep area and perch up by the wall. I hold his gaze as I lower the left strap of my swimsuit. He cuts through the water like *he's* Aquaman, and just as my fingertips grasp the material on my right shoulder, he's in front of me. He brushes my fingers away, replacing them with his own.

"Let me help you." Dizziness threatens when my breath hitches. He lowers the strap, taking his time to drag the material down my arm, and when my breasts are exposed, he pauses. Glancing at me, he asks, "Okay?"

"Yes." Placing my hands on his, I guide them to slide the swimsuit off my body. I lean against the wall and raise each foot, so he can pull it off completely. Laying my head against the cement, my eyelids heavy with lust, Leo leans in and places my suit somewhere behind me.

"Now what? Tell me what you want, baby."

His low voice only serves to fan the flames of desire. One of the best things about the water is it gives you a sense of weightlessness. With his fingertips running up my ribcage, I lift my leg and curl it around his hip. I give him time to back away, but he doesn't. He holds perfectly pliant and lets me pull him toward me.

Dragging my hands from the water, I slide them up his tattooed arms, over his muscled shoulders and traps, and curl around the back of his neck. He reads my cues and leans into me, stopping just shy of connecting our lips. It's the perfect moment for me to lift my other leg and wrap it around his waist.

"You. I want you, Leo," I whisper against his lips before I use my legs to pull him into me. My bare pussy bumps up against his lower abs. Our height difference is cock-blocking us right now, but I don't even care because Leo crashes his mouth to mine with a groan.

chapter twenty-nine

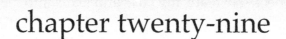

His hands brace against the edge of the pool as I wrap my body around his, indulging in our shared lust. Passion leaks from every pore of Leo's body as he breaks me down with one single kiss. My head feels light, dizzy, like I'm liable to detach and float away at any moment.

I know I need to take a breath. But honestly, it doesn't feel worth it. I'd rather go without air if it means stopping this kiss. He moves his hand from the edge and slides it under my ass, kneading my cheek as he lifts me up and settles me against him.

Oh. *Oh.* I moan into his mouth from the perfect angle he just created. I wiggle my hips, delighting in the delicious friction. The tip of his hard cock bumps against my clit with every roll. I chase that feeling, swirling my hips, and loving the way it sends little tingling ripples of pleasure shocks throughout my whole system.

My nerve endings spark with lust, lighting up like sparklers. My hands leave his neck and explore every bare inch of him, molding over every dip and bulge, every muscle carved into his body. We devour one another against the side of the pool for the setting sun and the rising moon to bear witness.

If I didn't keep at least one shred of rationale, I would beg him to fuck me right here. And as much as I want him to—as much as I'm desperate for it—I know the ramifications of having sex in a pool far outweigh any of the joy and pleasure.

He adjusts his hold on me, adding his other hand underneath my ass, spreading my cheeks and gently massaging them. His long hands reach my pussy from his grip underneath my thighs. Soft, almost tentative, fingers brush against me, and I arch my back so he has better access. My silent communication for more.

He doesn't need any more encouragement. Shifting me, he adjusts his hold once more and sinks a finger inside me. I gasp in his mouth at the feeling. My hips continue their grind against him, desperation increasing my tempo. One finger becomes two, the water around us turns choppy with our hasty movements.

I reach a hand down between us and I curl my fingers around his impressive cock. A little gasp leaves me at the sheer size of him in my hand. I don't have a lot of room, but I make it work, sliding my hand up and down, pausing to circle over the head.

"Harder, baby," he murmurs against my mouth.

His direction ignites that dark corner of my pleasure. So I tighten my fist on him and pump harder.

He grunts, a low, primal noise, and I bite his bottom lip softly in response.

We're chasing something together, him and I. And I want us both to arrive.

I rip my mouth away from him, panting and gasping for air. "Wait, wait."

He stops instantly, his eyes flash open. He looks drunk on lust— *on me*. A perverse sort of glee slithers in my veins, and I'm not too proud to admit that I like it.

No, *I love it*.

"I want to taste you," I say.

He doesn't say anything, just turns around and walks us toward the zero-gravity exit. My legs hug his waist, my arms around his shoulders. He carries me to a nearby beach lounger. This one's partially hidden behind a copse of trees. Not that there's anyone around to see us.

Where's Aries? A little thought slithers in my mind. Maybe I'll have time later to examine why that idea turns me on even more, but for now, I sink into Leo. He sits us down on the fully reclined lounger and runs his hands up and down my back, toying with the ends of my hair.

"You're going to sit on my face, and I'm going to eat that pretty pink pussy of yours until the whole fucking neighborhood hears who you belong to, yeah?"

Something darker and deeper rolls over me, like fog on an early morning. Arousal skates down my spine, and my nipples tighten even further under his words alone. Without conscious thought, my hips start moving, just a small side to side motion.

He leans back on the lounger, his palms heavy and hot on my thighs as I remain in his lap. With a gentle squeeze, he guides me up, on my knees, until I'm hovering right above his face. Little fissures of worry worm their way through all of my lust and excitement.

Leo caresses my thighs, drawing my attention to his expressive eyes. Right now, they're the darkest green I've ever seen, and raw need strains his face.

"Ride my face, baby." He encourages me to move closer. "Right there, just like that," he murmurs as I lower myself down.

Insecurity flashes for a single moment, worry about how I look. But then I feel his tongue licking a path up the entire length of me, and then I'm not thinking anything at all. He licks and sucks and swirls every last inch of me. He slides his hands around to my ass, and moves me against his face, gently rocking over him.

My eyes close at some point—I don't even remember when. My hands slide up my ribcage to cup my breasts and lightly pinch and pull on my nipples. That small bite of pain sends a thrill through me, ramping up my arousal further.

"Leo," I breathe out. My hips start their own rhythm against his face.

"That's right, baby, just like that," he murmurs, his voice low.

He slides two fingers inside of me, and it feels incredible. Then he does this motion, hitting something that has me blacking out for a moment. I tense up, my muscles flexing. It's a foreign feeling, but not an unwelcome one.

Leo groans, but I'm too focused on the way he's making me feel. He does it again, faster this time. Timing his tempo with his tongue swirling around my clit. He does that thing inside me again with his fingers, and my eyes slam shut. My head tips back, and a low moan is ripped from my very core.

It's toe-curling, muscle-freezing, blackout good. Even my breath stalls in my chest for a pure moment of bliss.

Coming down is hard when he doesn't let up. Tiny aftershocks of pleasure assault my nerve endings. I'm overstimulated but it's the right kind.

"No more," I beg, pushing away from his face. Leo takes one last long lick before he eases up and helps me sit back.

I sort of collapse backward, spent with my arm thrown over my eyes as I fight to regain my breath. My chest heaves as I make my way back down to Earth, and I peek at Leo from underneath my arm.

I take back every other time I said he has a calculated smirk. Those expressions have nothing on the way he looks right now. I wouldn't be more surprised if he starts walking around beating his chest, radiating pride. His expression is sheer satisfaction, and his face glistens with me all over him. And that only excites me more.

"Are you okay?" he asks.

"I'm perfect," I tell him with a wide grin spreading across my face.

"Good. You taste fucking delicious, Madison." His voice is low.

I use my elbows to lean up and take a peek at his hard cock resting against my thigh. It looks almost painfully hard, and I know exactly how I want to fix that. Shifting, so I'm on my knees, I lean over and kiss him. I taste myself on his tongue, and he groans into my mouth.

I break the kiss before we get carried away again and move down his body, placing soft kisses along his chest and abs. I wrap my fingers around his cock, stroking him.

I've only done this a few times before, and it's been a couple years since the last time. But it's like riding a bike, right?

With my little pep talk done, I lower my head and swirl my tongue around the head of his dick a few times. I lick his entire length before taking him in my mouth. A hiss leaves his lips, and it's the encouragement I needed. I stroke and lick and suck, determination riding me hard.

"Fuck, baby, it feels so good."

I shift my hips a little, his praise hitting me in a way that feels all too good. I moan around his thick cock, and that's the push that tips Leo over the cliff. He free falls, a long, low groan splitting the air as he comes down my throat.

I sit back on my heels and wipe the corner of my mouth. Warmth rises to my cheeks when Leo stares at me with something close to awe on his face.

"Holy fucking shit, Madison. That was incredible." He leans up, his abs flexing and seals his mouth to mine in a kiss that feels different from all the rest.

He breaks the kiss and rests his forehead against mine. And because the fates decided that we needed a comic relief moment, my stomach chooses that second to rumble.

Leo laughs, the sound carefree. "Let's get you some food. I think they left us dinner." He gathers me in his arms, despite my protests, and walks us inside the pool house to get dressed.

chapter thirty

Matteo

I stare at the faces of the men of the five families across the old wooden table in the back of a strip club they love to visit. We used to wash all the cash through this place, but it's been hit too many times, so I finally convinced my dad to move it to a more legitimate place.

I resist the urge to sigh or check my phone for the fifth time since we got here ten minutes ago. Dante and I got back to the city last night and checked in with a few of our guys, and asked around a bit. It was an information gathering trip, plus it helps boost loyalty when I see the guys and not just bark orders at them over the phone or using middle men. Something else my father doesn't understand.

Our impromptu check-in was twofold. We also needed information on any recent attacks and if anyone heard about my trip to the hospital. Luckily for me, word hadn't spread. Yet. I'm not ashamed, but it doesn't matter, because people will think I'm weak. And we can't very well usurp Angelo Rossi if I don't have the backing of our men.

And until then, I'm stuck in these fucking pointless meetings. There's no reason to call another one so soon, unless Angelo has information on whoever is inciting these attacks on us. Dante's large presence behind me reassures me in a way no words ever could. And I'm still fucking jumpy over being shot less than a week ago. That kind of shit takes me a month to work though my instincts blaring to shoot first, ask questions never to anyone who gets too close.

But that's the mentality of my father, and I'll be damned if I turn into him.

My shoulder throbs in time with my heartbeat, and a drop of sweat slides down my back. It's fucking hot in this dingy, outdated basement. The pain is manageable, but if Dad goes into one of his famous tirades right now, Dante and I are fucked. We don't have time to run interference. My head starts to ache, and I mentally curse the fucking Vitales for being late. Again.

Finally, Ralph Vitale and all three of his prick sons walk in and sit at the table.

"About fuckin' time." Dad glares at all of them.

Ralph shrugs. "It was last-minute. We had shit to do."

Dad stills completely, like time freezes. "The fuck you say to me?"

I suppress the groan. This posturing is such bullshit, and I'm on a tight fucking schedule if I want to make it to the white party tonight. I gave my girl my word, and I intend on keeping it. It's bad enough that Angelo decided to push the last-minute meeting by a day. It gave us extra time to follow up on some loose ends, but I'm ready to get the fuck outta here.

"Nothin', boss," Ralph mutters, his eyes closed to slits.

"That's what I fuckin' thought," Dad says, leaning back in his chair. He eyes everyone in the room. "Where are we with these people who insist on fucking up our lives? I want answers and names."

"Torched five more buildings and three more soldiers dropped on the lawns of our capos," Victor Gallo says.

Dad drums his fingers on the table. "They're making us look foolish. Have your men start shaking people down until they talk. I don't give a fuck how you get 'em, I want fucking answers."

I actually agree with him, which is fucking weird. Whoever is responsible is toying with us. If they can snatch our men off the streets and toss them on porches like packages without anyone noticing, then they most likely have help. My theory of a rat within the five families seems more plausible by the minute.

"People are scared, Angelo. We need a show of force and soon. Something to settle nerves. My wife is afraid to go to our favorite restaurant," Anthony Romano says.

Dad stills his hand. "Your wife's feelings are hardly worthy of bringing to the table."

Anthony scowls, his eyes narrowing on Dad. My heart beats louder in my ears as I watch it play out in front of me. There's a moment, a single beat where it feels like the air is sucked out of the room, swallowed by violence and rage.

Anthony sits back in his chair and tilts his head to the side. "Are you disrespecting my wife, Angelo?"

Dad smiles, a fucking cruel slash across his face. It's the one he flashes before he strikes. He chuckles, the sound sends chills down my back. "Disrespect? Nah, just pointing out facts. This is a *boys* club, Anthony, or have you forgotten?"

They glare at one another for a moment before Anthony grits out, "I haven't forgotten."

"I have my own nagging wife at home, I'm not interested in hearing about yours. Now, what did you have in mind for our little problem?"

Anthony shrugs a shoulder, jaw tight. "An eye for an eye."

His tone says there might be more than one thing he's referring to, and if I thought my mother was worth redemption, I might be worried for her. As it stands, she'll rot in hell alongside her beloved husband, and I'll never even bat an eye.

"I like where your head's at, Anthony." Dad smiles and slaps a palm on the table, the noise loud and jarring. "Let's start with the new cartel and the Russians."

"And if they're not responsible? It could start another war," Dominic Marino says.

Dad shrugs. "They're already our enemies. I want it done in forty-eight hours." He pauses, looking around the room at each man. "If no one has anything else to offer, I have some news." He doesn't even pause to see if anyone chimes in, he just railroads them.

My gut churns, acidic anxiety splashing around. It's fucking uncomfortable, and I don't know why the hell it's happening.

"In fact, it might just persuade that wife of yours to visit your favorite restaurant again. It seems we have cause for celebration.

My son has made quite the profitable arrangement."

Everything inside me freezes—the very cells in my body turn to stone as I try to process what he's saying. I feel the air move behind me, and I know that Dante is reacting the same way. The man's a stone statue normally, so for him to even shift the slightest bit is alarming. It's akin to a scream from him.

Murmurs break out, the mood tentative.

"It seems some girl from the city bewitched him enough to tie him down. They'll be at Holy Trinity before the year ends. Hell, he might even beat his brother there, eh, Matteo?"

Dad claps me on my injured shoulder with a feral sort of grin. Pain lances up my arm, and I grit my teeth through it. If I needed confirmation that he knows I was shot, here it is. Luckily for everyone, my mind is freefalling over the news of Rafe's supposed engagement.

There's no way he's talking about Maddie. *Right?*

I can't figure out what the fuck he thought he was doing by telling Dad about her—or why the fuck he thought an engagement was an answer.

The deeper, baser part of me fucking seethes at his betrayal. She was *my* fucking girl first, and if anyone gets to marry her, it's *me*.

I ignore the rational part of me that says she'd be better off with Rafe—the same protection but without any of the spotlight my wife would have. I've never claimed to be perfect, and she brings out the fucking irrational side of me.

Dad leers at me, taunting me. I need to get the fuck out of here and get back to the Hamptons. Maddie was right, I never should've left her there.

I maintain my blank expression despite the rage screaming inside me and stare at my father. "Maybe we should have a double wedding."

Dante chokes behind me, the noise small and lost in the chatter around the table. I share his sentiment. I don't know what the fuck possessed me to spill that, and I wish I could take it back instantly. Not because I won't make Madison Walsh my wife one day, but because I'm fairly certain Dad will kill all of us if we show up and try to marry the same girl.

"Two new daughters for me? Sounds perfect, son."

Revulsion pounds against my skin, threatening to unleash all over my father, but I offer him an insincere smirk instead.

"See, Anthony? Good news to bring home to your missus. Alright, I've got shit to do. Forty-eight hours, and I want our message delivered," Dad says with a manic smile. "Someone send me Cupcake and Cherry Pie."

I grit my teeth at the coincidental stage name of one of the dancers from the club. I don't have time to work through that shit now anyway. We have a fucking party to attend, and apparently, pick up clothes. The white party lives up to its name, and white is the antithesis of being in the family business. Dante ordered us clothes that we need to grab on the way out of town.

Chairs scrape against the cement floor as everyone gets up. Dante's at my side in an instant, his fists clenched and his face the same impenetrable mask.

"Oh, and son?"

I stop by the doorway, Dante at my back. We both look over our shoulders at the same time. "Bring your girl around this week. I want to meet her." Dad's smile spreads into something resembling the Cheshire Cat, you know, if he was a murdering psychopath.

I force a nod from my stiff neck and walk out the door without saying a word. I don't trust myself right now, I feel like I'm unraveling too fast. My plans are going to shit, and I haven't had enough time to regroup.

chapter thirty-one

Madison

It's been two days. Two days since Matteo and Dante left. Two days since Aries turned into a ghost. Two days since Leo and I had our moment in the pool.

And for the last two days. Leo and I have a few more moments. It's been amazing. I feel giddy and light in a way I haven't felt before.

Being in this big house, having the freedom to do whatever we wanted whenever we wanted made it feel like a vacation. Well, how I imagine a vacation is supposed to feel.

For years, every vacation we were on, it was me, my sister, and my mom. Sometimes, Lainey would join us for a little bit, and those were always my favorite parts. And occasionally, my mother would bring her newest boyfriend, which was always awkward and uncomfortable.

But it never felt like fun. There was no joy in the experience. No tiny sunflower that bloomed and grew, shifting and guiding you to your next adventure.

Vacations became less about fun and more about work—and not in the traditional sense. It's work to go on a vacation with my mother. And it's definitely work to go on a vacation with my mother *and* my sister—*without* my cousin.

Somewhere around fifteen, maybe even younger, I decided playing wingman to my mother was not a good look for either one of us. For her to bring home—to our shared hotel rooms and villas across the world—men who were barely legal felt like a violation of family-vacation protocol.

Not that I'm that familiar with them to begin with. Though I do have a fleeting memory of my whole family before my dad died driving to Disney World when we were young. I mostly remember the car ride was long and hot. My sister got carsick, so we couldn't do many rides, but I have this sort of fondness, nostalgia even toward Disney World ever since.

And on the opposite end of that vacation spectrum, is the quicksand of dread threatening to swallow me whole anytime someone mentions going on vacation.

But these last two days, they've been amazing. I haven't heard from Mary or Lainey, but I trust Dante and Matteo to keep their word to look out for them, and to let me know if there's anything I need to know. For now, I'm operating under the assumption that they're safe and they're fine, just busy maybe.

Leo and I have shared every meal and nearly every minute

together for the last two days.

It's been strangely incredible. Strange only because I've never spent so much time with someone who wasn't related to me. And incredible because I feel like we're learning new things about each other. Every day, every hour, sometimes. There was an unspoken agreement between us that we'd make every moment here count but without the pressure of other eyes.

True to his word, he started me on a few Marvel movies. Meanwhile, I talked him into watching one of my favorite musicals. He was a good sport about it, and I don't care what he tries to say, I heard him humming a song from the musical last night.

After two days of unencumbered time away, reality comes crashing in the form of a party. I feel like there's probably irony somewhere in there.

So for now, this is our next step. I've been to the infamous white party in the Hamptons before. For all the hype, it's not as glamorous as you would think. It's just another party for the wealthy and powerful to subtly flex on one another. I'm sure there are a ton of deals that get made at this party every year—charities funded, endorsements secured, convenient persuasions.

But they're true to their word. If you're not wearing all white—you're not getting in. The private security inside these parties is insane. They kind of have to be with all the different people there. I'm pretty sure most people bring at least one personal security, and luckily for me, I'll have four.

Dante and Matteo are on their way here, but we're meeting them at the party. They're stuck in some traffic, and apparently, Aries's plan hinges on Leo and I being seen together first. At least I get to show off this dress.

It's a gorgeous long white chiffon dress. I found it in a box on my bed this morning. There was no note, but considering Leo was standing next to me and looked just as surprised, it wasn't him. So that leaves Aries, unless Dante or Matteo somehow had it delivered.

I finger the soft, sheer chiffon sleeves that gather at the wrist. It's a soft white, leaning more toward warm cream than the harsh stark white. The bodice is in the same color and molds to my torso, a chiffon overlay over the entire thing. The neckline is more modest, only showing the barest hint of my breasts.

Several layers of chiffon make up the maxi-style skirt, going all the way to the floor. They swish and swirl when I walk, and it makes me feel like some sort of princess.

But my favorite part about this dress is the double thigh-high slit, and with every step, a peek of my leg flashes.

It has the old Hollywood glamour vibe. Understated from far away, but still alluring, and when you get closer, you get to appreciate its beauty. Perhaps the most important part is that I feel amazing in it.

It fits like it was made for me, which shouldn't be surprising considering who got it for me. I slip my feet into the pair of white open toed heels I found in a box next to the dress box.

I smooth my hair back, one final time and give myself a once over in the bathroom mirror. My hair hangs in loose, bouncy waves. I thought it'd be a nice touch to the dress which offers so much movement already.

"Ready?" Leo asks from his perch against the doorway.

Something tightens inside my chest when I look over at him. Hope. Hope has sprouted and grown inside me, wrapping itself around my heart and infusing in my soul. There's a part of me that recognizes that irreparable damage has already been done. But I'm too far down the rabbit hole to stop even if I wanted to. Which I don't.

I flash him a smile. "You clean up nice."

"Oh, this?" he asks as he tugs the shoulder of his white linen dress shirt.

He's wearing matching white linen pants and white Nike sneakers. His hair is styled in that artfully messy way that I'm sure he didn't spend nearly as much time as people would think.

"Where's Aries?" I ask, walking toward Leo.

"Right here." His voice comes from the bedroom behind Leo.

Aries. My mystery man—who I haven't seen in two days. I narrow my eyes on him, a little irritated that he looks so good while I'm so annoyed with him. I can't explain my annoyance other than I don't know why he hasn't been around.

"Where have you been?" I ask, folding my arms across my chest.

He cocks a brow. "I told you I had calls to make."

"That was two days ago, Aries. What the hell?" I huff a breath.

He slides his hands in the pockets of his white suit. It's not quite linen but some other light material. He tips his chin up and looks down at me.

"You seemed occupied enough. Are you sure you even noticed I was gone?"

My intuition perks up at the shift in his tone. Is he . . . jealous? Aries is as much a mystery to me now as he was when I first met him.

I sigh and unfold my arms, and step toward him. He holds his ground and continues to look at me with a neutral sort of expression on his face.

"I wanted to spend time with you," I whisper.

"Huh. That's so strange. Was that before or after you rode my brother's face out in the backyard?"

"Fuck you, man," Leo snaps.

Warmth stamps my cheeks and the top of my chest as embarrassment and anger war inside me.

Anger wins.

I focus on the spot to the side of him, right next to the TV hanging on the wall to give myself a moment to collect my thoughts. Shifting my glare to his face, I say, "That's not fair, and that's not how this works. You don't get to just say those kinds of things to me."

"Oh yeah? What kinds of things can I say then?"

I flash him a dark look, hurt piercing my chest. "Why are you doing this?"

"Doing what?"

My eyebrows reach my hairline as I stare at him. "Acting like—like—like such an asshole."

He grins, but there's no mirth in it whatsoever. "Didn't you hear, baby girl? I am an asshole."

He flashes his teeth at me in a feral sort of grin.

"Come on, man. You've been drinking tonight or get a bad batch of something? What's going on?" Leo asks him from his perch against the wall.

Aries shrugs his shoulders. "No, I'm just trying to find out my place here."

Ah, there it is. The tiniest shred of vulnerability snuck through his tough exterior.

I look over my shoulder at Leo. "Can you give us a minute, please?"

"I don't know. I don't like the way he's talking to you. Maybe I should—"

"It's fine, Leo," I say.

"Fuck you," Aries snaps at the same time.

I press a palm to Aries's chest, his heart racing underneath my touch. "I'm fine, Leo. We'll meet you downstairs."

He stares at his brother for a moment, jaw tight and eyes narrowed. He looks back at me, his face instantly softening. "I'll be right outside."

I nod my agreement and then slide my other palm up his chest, resting them against his heart. "Why don't you tell me what's really going on?"

He takes his hands out of his pockets and sets them against my hips, branding me with his touch. "I already told you."

I tip my head back and glare at him. "How long are we going to do this? It's not who you are."

"You don't even know who I am. Shit, my brothers don't even know who I am. I don't even know who I am. I've spent the better part of my life molding myself to fit whoever my next mark was, to be what they needed, so I could get what *I* needed." He removes his hands from my hips and splays his arms out wide. "So maybe this is who I am?"

I step into him further, tapping my fingers against his chest. "Well, I *do* know who you are. In here."

He scoffs, but stops when I slide my hands up over his chest and around his neck. I pull him closer to me and push up onto my toes.

"It's true," I murmur, our mouths an inch apart. "My soul recognizes yours in a way I've never experienced before. Ever. And I had hoped that we could let our bodies catch up these last two days."

He opens his mouth, but his face is still tense, so I know I'm not going to like whatever comes out of it. Instead, I brush my mouth against his lower lip. His hands tighten against my waist with a sharp exhale. His palms slide up my ribcage, stopping just beneath my breasts.

"Did you wish it was my hands on you instead of my brother's?" There's acid in his tone, and I have a choice here. I can respond with something to neutralize it, or I can set it on fucking fire.

I tug his bottom lip with my teeth for a moment. "No, I wished for your hands *alongside* your brother's."

A low growl is the only warning I get before he slams his mouth to mine. His tongue demands entrance, and I happily oblige him. His hand slides down to slip beneath the slit in my skirt and grab my thigh, hauling me against him. I gasp into his mouth, my heart racing as my body demands air.

I break the kiss, tipping my head back and gulping air into my kiss-starved lungs. He drags his mouth down the column of my neck, nipping against my skin.

A throat clearing stalls our movements, but we're still locked in our embrace. "I'm glad you worked your shit out, but if we want to keep our timeline, we need to leave now," Leo says.

"We'll be right down," I pant.

Aries takes his time putting my leg down, sliding his lips along my skin and letting his fingertips linger on my thigh. He takes a half-step back, just enough for common sense to trickle in. He doesn't offer me any platitudes, just watches me with a contemplative look on his face.

I rearrange my dress and fluff my hair, my skin heating under his watchful gaze. "Ready."

He grabs my hand in his and links our fingers, and together, we walk downstairs.

chapter thirty-two

Madison

Leo and I walk inside hand in hand, greeted by women dressed in short white cocktail dresses strategically placed around the entryway. They hold white trays with delicate champagne flutes, painted fake smiles on their faces. Leo snags two from the girl nearest to us and hands one to me. "Thank you." The woman dips her head, never making eye contact with either one of us.

The entryway is done in shades of cream, and I can't tell if it's ironic after its famed summer event or simply coincidence. From the stonework floor to the white chandelier and the cream-colored paint on the walls. Lantern-like sconces hang in between four open archways, illuminating the space with a soft pale glow. We walk through the middle arch, the one that leads to the backyard and the main party space. It's always in the same location every year, or so I'm told. But this is definitely the same location as the time I was here.

Humid night air and general merriment greet us as soon as we cross through the archway and into the backyard. Large green trees frame each side, giving the backyard a magical garden feel. We nod and smile politely at everyone we pass, never really stopping on our way to the tent, per Aries's instructions.

Get to your table, he said. That's a simple enough task, right? He drove separately, although he tailed us close the entire way here. Something about not wanting to tip our hand. I sip the champagne, letting the bubbles fizzle on my tongue and distract me from the nerves scratching my veins.

It's a white monstrosity, big enough to look more like a building and less like a tent. It's sort of a cross between a greenhouse and an atrium, with light gauzy walls and a clear roof.

Men in white suits on either side of the doorway greet us with nods as we walk inside. The walls, a soft white gauzy fabric on both the outside and inside offer a little breeze to wind its way through. Strings of white twinkling lights are strung up along the structural beams of the transparent ceiling.

It looks like an explosion of stars against the deep night sky. It's a sharp contrast to all the sheer white around us. White marble flooring, white round tables with white tablecloths, white flowers, and white vases for flower arrangements. White small bar tables and stools along the edge of the wall, a white bar with four bartenders—all dressed in, you guessed it, white.

There's a stage on the opposite end of the bar, where I'm sure someone will be spinning records before the night is out.

It's an overload of the color white, a shock to the system, blinding me. Ironically, it only makes the very colorful food going around on trays all the more vibrant.

My stomach rumbles, reminding me that I haven't eaten in a while. I was too nervous to eat before we left, and now, I'm regretting that decision.

"Let's find our table and get this shit over with," Leo murmurs.

I nod and squeeze his hand. "I couldn't agree more."

We make our way around the tables, weaving through the chairs and the people laughing and chatting. I recognize more than a few faces. Some I've met and some I've only seen from afar. I keep an eye out for Blaire, half expecting her to pop out in front of me at any moment.

When we arrived and gave our names, they gave us our table name. Black Pearl Louis XIII. It wasn't until I heard a group of people say they're seated at Diamond Jubilee and Sapphire Revelation that I realized the tables are named after rare, expensive drinks.

Our table is easy enough to find, about halfway between the bar and the stage. We're the first ones to arrive, and that suits me just fine. My nerves are tight, sparking too often. Leo pulls out the chair for me, tension radiating from him like a low vibration. Seems I'm not the only one on edge tonight.

I carefully sit down, making sure not to wrinkle the chiffon too much. The chairs are soft, almost like a velvet quilted cushion and more comfortable than I thought they'd be.

The soft subtle floral scent washes over me. Our centerpiece is a bouquet of cream-colored roses. I smooth my fingertips over a petal, letting the softness ground me to this moment. I resist the urge to continue looking for people every few moments. They said they would be here, so I just have to trust that they'll be here. And the guys will call Leo if something's wrong.

Ten minutes go by, and then someone gets on stage and grabs the mic. "Alright everybody, I'm here to officially welcome you to the white party. Now you know we like our rules here—the dress code, anyone?" He pauses and laughs awkwardly. "Well, it's time to eat. Once dinner is served, you're free to enjoy yourselves the rest of the night. We have a special guest spinning for us tonight. Until then, enjoy the food. It's catered by a few different world-renowned chefs who came together today to create a completely custom, collaborative menu. Let's give them a round of applause."

Polite clapping fills the air, and the speaker beams. He doesn't look familiar to me, but that doesn't mean anything. "All right. Enjoy your meal."

I take another sip of champagne and settle back against my chair, content to casually people-watch. I don't know exactly when Aries's plan starts, but I know that Leo and I have to be seen for a little bit first. Our table starts to fill up, Leo greets everybody with a polite nod. His knee bounces underneath the table, his anxiety making itself known.

I place a palm against the bouncing knee, slowly running it up and down. Just a small motion of my fingertips, hoping to soothe him a little.

Leo leans into me, bringing his mouth close to my ear. "Did he say how long?"

I shake my head. "No, but I hope soon."

He places a soft, chaste kiss on the underside of my jaw, right below my ear. "Me too," he whispers. "There are much better ways I'd like to spend my evening with you."

A smile curls the corner of my lips up. An affectionate and

charming Leo is something that I've grown quite fond of over the last couple of days. I squeeze my hand still on his knee and reach for my champagne flute with my other hand.

My fingers brush the cool glass and stall as I stare in horror at the face sitting across from me.

"Senator Hardin." His name is a whisper, chalky and rotted on my tongue. The color drains from my face and my head feels light and woozy.

"Maddie, are you okay?" Leo asks.

My heart beats so fast it feels like it's going to punch outside my chest.

"What is it?" he asks.

I turn and look at him, just that small movement has my head feeling like it weighs a thousand pounds. "It's him." My words are barely audible, a whisper of sound from my lips. But it's all Leo needs. He scoots his chair closer, so now our seats touch, and drapes his arm across my lap. It's a move that's clearly protective. He tilts his chin back, and I stare, transfixed at the transformation before me.

My affectionate, charming Leo is temporarily tucked away, and Leonardo Rossi, brother of the underboss, the son of the boss of the mob stares down the man who inadvertently had me kidnapped and drugged.

I lean my head against his shoulder, turning my face and letting my hair slide over it, so nobody can see my lips move. "Hold it in, Leo. We can't do anything, not yet."

He nods, but he doesn't say anything else. It's enough.

"Ah, Miss Walsh, is it? I do believe we've met a time or two."

I nod, just this side of frantic. "It's nice to see you again," I choke the words out.

"You too, dear," he says, a strained smile on his face before he turns to engage his companions in idle chatter.

Meanwhile, I'm internally freaking out. What the actual fuck is going on? "Is this part of the plan?" I whisper-shout in Leo's ear.

His jaw tightens as he says, "I have no idea."

We sit in uncomfortable silence for another few minutes before I feel him. There's a shift in the air, like my soul is calling out to one of its mates.

"Is this seat taken?" Aries's smooth voice is on my right.

I turn to look at him, eager for reassurance. He glances at me for a split second, flashing me a private smile, before he trains his gaze on the senator across from me. Aries takes his time sliding out the chair and folding his long body into it.

I hazard a glance at the senator, pleasantly surprised to see his pallor turning ashen. If it's wrong to get satisfaction from this, then I accept it. It's worth the moral repercussions to see him sweat—literally.

"Rafe Rhodes? Is that you?" Senator Hardin's voice wobbles on the end as sweat beads along his brow.

He flashes the senator a too-wide grin, a taunt. "In the flesh. Have you met my wife yet?" Aries places an arm around the back of my chair, and I choke on absolutely nothing. Reaching for my champagne glass, I take a sip and wave off Leo's concern. My brows hit my hairline as I stare at Aries.

He chuckles and plays with the ends of my hair, his fingertips swirling circles on my shoulders. "Oh, forgive me. We're not technically married yet, but I'm just so goddamn excited to bind the love of my life to me, I get carried away sometimes. I'm liable to snap if someone so much as sneezes on her, ya know?"

Senator Hardin grunts something too low for me to hear as he dabs his face with a napkin.

Aries looks at him. "You ever love someone so much that it has the potential to drive you to *murder*, Senator Hardin?"

My heart pounds and my adrenaline spikes. I don't know if this is all an act or what the hell is going on, but I kind of hate myself for getting excited at his words. Murder shouldn't be a declaration of love, and yet, from Aries, like this, it feels a whole hell of a lot like it.

Senator Hardin pushes back his chair abruptly and stands up. "Excuse me. I forgot I have a pressing matter to attend to."

Aries tips his chin up. "I'll be seeing you, Hardin."

I didn't think it was possible, but his face pales even further. When he doesn't come back for five minutes, I let myself relax. After ten, I finally lean into Aries.

"Now what?"

"Now, we enjoy our evening," Aries says before he sips his own champagne.

"That's it?" My brows arch high and my mouth parts. "What was all that marriage stuff?"

He brings his face close to mine, skimming his nose along mine and whispering against my lips, "Would it be so bad if we got married?"

My breath hitches, and for the first time in a long time, I'm speechless.

"By the way, you look absolutely gorgeous tonight. I haven't had a chance to tell you. In fact, murder may be off the table for tonight, but I make no promises about rearranging a few faces if these men around here don't start keeping their eyes to themselves."

"That's . . . a lot to unpack in that statement," I murmur with a smile.

Waiters bring salads out, interrupting our brief moment, even though my stomach approves. Chatter mixes with the sounds of forks and knives on china as everyone tucks into their plates. I finish my salad, a delicious strawberry and fig on a bed of arugula, and sit back in my chair, wine glass in hand. I opted for white wine with my meal tonight. I love champagne, but any more than one glass, and I have a headache.

"How's your food?" Leo asks, placing a hand on my thigh. His fingers slip through the high slit and land on my bare upper thigh.

My breath hitches at the feeling of his rough fingertips on my sensitive skin. He slowly traces my skin, small brushes up and down, and I zero-in on it.

"You okay, Raven?" Aries asks from my other side.

I cut a look at him, shifting my weight and inadvertently spreading my legs open another inch. I mean, I think I inadvertently did that, but now that I'm thinking about—and I *am* thinking about it—I'm not sure I didn't do it purposely.

"Hmm? Oh, I'm fine." If my voice is breathy, they don't comment on it.

Waiters come around to clear our salad plates, replacing with a small bowl of soup. It looks like roasted butternut squash, and normally, I'd be excited to try it. But I feel a warm palm on my right thigh, fingers stretching to dip underneath the slit of my dress.

I hold myself very still, trying my best to calm my breathing so no one notices anything's amiss. Both Leo and Aries dive in to eat their soup, and almost like it was choreographed, I witness the gauntlet thrown over my soup bowl.

Both brothers toss each other a look full of determination. And that's all the warning I get before both hands start their exploration.

It's exquisite torture.

It feels amplified by a hundred, every light touch and soft caress brings more warmth to my face and chest. I sip my wine and adjust my posture, slouching down and spreading my thighs open wider. If they're going to compete in a competition where I get to come, then I'm one hundred percent in.

In a perfect twist of fate, the fact that we're completely surrounded by people and no one can see anything underneath the floor-length tablecloths ramps up my desire.

I'm slick before they even touch me, lust flooding my bloodstream like a tsunami. Like it was a coordinated attack, they slide their fingers underneath my thong, on either side of my clit, up and down and up and down. They tease me with one hand while they eat their soup with the other.

"Oh, dear. Are you alright? You look flushed," a woman to Aries's left says.

"She had a little too much champagne earlier. Isn't that right, Raven?" His eyes sparkle with mirth.

He's enjoying watching me squirm a little too much, so I decide to up the ante. With a smile and a nod, I lay my left hand on top of Leo's under the table and pick up my soup spoon with my right hand. I guide Leo's fingers inside me, and he goes all too willingly. I push and pull on his hand, encouraging him to fuck me with two fingers.

My breath hitches, and my toes flex as I start barreling toward bliss. My thigh muscles strain, small tremors shaking them. It's enough to get Aries's attention. He narrows his eyes at me as I dip the spoon into the soup and bring it to my lips, shaking hand and all. Aries takes the bait and pinches my clit with the perfect amount of pressure to instantly command an orgasm. I clench the spoon in my hand, slam my eyes closed, and bite my lip to muffle the groan of ecstasy that drips from my lips.

"Are you sure you're alright?" the same woman asks, her brow creased.

I clear my throat and dip my spoon back in the soup. "Yep, just really good soup."

chapter thirty-three

Madison

I scoot my chair back, a generic excuse on my lips, and head toward the bathroom.

"I'll come with you," Leo offers, tossing his napkin on the table.

"I'm fine. Really. I'll be right back," I murmur. I hesitate for a moment, the instinct to brush my lips across his forehead rides me hard. The only reason I don't is because I have the same instinct for Aries. Considering they both just made me come in a roomful of people, I'm trying not to pad the rumor mill if we can help it. I'm not ashamed, but I also want to make sure we do make these sorts of things a group decision.

I pass a couple bathrooms, walking to the one closer to the entrance. It's bigger and further away from the party, a perfect spot for me to collect myself.

I clench my thighs as I walk into the bathroom, fear of my soaked panties leaking on the delicate chiffon skirt. A woman reapplies her lipstick in the mirror, and I flash her a polite smile as I go into a stall. After locking the door, I just stand there for a second and blow out a breath.

Holy shit.

Holy fucking shit.

I can't believe I just did that.

Actually, I kinda can, I think with a wide grin. It was exhilarating and exciting, and it felt amazing. I take a few moments to clean myself up the best I can. Wet underwear isn't ideal, but it beats going without at a function like this. Especially in this dress.

I exit the stall and wash my hands. I don't hear anyone over the sound of the water, so when I feel hands on my shoulders, I jump. My gaze flies to the mirror and the person behind me. Cold terror sinks into my body like thick mud.

"Charles."

Charles Pinkerton, asshole extraordinaire, stands behind me, his eyes glassy and wide, his hair standing on its end in a way that I don't think is intentional. His hands curl around my biceps in a punishing grip as he sneers at me.

"Well if it isn't little miss prude. How lucky am I that I ran into you again so soon after the masquerade ball?" His eyes go wide, pupils blown. He looks manic, and I'd be willing to bet he's fucked-up on too many different things right now.

I shift my shoulders and try to get out from underneath his grip. "Get off of me. What are you even doing here? This is the women's restroom."

"I fucking know where I am. I called your name twice and you kept walking. Don't fucking ignore me," he snaps, shoving me.

The countertop digs into my hips and lower belly painfully. And I have this moment of clarity. It's a sense that most women have developed and honed, something instinctual and built into our very skin and bones and muscles.

"You're fucked-up, Charles. Just get out of here, and we can forget about it."

"You don't tell me what to do, you frigid bitch. *I* tell *you*."

I stem the rising tide of panic and force my body to still, even though it goes against my fight or flight instinct. Just like I knew he would, Charles leans into me further, leering at me in a way that I'll never forget for as long as I live.

I force my gaze to his in the mirror. "What do you want, Charles?"

He shifts his hold, banding one arm around my throat and tugging on my hair with the other. "See, the thing is, I don't like playing this game with you anymore."

"I'm not playing a game, Charles." I grab his forearm, unwilling to let him choke me out.

"Stop," he yells, tightening his hold. "Stop saying my name like that." His voice lowers into something softer, and that's infinitely scarier.

"I don't know what you're talking about, but I don't want to be in here with you. Okay? So you're going to let me go. My boyfriend is waiting for me."

He laughs, the noise caustic, loud over the water I left running. It echoes around us, sending another shiver of fear over me. I grip the edge of the counter, pushing against him just enough so he can't overpower me and bend me over. I know if he gets me into that situation, it'll be infinitely harder to get out of.

"Oh? Well, I cashed in a favor, and Dale's keeping him busy at the table for me. Isn't that nice of him?" He leans in and smells my hair, an audible sniff that sets off a chain reaction in my body. The tremble begins in my fingers and spreads to the rest of my body.

Water laps against my fingertips, and a quick glance down confirms it. The sink is overflowing, the water pouring from the faucet too fast for the drain to keep up. It spills over the sink and onto the counter, dripping onto the floor and soaking my dress in a second.

It's the sign I was waiting for, I guess.

I will my tense muscles to relax further, releasing my hold on the countertop and pray that it doesn't backfire.

"Ah, see, that's not so bad, is it?" He runs his nose into my hair and groans, fitting the front of his body to my back.

I swallow down the bile rising in my throat, and with a quick prayer on my lips, I turn my head toward him. Triumph beams from his gaze, his face joyous and his smile wide. He gives me a little space, turning me around, and just as he leans into me, I bring my knee up and slam it as hard as I can against his dick.

"You fucking bitch," he wails.

Before I even have time to process his words, he backhands me. The force of his swing sends me crashing into the counter, my head hitting the edge of the sink hard enough that stars dance in front of my eyes. With one hand on his crotch, he lunges for me, murder in his eyes. It has to be the drugs, whatever he's on has him bypassing the normal pain he'd be feeling from a knee to the balls.

I shove him hard, slapping his hands away from me as I scramble to get out of his reach. Desperation to flee mounts higher and steals my breath. "Get the fuck off of me."

"You belong to me, Madison!" he roars, lunging for me again.

I step backward, skirting his outreached hands, and I trip over my dress. I land on my ass with a painful thump and watch in fascination as Charles trips over his own foot, slips on water and falls. His head hits the counter with a sickening thunk, and he falls to the floor motionless.

I hug my knees to my chest and wrap an arm around them, never blinking from my stare at Charles Pinkerton's lifeless body.

chapter thirty-four

Madison

"Maddie! Maddie! Open this fucking door right now, or I'm going to break it down."

I recognize Leo's voice, and I scramble over to the restroom door, careful to keep an eye on Charles's body. I unlock the door, and there he is. One of my dark knights. A sob bubbles up in my throat, like just seeing him unlocks the gate holding back my emotions.

He gathers me into his arms in an instant. "Jesus, Maddie. Are you okay? Are you hurt?" He runs his hands over my arms and back.

I bury my face in his neck and let the terror leave my body.

"He's dead."

He pulls me back, my hair messy and sticking to him. He scans my face with dipped brows. "Who is?"

"Charles Pinkerton cornered me, and he—he was—"

"Shh. Okay. It's okay. Rafe will be here soon, and he'll know what to do, okay?"

His eyes are soft and kind and so fucking understanding that another wave of tears slide down my cheeks.

"Shh, it's alright. I'm here, okay? Are you sure he's dead?"

I shake my head. "He slipped and hit his head on the counter, and now he's not moving. I was trying to get away."

He pushes my hair behind my ear, the touch so tender, it makes my heart ache. "Okay, let's go check, okay?" He grabs my hand and leads me back into the sink area. "You stay here," he says as he stops by the wall furthest from Charles.

Leo turns off the water and steps around Charles until he's close to his head. Charles's eyes are closed, but I don't see his chest moving.

I had gotten so used to the sound of water running, that it takes me a moment to realize that voices are getting louder. "Someone's coming," I hiss.

Leo stands up, panic tightening his eyes. He holds out his hand and says, "Let's go."

"You're not going anywhere until you tell me what the fuck happened to my nephew," a voice I don't recognize says.

We spin around and face the four men crowding the only exit. Hopelessness fills my gut like a black hole. Three of them are built like pro football players, hands clasped and standing shoulder to shoulder. There's no way we'll make it out of here without going out that door. I've never needed a fire safety exit more than I do right now. I swallow around the lump in my throat.

Leo steps in front of me, shielding their view. "Yeah, well your nephew's a piece of shit rapist. As far as I'm concerned, he got what he deserved." His voice is like ice, a sharpened point used against these unknown men.

I step into his back, leaning my forehead against his back. Charles didn't rape me, but I can't deny that he scared me, he made me think he was going to. He cornered me and overpowered me in the fucking women's bathroom, for goodness's sake.

"Sounds like a confession to me, boys. Let's save the sheriff a trip and take him ourselves," Charles's uncle says, looking at the three men behind him while holding his hand out, palm up.

"Fuck you," Leo spits at them.

The three men, bodyguards if I had to guess, are silent as they stare at us with impassive looks on their faces.

"Now, now, boy. You don't want me to take the girl too, do you? I'll be so preoccupied keeping you in line, my colleagues here will have to watch over her," Charles's uncle says.

He's so nonchalant, like he's asking if you want cream and sugar in your coffee and not something far more sinister. Almost like a premeditated move, the bodyguards all peel back one side of their suitcoats, showing us their concealed weapons. The threat is more than clear.

Leo's fingers flutter for a moment, his muscles incredibly tense. "Fuck. You. You'll have to kill me before I let you touch her."

"That can be arranged. Let's go. I've got more important things to do."

"No, don't!" I yell, trying to step out from behind him. "Leo didn't do anything." My head spins as nausea threatens to bring up the soup I barely remember tasting. Fear holds me in its dark clutches, dragging me underneath its tidal wave of inky despair.

"Shh, baby," Leo says, keeping me behind him, protected. "It'll be alright. You wait for Aries, yeah? He'll sort everything out."

I fist his shirt, my heart slamming against my ribs in protest. "No, it was an accident. Charles slipped, and you weren't even in—"

Leo spins around and palms my face between his hands. "Listen to me, Maddie. You find *Aries*, and you tell him what happened. No one else, okay?"

He emphasizes my nickname for his brother, and it clicks. I glance over his shoulder at the men watching me with cruel faces and fear roots me to the spot. "Okay, Leo. Just . . . just hold on, okay?"

Leo's gaze scans my face, running over it fast and soft like he's memorizing it. "Alright, baby. Get to Aries. And Maddie?"

"Yeah?" I whisper, holding onto his wrists.

"I love you," he breaths against my mouth before sealing his declaration of love with a kiss. It's over before it even really begins, and I hope to god or anyone listening, that it's not a parallel to our relationship.

"I love you, too," I murmur. "I'll come for you, and we'll sort it out. I promise."

"I know, baby. I know." He gives me a breathtaking smile that makes my heart ache.

"That's enough, Romeo." Someone grabs him by the shoulder and yanks him away from me.

I take a step toward him when he cuts me a look. I nod, letting him know that I'll get Aries as soon as they're out of sight.

"Let's go boys," Charles's uncle says as what looks like a bodyguard leads Leo out of the room. "We'll let someone else take care of Charles."

In another second, they're gone, and like a flip has been switched, I'm out the door in the flash. I slip and trip on my wet dress, the chiffon ripped and clinging to my legs. I turn around the corner and collide with Aries.

"Raven."

"Oh my god. We have to go. We have to go right now," I cry, tugging on his jacket and leading him the direction I think they went. My breaths come in heavy as terror lodges itself in my throat, making it hard to get enough oxygen.

"Whoa, whoa, whoa, slow down. What's going on?" He stops moving.

"We don't have time for explanations. Leo is in trouble. And it's my fault—well, it's fucking Charles Pinkerton's fault. But he's dead, and they took Leo, and we have to get him before they put him in jail." My words are choppy and quick, a testament to how my mind keeps spinning out of control. I grab his hand and march down the hallway. "Let's go."

"Okay. Where are they taking him?"

"Charles's uncle said they're taking him to the sheriff."

"That doesn't make sense. There's no sheriff here."

My steps slow to a halt. "How can that be? Every town has a sheriff."

"Not if your collective net worth outweighs any sort of lawful jurisdiction." He rubs his jaw for a moment before he fishes his phone out of his pocket, never taking his eyes off of me.

"I don't care what speed Dante has to go, you fucking get here now. Our brother's life depends on it." He hangs up before Matteo gets a word in, pocketing his phone once more. "Okay. Let's take a breath. Are you okay?"

I swallow against the sob that's been stuck in my throat for a while and just nod. "I'll be fine. I'm more worried about Leo."

Aries looks at me for another moment. "Alright. Who took him?"

"I don't know his name. Just said he was Charles Pinkerton's uncle."

Aries drags a hand down his face and curses under his breath. "What is it? What's wrong?"

He looks at me then. "Charles Pinkerton takes his mom's last name, old money or some shit. But his dad's side of the family is in a west coast connected family."

"What does that mean?" I feel lightheaded, blackness encroaching on my vision from the sides.

"The Santorinis run the Las Vegas mob. And Vito Santorini hates Angelo Rossi enough to kill his youngest son just for the fun of it."

"What?" I gasp, terror lodging itself so far deep in my soul that I fear I'll never eradicate it.

"It means we have twenty-four hours to find Leo, or he's dead."

TO BE CONTINUED . . .

Read what happens next in Vicious Reign!
Grab it at books2read.com/viciousreign

penelope black

A NOTE TO READERS

Are you still with me? I know that cliffhanger is a little high, but I promise I won't leave you dangling there for too long! And my DMs are always open if you need to slide in there and proverbially throw your kindle at me! ;)
Maddie's story continues in Twisted Queen! Read it here:
books2read.com/twistedqueen

* * *

I would be honored if you had the time to leave a brief review of this book! Reviews are the lifeblood of a book, and I would appreciate it so much. Until next time!

xoxo

—pen

Stay in the loop!

Join my Facebook group, Penelope's Black Hearts
Follow me on Instagram @authorpenelopeblack

penelope black

ACKNOWLEDGMENTS

Thank you to my readers! Thank you for hanging in there with me on all those cliffs too, sending all of you air hugs for that!

Thank you to my husband who's always the first one to champion me. And I love that you're always shouting, "My wife's a romance author!" with pride to anyone you pass on the street. He literally told our new neighbors about my books ten minutes after we met! You're the best, and I love to so much.

To my tiny humans: I love you both more than all the stars in the sky. And you have to wait until you're older to read Mommy's books.

To my wonderful family who's encouraged and supported me—thank you, thank you! And thank you to each and every one of you who read my books. I'm looking at you, Grandma + Grandpa!

To my amazing beta readers, I'm so thankful for each of you. Your kindness and support means the world to me.

To all the bookstagrammers and bloggers and readers that send me messages and create beautiful edits for my books—I'm still in awe. Thank you so, so much. On my most insecure days, I pull up your edits and kind words and never fails to reignite my spark.

Thank you to the amazing babes on my ARC team! I'm so grateful to have you in my corner!

To Savy—I'd be lost without you, girl. One day, I'm going to hop on a plane and then tackle-hug you.

And finally, I want to thank each and every author who has been so kind and wonderful while I asked a million questions. There are far too many of you to thank, and for that alone, I'm forever grateful. There are a lot of wonderful people in this community, and I'm so glad to be apart of it.

MORE FROM PENELOPE BLACK

The Brotherhood Trilogy
Wolf
Rush
Sully

The Five Families
Gilded Princess
Twisted Queen
Vicious Reign (coming soon)

penelope black

penelope black

Made in United States
Orlando, FL
28 June 2023